The Gold Bag

By Carolyn Wells

Originally published in 1911

The Gold Bag

© 2013 Resurrected Press
www.ResurrectedPress.com

Published by Resurrected Press

This classic book was handcrafted by Resurrected Press. Resurrected Press is dedicated to bringing high quality classic books back to the readers who enjoy them. These are not scanned versions of the originals, but, rather, quality checked and edited books meant to be enjoyed!

Please visit ResurrectedPress.com to view our entire catalogue!

ISBN 13: 978-1-937022-63-1

Printed in the United States of America

RESURRECTED PRESS CLASSIC MYSTERY CATALOGUE

Journeys into Mystery
Travel and Mystery in a More Elegant Time

The Edwardian Detectives
Literary Sleuths of the Edwardian Era

Gems of Mystery
Lost Jewels from a More Elegant Age

Anne Austin
One Drop of Blood
The Black Pigeon
Murder at Bridge

E. C. Bentley
Trent's Last Case: The Woman in Black

Ernest Bramah
Max Carrados Resurrected:
The Detective Stories of Max Carrados

Agatha Christie
The Secret Adversary
The Mysterious Affair at Styles

Octavus Roy Cohen
Midnight

Freeman Wills Croft
The Ponson Case
The Pit Prop Syndicate

J. S. Fletcher

Arthur Griffiths
The Passenger From Calais
The Rome Express

Fergus Hume
The Mystery of a Hansom Cab
The Green Mummy
The Silent House
The Secret Passage

Edgar Jepson
The Loudwater Mystery

A. E. W. Mason
At the Villa Rose

A. A. Milne
The Red House Mystery

Baroness Emma Orczy
The Old Man in the Corner

Edgar Allan Poe
The Detective Stories of Edgar Allan Poe

Arthur J. Rees
The Hampstead Mystery
The Shrieking Pit
The Hand In The Dark
The Moon Rock
The Mystery of the Downs

Mary Roberts Rinehart
Sight Unseen and The Confession

Dorothy L. Sayers
Whose Body?

Sir William Magnay
The Hunt Ball Mystery

Mabel and Paul Thorne
The Sheridan Road Mystery

Louis Tracy
The Strange Case of Mortimer Fenley
The Albert Gate Mystery
The Bartlett Mystery
The Postmaster's Daughter
The House of Peril
The Sandling Case: What Would You Have Done?

Charles Edmonds Walk
The Paternoster Ruby

John R. Watson
The Mystery of the Downs
The Hampstead Mystery

Edgar Wallace
The Daffodil Mystery
The Crimson Circle

Carolyn Wells
Vicky Van
The Man Who Fell Through the Earth
In the Onyx Lobby
Raspberry Jam
The Clue
The Room with the Tassels
The Vanishing of Betty Varian
The Mystery Girl
The White Alley
The Curved Blades
Anybody but Anne
The Bride of a Moment

FOREWORD

Published in 1911, *The Gold Bag*, is one of Carolyn Wells' first mysteries. She was, however, already a well known humorist and poet when she decided to turn her hand to the mystery genre after reading a book by that pioneering American mystery writer Anna Katherine Green. Yet from the beginning, Wells, rather than being a mere imitator, had her own personal style.

While detective fiction at this time followed the mode of the Sherlock Holmes stories in being primarily concerned with finding the solution to an intricate puzzle based on a set of clues, Wells was much more concerned with the interaction of the various characters, and in particular their reactions and the reactions of those around them, to being the prime suspect. For Wells, clues were just so much window dressing, necessary in a mystery, but only a backdrop to the social dramas playing out in her books.

In her early mysteries, those written at the tail end of the Edwardian era, the period before the First World War, much of this drama deals with the place and role of women in that world, particularly women in the wealthy East Coast society that was the scene of much of her fiction. At a time when women had yet to achieve the vote, such women, while pampered and surrounded with luxuries, were also subject to the whims of their fathers, husbands and guardians. Yet at the same time, modern advances were exposing such women to a wider world, a world that promised opportunities. It was the tension between these two realities that Wells often chose to explore in her mysteries.

The primary purpose of Murder, the crime in most of her books, was to serve as a catalyst, something to put her heroines in jeopardy when suspected of the crime and thus reveal these tensions. Because her focus was on these social issues, Wells often did not particularly "play fair" with her readers. She has been accused, with some justice, of overreliance on the use of architectural features such as secret passages and concealed doors for the solution to her crimes. Clues are often presented and then revealed to be irrelevant to the crime. While these criticisms may be true, they ignore the point that "the puzzle" was never the important feature of a Wells' story. It is the reaction of the characters in the story to the crisis of the crime that is of concern. The mystery is just a device to keep the reader interested until the end.

The Gold Bag features a detective that was to appear in many of Wells' mysteries, Fleming Stone. While possessed of that trait common to detectives of the time, the ability to make brilliant deductions from scant evidence, Fleming Stone is unusual, in that he typically appears only in the last two or three chapters after other characters have seemingly explored and discounted all of the evidence. Stone then makes an appearance, make a cursory examination of the crime scene and reveals the culprit. It is before his appearance, that most of the drama takes place, when the true natures of the characters are revealed for good or ill.

An interesting aspect of The Gold Bag is that Wells pokes fun at the deductive sort of detective. After Stone, in a cameo appearance in the first chapter, gives an unverified example of such a deduction based on a pair of shoes at a shoe shine stand, Burroughs, the detective called in on the case and the narrator of the story tries unsuccessfully to emulate this feat with his fellow passengers on the train trip to the scene of the crime. Proving himself to be an abject failure at this sort of deduction he vows to confine his detection to the facts.

Though a prolific and successful mystery writer, Carolyn Wells is, today, sadly neglected. Yet her novels can be both entertaining as mysteries and interesting in what they reveal about the society of the time. It is with pleasure that Resurrected Press brings you this new edition of *The Gold Bag.*

About the Author

Carolyn Wells, June 18, 1862 March 26, 1942 was an American writer and poet. She was best known for her books of poetry and humor until around 1910 she read one of Anna Katherine Green's mysteries and took up the genre. Many of her mysteries featured the detective Fleming Stone. She was married to Hadwin Houghton, heir to the Houghton-Mifflin publishing company. She was a collector of poetry by other authors, and, upon her death, she bequeathed her collection of the works of Walt Witman to the Library of Congress.

Greg Fowlkes
Editor-In-Chief
Resurrected Press
www.ResurrectedPress.com

TABLE OF CONTENTS

CHAPTER 1: THE CRIME IN WEST SEDGWICK

Though a young detective, I am not entirely an inexperienced one, and I have several fairly successful investigations to my credit on the records of the Central Office.

The Chief said to me one day: "Burroughs, if there's a mystery to be unravelled; I'd rather put it in your hands than to trust it to any other man on the force.

"Because," he went on, "you go about it scientifically, and you never jump at conclusions, or accept them, until they're indubitably warranted."

I declared myself duly grateful for the Chief's kind words, but I was secretly a bit chagrined. A detective's ambition is to be, considered capable of jumping at conclusions, only the conclusions must always prove to be correct ones.

But though I am an earnest and painstaking worker, though my habits are methodical and systematic, and though I am indefatigably patient and persevering, I can never make those brilliant deductions from seemingly unimportant clues that Fleming Stone can. He holds that it is nothing but observation and logical inference, but to me it is little short of clairvoyance.

The smallest detail in the way of evidence immediately connotes in his mind some important fact that is indisputable, but which would never have occurred to me. I suppose this is largely a natural bent of his brain, for I have not yet been able to achieve it, either by study or experience.

Of course I can deduce some facts, and my colleagues often say I am rather clever at it, but they don't know

Fleming Stone as well as I do, and don't realize that by comparison with his talent mine is insignificant.

And so, it is both by way of entertainment, and in hope of learning from him, that I am with him whenever possible, and often ask him to "deduce" for me, even at risk of boring him, as, unless he is in the right mood, my requests sometimes do.

I met him accidentally one morning when we both chanced to go into a basement of the Metropolis Hotel in New York to have our shoes shined.

It was about half-past nine, and as I like to get to my office by ten o'clock, I looked forward to a pleasant half-hour's chat with him. While waiting our turn to get a chair, we stood talking, and, seeing a pair of shoes standing on a table, evidently there to be cleaned, I said banteringly:

"Now, I suppose, Stone, from looking at those shoes, you can deduce all there is to know about the owner of them."

I remember that Sherlock Holmes wrote once, "From a drop of water, a logician could infer the possibility of an Atlantic or a Niagara without having seen or heard of one or the other," but when I heard Fleming Stone's reply to my half-laughing challenge, I felt that he had outdone the mythical logician. With a mild twinkle in his eye, but with a perfectly grave face, he said slowly,

"Those shoes belong to a young man, five feet eight inches high. He does not live in New York, but is here to visit his sweetheart. She lives in Brooklyn, is five feet nine inches tall, and is deaf in her left ear. They went to the theatre last night, and neither was in evening dress."

"Oh, pshaw!" said I, "as you are acquainted with this man, and know how he spent last evening, your relation of the story doesn't interest me."

"I don't know him," Stone returned; "I've no idea what his name is, I've never seen him, and except what I can read from these shoes I know nothing about him."

I stared at him incredulously, as I always did when confronted by his astonishing "deductions," and simply said,

"Tell this little Missourian all about it."

"It did sound well, reeled off like that, didn't it?" he observed, chuckling more at my air of eager curiosity than at his own achievement. "But it's absurdly easy, after all. He is a young man because his shoes are in the very latest, extreme, not exclusive style. He is five feet eight, because the size of his foot goes with that height of man, which, by the way, is the height of nine out of ten men, any way. He doesn't live in New York or he wouldn't be stopping at a hotel. Besides, he would be down-town at this hour, attending to business."

"Unless he has freak business hours, as you and I do," I put in.

"Yes, that might be. But I still hold that he doesn't live in New York, or he couldn't be staying at this Broadway hotel overnight, and sending his shoes down to be shined at half-past nine in the morning. His sweetheart is five feet nine, for that is the height of a tall girl. I know she is tall, for she wears a long skirt. Short girls wear short skirts, which make them look shorter still, and tall girls wear very long skirts, which make them look taller."

"Why do they do that?" I inquired, greatly interested.

"I don't know. You'll have to ask that of some one wiser than I. But I know it's a fact. A girl wouldn't be considered really tall if less than five feet nine. So I know that's her height. She is his sweetheart, for no man would go from New York to Brooklyn and bring a lady over here to the theatre, and then take her home, and return to New York in the early hours of the morning, if he were not in love with her. I know she lives in Brooklyn, for the paper says there was a heavy shower there last night, while I know no rain fell in New York. I know that they were out in that rain, for her long skirt became muddy, and in turn muddied the whole upper of his left shoe. The fact that only the left shoe is so soiled proves that he walked only at her right side, showing that she must be deaf in her left ear, or he would have walked part of the time on that side. I know that they went to the theatre in New York, because he is still sleeping at this hour, and has sent his boots down to be cleaned, instead of coming down with them on his feet to be shined here. If he had been merely calling on the girl in Brooklyn, he would have been home early, for they do not sit up late in that borough. I know they went to the theatre, instead of to the opera or a ball, for they did not go in a cab, otherwise her skirt would not have become muddied. This, too, shows that she wore a cloth skirt, and as his shoes are not patent leathers, it is clear that neither was in evening dress."

I didn't try to get a verification of Fleming Stone's assertions; I didn't want any. Scores of times I had known him to make similar deductions and in cases where we afterward learned the facts, he was invariably correct. So, though we didn't follow up this matter, I was sure he was right, and, even if he hadn't been, it would not have weighed heavily against his large proportion of proved successes.

We separated then, as we took chairs at some distance from each other, and, with a sigh of regret that I could never hope to go far along the line in which Stone showed such proficiency, I began to read my morning paper.

Fleming Stone left the place before I did, nodding a good-by as he passed me, and a moment after, my own foot-gear being in proper condition, I, too, went out, and went straight to my office.

As I walked the short distance, my mind dwelt on Stone's quick-witted work. Again I wished that I possessed the kind of intelligence that makes that sort of thing so easy. Although unusual, it is, after all, a trait of many minds, though often, perhaps, unrecognized and undeveloped by its owner. I dare say it lies dormant in men who have never had occasion to realize its value.

Indeed, it is of no continuous value to anyone but a detective, and nine detectives out of ten do not possess it.

So I walked along, envying my friend Stone his gift, and reached my office just at ten o'clock as was my almost invariable habit.

"Hurry up, Mr. Burroughs!" cried my office-boy, as I opened the door. "You're wanted on the telephone."

Though a respectful and well-mannered boy, some excitement had made him a trifle unceremonious, and I looked at him curiously as I took up the receiver.

But with the first words I heard, the office-boy was forgotten, and my own nerves received a shock as I listened to the message. It was from the Detective Bureau with which I was connected, and the superintendent himself was directing me to go at once to West Sedgwick, where a terrible crime had just been discovered.

"Killed!" I exclaimed; "Joseph Crawford?"

"Yes; murdered in his home in West Sedgwick. The coroner telephoned to send a detective at once and we want you to go."

"Of course I'll go. Do you know any more details?"

"No; only that he was shot during the night and the body found this morning. Mr. Crawford was a big man, you know. Go right off, Mr. Burroughs; we want you to lose no time."

Yes; I knew Joseph Crawford by name, though not personally, and I knew he was a big man in the business world, and his sudden death would mean excitement in Wall Street matters. Of his home, or home-life, I knew nothing.

"I'll go right off," I assured the Chief, and turned away from the telephone to find Donovan, the office-boy, already looking up trains in a timetable.

"Good boy, Don," said I approvingly; "what's the next train to West Sedgwick, and how long does it take to get there?"

"You kin s'lect the ten-twenty, Mr. Burruz, if you whirl over in a taxi an' shoot the tunnel," said Donovan, who was rather a graphic conversationalist. "That'll spill you out at West Sedgwick 'bout quarter of 'leven. Was he moidered, Mr. Burruz?"

"So they tell me, Don. His death will mean something in financial circles."

"Yessir. He was a big plute. Here's your time-table, Mr. Burruz. When'll you be back?"

"Don't know, Don. You look after things."

"Sure! everything'll be took care of. Lemme know your orders when you have 'em."

By means of the taxi Don had called and the tunnel route as he had suggested, I caught the train, satisfied that I had obeyed the Chief's orders to lose no time.

Lose no time indeed! I was more anxious than any one else could possibly be to reach the scene of the crime before significant clues were obliterated or destroyed by bungling investigators. I had had experience with the police of suburban towns, and I well knew their two principal types. Either they were of a pompous, dignified demeanor, which covered a bewildered ignorance, or else they were overzealous and worked with a misdirected energy that made serious trouble for an intelligent detective. Of course, of the two kinds I preferred the former, but the danger was that I should encounter both.

On my way I diverted my mind, and so partly forgot my impatience, by endeavoring to "deduce" the station or occupation of my fellow passengers.

Opposite me in the tunnel train sat a mild-faced gentleman, and from the general, appearance of his head and hat I concluded he was a clergyman. I studied him unostentatiously and tried to find some indication of the denomination he might belong to, or the character of his congregation, but as I watched, I saw him draw a sporting paper from his pocket, and turning his hand, a hitherto unseen diamond flashed brilliantly from his little finger. I hastily, revised my judgment, and turning slightly observed the man who sat next me. Determined to draw only logical inferences, I scrutinized his coat, that garment being usually highly suggestive to our best regulated detectives. I noticed that while the left sleeve was unworn and in good condition, the right sleeve was frayed at the inside edge, and excessively smooth and shiny on the inner forearm. Also the top button of the coat was very much worn, and the next one slightly.

"A-ha!" said I to myself, "I've nailed you, my friend. You're a desk-clerk, and you write all day long, standing at a desk. The worn top button rubs against your desk as you stand, which it would not do were you seated."

With a pardonable curiosity to learn if I were right, I opened conversation with the young man. He was not unwilling to respond, and after a few questions I learned, to my chagrin, that he was a photographer. Alas for my deductions! But surely, Fleming Stone himself would not have guessed a photographer from a worn and shiny coat-sleeve. At the risk of being rudely personal, I made some reference to fashions in coats. The young man smiled and remarked incidentally, that owing to certain circumstances he was at the moment wearing his brother's coat.

"And is your brother a desk clerk?" inquired I almost involuntarily:

He gave me a surprised glance, but answered courteously enough, "Yes;" and the conversation flagged.

Exultantly I thought that my deduction, though rather an obvious one, was right; but after another furtive glance at the young man, I realized that Stone would have known he was wearing another's coat, for it was the most glaring misfit in every way.

Once more I tried, and directed my attention to a middle-aged, angular-looking woman, whose strong, sharp-featured face betokened a prim spinster, probably at the head of a girls' school, or engaged in some clerical work. However, as I passed her on my way to leave the train I noticed a wedding-ring on her hand, and heard her say to her companion, "No; I think a woman's sphere is in her own kitchen and nursery. How could I think otherwise, with my six children to bring up?" After these lamentable failures, I determined not to trust much to deduction in the case I was about to investigate, but to learn actual facts from actual evidence.

I reached West Sedgwick, as Donovan had said, at quarter before eleven. Though I had never been there before, the place looked quite as I had imagined it. The railway station was one of those modern attractive structures of rough gray stone, with picturesque projecting roof and broad, clean platforms. A flight of stone steps led down to the roadway, and the landscape in every direction showed the well-kept roads, the well-grown trees and the carefully-tended estates of a town of suburban homes. The citizens were doubtless mainly men whose business was in New York, but who preferred not to live there.

The superintendent must have apprised the coroner by telephone of my immediate arrival, for a village cart from the Crawford establishment was awaiting me, and a smart groom approached and asked if I were Mr. Herbert Burroughs.

A little disappointed at having no more desirable companion on my way to the house, I climbed up beside the driver, and the groom solemnly took his place behind. Not curiosity, but a justifiable desire to learn the main facts of the case as soon as possible, led me to question the man beside me.

I glanced at him first and saw only the usual blank countenance of the well-trained coachman.

His face was intelligent, and his eyes alert, but his impassive expression showed his habit of controlling any indication of interest in people or things.

I felt there would be difficulty in ingratiating myself at all, but I felt sure that subterfuge would not help me, so I spoke directly.

"You are the coachman of the late Mr. Crawford?"

"Yes, sir."

I hadn't really expected more than this in words, but his tone was so decidedly uninviting of further conversation that I almost concluded to say nothing more. But the drive promised to be a fairly long one, so I made another effort.

"As the detective on this case, I wish to hear the story of it as soon as I can. Perhaps you can give me a brief outline of what happened."

It was perhaps my straightforward manner, and my quite apparent assumption of his intelligence, that made the man relax a little and reply in a more conversational tone.

"We're forbidden to chatter, sir," he said, "but, bein' as you're the detective, I s'pose there's no harm. But it's little we know, after all. The master was well and sound last evenin', and this mornin' he was found dead in his own office-chair."

"You mean a private office in his home?"

"Yes, sir. Mr. Crawford went to his office in New York 'most every day, but days when he didn't go, and evenin's and Sundays, he was much in his office at home, sir."

"Who discovered the tragedy?"

"I don't rightly know, sir, if it was Louis, his valet, or Lambert, the butler, but it was one or t'other, sir."

"Or both together?" I suggested.

"Yes, sir; or both together."

"Is any one suspected of the crime?"

The man hesitated a moment, and looked as if uncertain what to reply, then, as he set his jaw squarely, he said:

"Not as I knows on, sir."

"Tell me something of the town," I observed next, feeling that it was better to ask no more vital questions of a servant.

We were driving along streets of great beauty. Large and handsome dwellings, each set in the midst of extensive and finely-kept grounds, met the view on either aide. Elaborate entrances opened the way to wide sweeps of driveway circling green velvety lawns adorned with occasional shrubs or flower-beds. The avenues were wide, and bordered with trees carefully set out and properly trimmed. The streets were in fine condition, and everything betokened a community, not only wealthy, but intelligent and public-spirited. Surely West Sedgwick was a delightful location for the homes of wealthy New York business men.

"Well, sir," said the coachman, with unconcealed pride, "Mr. Crawford was the head of everything in the place. His is the handsomest house and the grandest grounds. Everybody respected him and looked up to him. He hadn't an enemy in the world."

This was an opening for further conjecture as to the murderer, and I said: "But the man who killed him must have been his enemy."

"Yes, sir; but I mean no enemy that anybody knew of. It must have been some burglar or intruder."

Though I wanted to learn such facts as the coachman might know, his opinions did not interest me, and I again turned my attention to the beautiful residences we were passing.

"That place over there," the man went on, pointing with his whip, "is Mr. Philip Crawford's house—the brother of my master, sir. Them red towers, sticking up through the trees, is the house of Mr. Lemuel Porter, a great friend of both the Crawford brothers. Next, on the left, is the home of Horace Hamilton, the great electrician. Oh, Sedgwick is full of well-known men, sir, but Joseph Crawford was king of this town. Nobody'll deny that."

I knew of Mr. Crawford's high standing in the city, and now, learning of his local preeminence, I began to think I was about to engage in what would probably be a very important case.

CHAPTER 2: THE CRAWFORD HOUSE

"Here we are, sir," said the driver, as we turned in at a fine stone gateway. "This is the Joseph Crawford place."

He spoke with a sort of reverent pride, and I afterward learned that his devotion to his late master was truly exceptional.

This probably prejudiced him in favor of the Crawford place and all its appurtenances, for, to me, the estate was not so magnificent as some of the others we had passed. And yet, though not so large, I soon realized that every detail of art or architecture was perfect in its way, and that it was really a gem of a country home to which I had been brought.

We drove along a curving road to the house, passing well-arranged flower beds, and many valuable trees and shrubs. Reaching the porte cochere the driver stopped, and the groom sprang down to hand me out.

As might be expected, many people were about. Men stood talking in groups on the veranda, while messengers were seen hastily coming or going through the open front doors.

A waiting servant in the hall at once ushered me into a large room.

The effect of the interior of the house impressed me pleasantly. As I passed through the wide hall and into the drawing-room, I was conscious of an atmosphere of wealth tempered by good taste and judgment.

The drawing-room was elaborate, though not ostentatious, and seemed well adapted as a social setting for Joseph Crawford and his family. It should have been inhabited by men and women in gala dress and with smiling society manners.

It was therefore a jarring note when I perceived its only occupant to be a commonplace looking man, in an ill-cut and ill-fitting business suit. He came forward to greet me, and his manner was a trifle pompous as he announced, "My name is Monroe, and I am the coroner. You, I think, are Mr. Burroughs, from New York."

It was probably not intentional, and may have been my imagination, but his tone seemed to me amusingly patronizing.

"Yes, I am Mr. Burroughs," I said, and I looked at Mr. Monroe with what I hoped was an expression that would assure him that our stations were at least equal.

I fear I impressed him but slightly, for he went on to tell me that he knew of my reputation as a clever detective, and had especially desired my attendance on this case. This sentiment was well enough, but he still kept up his air and tone of patronage, which however amused more than irritated me.

I knew the man by hearsay, though we had never met before; and I knew that he was of a nature to be pleased with his own prominence as coroner, especially in the case of so important a man as Joseph Crawford.

So I made allowance for this harmless conceit on his part, and was even willing to cater to it a little by way of pleasing him. He seemed to me a man, honest, but slow of thought; rather practical and serious, and though overvaluing his own importance, yet not opinionated or stubborn.

"Mr. Burroughs," he said, "I'm very glad you could get here so promptly; for the case seems to me a mysterious one, and the value of immediate investigation cannot be overestimated."

"I quite agree with you," I returned. "And now will you tell me the principal facts, as you know them, or will you depute some one else to do so?"

"I am even now getting a jury together," he said, "and so you will be able to hear all that the witnesses may say in their presence. In the meantime, if you wish to visit the scene of the crime, Mr. Parmalee will take you there."

At the sound of his name, Mr. Parmalee stepped forward and was introduced to me. He proved to be a local detective, a young man who always attended Coroner Monroe on occasions like the present; but who, owing to the rarity of such occasions in West Sedgwick, had had little experience in criminal investigation.

He was a young man of the type often seen among Americans. He was very fair, with a pink complexion, thin, yellow hair and weak eyes. His manner was nervously alert, and though he often began to speak with an air of positiveness, he frequently seemed to weaken, and wound up his sentences in a floundering uncertainty.

He seemed to be in no way jealous of my presence there, and indeed spoke to me with an air of comradeship.

Doubtless I was unreasonable, but I secretly resented this. However I did not show my resentment and endeavored to treat Mr. Parmalee as a friend and co-worker.

The coroner had left us together, and we stood in the drawing-room, talking, or rather he talked and I listened. Upon acquaintance he seemed to grow more attractive. He was impulsive and jumped at conclusions, but he seemed to have ideas, though they were rarely definitely expressed.

He told me as much as he knew of the details of the affair and proposed that we go directly to the scene of the crime.

As this was what I was impatient to do, I consented.

"You see, it's this way," he said, in a confidential whisper, as we traversed the long hall: "there is no doubt in any one's mind as to who committed the murder, but no name has been mentioned yet, and nobody wants to be the first to say that name. It'll come out at the inquest, of course, and then—"

"But," I interrupted, "if the identity of the murderer is so certain, why did they send for me in such haste?"

"Oh, that was the coroner's doing. He's a bit inclined to the spectacular, is Monroe, and he wants to make the whole affair as important as possible."

"But surely, Mr. Parmalee, if you are certain of the criminal it is very absurd for me to take up the case at all."

"Oh, well, Mr. Burroughs, as I say, no name has been spoken yet. And, too, a big case like this ought to have a city detective on it. Even if you only corroborate what we all feel sure of, it will prove to the public mind that it must be so."

"Tell me then, who is your suspect?"

"Oh, no, since you are here you had better investigate with an unprejudiced mind. Though you cannot help arriving at the inevitable conclusion."

We had now reached a closed door, and, at Mr. Parmalee's tap, were admitted by the inspector who was in charge of the room.

It was a beautiful apartment, far too rich and elaborate to be designated by the name of "office," as it was called by every one who spoke of it; though of course it was Mr. Crawford's office, as was shown by the immense table-desk of dark mahogany, and all the other paraphernalia of a banker's work-room, from ticker to typewriter.

But the decorations of walls and ceilings, the stained glass of the windows, the pictures, rugs, and vases, all betokened luxurious tastes that are rarely indulged in office furnishings. The room was flooded with sunlight. Long French windows gave access to a side veranda, which in turn led down to a beautiful terrace and formal garden. But all these things were seen only in a hurried glance, and then my eyes fell on the tragic figure in the desk chair.

The body had not been moved, and would not be until after the jury had seen it, and though a ghastly sight, because of a bullet-hole in the left temple, otherwise it looked much as Mr. Crawford must have looked in life.

A handsome man, of large physique and strong, stern face, he must have been surprised, and killed instantly; for surely, given the chance, he would have lacked neither courage nor strength to grapple with an assailant.

I felt a deep impulse of sympathy for that splendid specimen of humanity, taken unawares, without having been given a moment in which to fight for his life, and yet presumably seeing his murderer, as he seemed to have been shot directly from the front.

As I looked at that noble face, serene and dignified in its death pallor, I felt glad that my profession was such as might lead to the avenging of such a detestable crime.

And suddenly I had a revulsion of feeling against such petty methods as deductions from trifling clues.

Moreover I remembered my totally mistaken deductions of that very morning. Let other detectives learn the truth by such claptrap means if they choose. This case was too large and too serious to be allowed to depend on surmises so liable to be mistaken. No, I would search for real evidence, human testimony, reliable witnesses, and so thorough, systematic, and persevering should my search be, that I would finally meet with success.

"Here's the clue," said Parmelee's voice, as he grasped my arm and turned me in another direction.

He pointed to a glittering article on the large desk.

It was a woman's purse, or bag, of the sort known as "gold-mesh." Perhaps six inches square, it bulged as if overcrowded with some feminine paraphernalia.

"It's Miss Lloyd's," went on Parmalee. "She lives here, you know—Mr. Crawford's niece. She's lived here for years and years."

"And you suspect her?" I said, horrified.

"Well, you see, she's engaged to Gregory Hall he's Mr. Crawford's secretary—and Mr. Crawford didn't approve of the match; and so—"

He shrugged his shoulders in a careless fashion, as if for a woman to shoot her uncle were an everyday affair.

But I was shocked and incredulous, and said so.

"Where is Miss Lloyd?" I asked. "Does she claim ownership of this gold bag?"

"No; of course not," returned Parmalee. "She's no fool, Florence Lloyd isn't! She's locked in her room and won't come out. Been there all the morning. Her maid says this isn't Miss Lloyd's bag, but of course she'd say that."

"Well, that question ought to be easily settled. What's in the bag?"

"Look for yourself. Monroe and I ran through the stuff, but there's nothing to say for sure whose bag it is."

I opened the pretty bauble, and let the contents fall out on the desk.

A crumpled handkerchief, a pair of white kid gloves, a little trinket known as a "vanity case," containing a tiny mirror and a tinier powder puff; a couple of small hairpins, a newspaper clipping, and a few silver coins were all that rewarded my trouble.

Nothing definite, indeed, and yet I knew if Fleming Stone could look at the little heap of feminine belongings, he would at once tell the fair owner's age, height, and weight, if not her name and address.

I had only recently assured myself that such deductions were of little or no use, and yet, I could not help minutely examining the pretty trifles lying on the desk. I scrutinized the handkerchief for a monogram or an initial, but it had none. It was dainty, plain and fine, of sheer linen, with a narrow hem. To me it indicated an owner of a refined, feminine type, and absolutely nothing more. I couldn't help thinking that even Fleming Stone could not infer any personal characteristics of the lady from that blank square of linen.

The vanity case I knew to be a fad of fashionable women, and had that been monogrammed, it might have proved a clue. But, though pretty, it was evidently not of any great value, and was merely such a trifle as the average woman would carry about.

And yet I felt exasperated that with so many articles to study, I could learn nothing of the individual to whom they belonged. The gloves were hopeless. Of a good quality and a medium size, they seemed to tell me nothing. They were but slightly soiled, and apparently might have been worn once or twice. They had never been cleaned, as the inside showed no scrawled hieroglyphics. But all of these conclusions pointed nowhere save to the average well-groomed American woman.

The hair-pins and the silver money were equally bare of suggestion, but I hopefully picked up the bit of newspaper.

"Surely this newspaper clipping must throw some light," I mused, but it proved to be only the address of a dyeing and cleaning establishment in New York City.

"This is being taken care of?" I said, and the burly inspector, who up to now had not spoken, said:

"Yes, sir! Nobody touches a thing in this room while I'm here. You, sir, are of course an exception, but no one else is allowed to meddle with anything."

This reminded me that as the detective in charge of this case, it was my privilege—indeed, my duty—to examine the papers and personal effects that were all about, in an effort to gather clues for future use.

I was ignorant of many important details, and turned to Parmelee for information.

That young man however, though voluble, was, inclined to talk on only one subject, the suspected criminal, Miss Florence Lloyd.

"You see, it must be her bag. Because who else could have left it here? Mrs. Pierce, the only other lady in the house, doesn't carry a youngish bag like that. She'd have a black leather bag, more likely, or a— or a—"

"Well, it really doesn't matter what kind of a bag Mrs. Pierce would carry," said I, a little impatiently; "the thing is to prove whether this is Miss Lloyd's bag or not. And as it is certainly not a matter of conjecture, but a matter of fact, I think we may leave it for the present, and turn our attention to other matters."

I could see that Parmalee was disappointed that I had made no startling deductions from my study of the bag and its contents, and, partly owing to my own chagrin at this state of affairs, I pretended to consider the bag of little consequence, and turned hopefully to an investigation of the room.

The right-hand upper drawer of the double-pedestalled desk was open. Seemingly, Mr. Crawford had been engaged with its contents during the latter moments of his life.

At a glance, I saw the drawer contained exceedingly valuable and important papers.

With an air of authority, intentionally exaggerated for the purpose of impressing Parmalee, I closed the drawer, and locked it with the key already in the keyhole.

This key was one of several on a key-ring, and, taking it from its place, I dropped the whole bunch in my pocket. This action at once put me in my rightful place. The two men watching me unconsciously assumed a more deferential air, and, though they said nothing, I could see that their respect for my authority had increased.

Strangely enough, after this episode, a new confidence in my own powers took possession of me, and, shaking off the apathy that had come over me at sight of that dread figure in the chair, I set methodically to work to examine the room.

Of course I noted the position of the furniture, the state of the window-fastenings, and such things in a few moments. The many filing cabinets and indexed boxes, I glanced at, and locked those that had keys or fastenings.

The inspector sat with folded hands watching me with interest but saying nothing. Parmalee, on the other hand, kept up a running conversation, sometimes remarking lightly on my actions, and again returning to the subject of Miss Lloyd.

"I can see," he said, "that you naturally dislike to suspect a woman, and a young woman too. But you don't know Miss Lloyd. She is haughty and wilful. And as I told you, nobody has mentioned her yet in this connection. But I am speaking to you alone, and I have no reason to mince matters. And you know Florence Lloyd is not of the Crawford stock. The Crawfords are a fine old family, and not one of them could be capable of crime. But Miss Lloyd is on the other side of the house, a niece of Mrs. Crawford; and I've heard that the Lloyd stock is not all that could be desired. There is a great deal in heredity, and she may not be responsible..."

I paid little attention to Parmalee's talk, which was thrown at me in jerky, desultory sentences, and interested me not at all. I went on with my work of investigation, and though I did not get down on my knees and examine every square inch of the carpet with a lens, yet I thoroughly examined all of the contents of the room. I regret to say, however, that I found nothing that seemed to be a clue to the murderer.

Stepping out on the veranda, I looked for footprints. The "light snow" usually so helpful to a detective had not fallen, as it was April, and rather warm for the season. But I found many heel marks, apparently of men's boots; yet they were not necessarily of very recent date, and I don't think much of foot-print clues, anyhow.

Then I examined the carpet, or, rather, the several rugs which ornamented the beautiful polished floor.

I found nothing but two petals of a pale yellow rose. They were crumpled, but not dry or withered, and could not have been long detached from the blossom on which they grew.

Parmalee chanced to have his back toward me as I spied them, and I picked them up and put them away in my pocket-book without his knowledge. If the stolid inspector saw me, he made no sign. Indeed, I think he would have said nothing if I had carried off the big desk itself. I looked round the room for a bouquet or vase of flowers from which the petals might have fallen, but none was there.

This far I had progressed when I heard steps in the hall, and a moment later the coroner ushered the six gentlemen of his jury into the room.

CHAPTER 3: THE CORONER'S JURY

It was just as the men came in at the door, that I chanced to notice a newspaper that lay on a small table. I picked it up with an apparent air of carelessness, and, watching my chance, unobserved by Parmalee, I put the paper away in a drawer, which I locked.

The six men, whom Coroner Monroe named over to me, by way of a brief introduction, stepped silently as they filed past the body of their late friend and neighbor.

For the jurymen had been gathered hastily from among the citizens of West Sedgwick who chanced to be passing; and as it was after eleven o'clock, they were, for the most part, men of leisure, and occupants of the handsome homes in the vicinity.

Probably none of them had ever before been called to act on a coroner's jury, and all seemed impressed with the awfulness of the crime, as well as imbued with a personal sense of sorrow.

Two of the jurors had been mentioned to me by name, by the coachman who brought me from the station. Horace Hamilton and Lemuel Porter were near-by neighbors of the murdered man, and; I judged from their remarks, were rather better acquainted with him than were the others.

Mr. Hamilton was of the short, stout, bald-headed type, sometimes called aldermanic. It was plainly to be seen that his was a jocund nature, and the awe which he felt in this dreadful presence of death, though clearly shown on his rubicund face, was evidently a rare emotion with him. He glanced round the room as if expecting to see everything there materially changed, and though he looked toward the figure of Mr. Crawford now and then, it was with difficulty, and he averted his eyes as quickly as possible. He was distinctly nervous, and though he listened to the remarks of Coroner Monroe and the other jurors, he seemed impatient to get away.

Mr. Porter, in appearance, was almost the exact reverse of Mr. Hamilton. He was a middle-aged man with the iron gray hair and piercing dark eyes that go to make up what is perhaps the handsomest type of Americans. He was a tall man, strong, lean and sinewy, with a bearing of dignity and decision. Both these men were well-dressed to the point of affluence, and, as near neighbor and intimate friends of the dead man, they seemed to prefer to stand together and a little apart from the rest.

Three more of the jurors seemed to me not especially noticeable in any way. They looked as one would expect property owners in West Sedgwick to look. They listened attentively to what Mr. Monroe said, asked few or no questions, and seemed appalled at the unusual task they had before them.

Only one juror impressed me unpleasantly. That was Mr. Orville, a youngish man, who seemed rather elated at the position in which he found himself. He fingered nearly everything on the desk; he peered carefully into the face of the victim of the crime, and he somewhat ostentatiously made notes in a small Russia leather memorandum book.

He spoke often to the coroner, saying things which seemed to me impertinent, such as, "Have you noticed the blotter, Mr. Coroner? Very often, you know, much may be learned from the blotter on a man's desk."

As the large blotter in question was by no means fresh, indeed was thickly covered with ink impressions, and as there was nothing to indicate that Mr. Crawford had been engaged in writing immediately before his death, Mr. Orville's suggestion was somewhat irrelevant. And, too, the jurors were not detectives seeking clues, but were now merely learning the known facts.

However, Mr. Orville fussed around, even looking into the wastebasket, and turning up a corner of a large rug as if ferreting for evidence.

The others exhibited no such minute curiosity, and, after a few moments, they followed the coroner out of the room.

Then the doctor and his assistants came to take the body away, and I went in search of Coroner Monroe, eager for further information concerning the case, of which I really, as yet, knew but little.

Parmalee went with me and we found Mr. Monroe in the library, quite ready to talk with us.

"Mr. Orville seems to possess the detective instinct himself," observed Mr. Parmalee, with what seemed like a note of jealousy in his tone.

"The true detective mind," returned Mr. Monroe, with his slow pomposity, "is not dependent on instinct or intuition."

"Oh, I think it is largely dependent on that," I said, "or where does it differ from the ordinary inquiring mind?"

"I'm sure you will agree with me, Mr. Burroughs," the coroner went on, almost as if I had not spoken, "that it depends upon a nicely adjusted mentality that is quick to see the cause back of an effect."

To me this seemed a fair definition of intuition, but there was something in the unctuous roll of Mr. Monroe's words that made me positive he was quoting his somewhat erudite speech, and had not himself a perfectly clear comprehension of its meaning.

"It's guessing," declared Parmalee, "that's all it is, guessing. If you guess right, you're a famous detective; if you guess wrong, you're a dub. That's all there is about it."

"No, no, Mr. Parmalee,"—and Mr. Monroe slowly shook his finger at the rash youth—"what you call guessing is really divination. Yes, my dear sir, it is actual divination."

"To my mind," I put in, "detective divination is merely minute observation. But why do we quibble over words and definitions when there is much work to be done? When is the formal inquest to be held, Mr. Monroe?"

"This afternoon at two o'clock," he replied.

"Then I'll go away now," I said, "for I must find an abiding place for myself in West Sedgwick. There is an inn, I suppose."

"They'll probably ask you to stay here," observed Coroner Monroe, "but I advise you not to do so. I think you'll be freer and less hampered in your work if you go to the inn."

"I quite agree with you," I replied. "But I see little chance of being invited to stay here. Where is the family? Who are in it?"

"Not many. There is Miss Florence Lloyd, a niece of Mr. Crawford. That is, she is the niece of his wife. Mrs. Crawford has been dead many years, and Miss Lloyd has kept house for her uncle all that time. Then there is Mrs. Pierce, an elderly lady and a distant relative of Mr. Crawford's. That is all, except the secretary, Gregory Hall, who lives here much of the time. That is, he has a room here, but often he is in New York or elsewhere on Mr. Crawford's business."

"Mr. Crawford had an office both here and in New York?" I asked.

"Yes; and of late years he has stayed at home as much as possible. He went to New York only about three or four days in the week, and conducted his business from here the rest of the time. Young Hall is a clever fellow, and has been Mr. Crawford's righthand man for years."

"Where is he now?"

"We think he's in New York, but haven't yet been able to locate him at Mr. Crawford's office there, or at his club. He is engaged to Miss Lloyd, though I understand that the engagement is contrary to Mr. Crawford's wishes."

"And where is Miss Lloyd,—and Mrs. Pierce?"

"They are both in their rooms. Mrs. Pierce is prostrated at the tragedy, and Miss Lloyd simply refuses to make her appearance."

"But she'll have to attend the inquest?"

"Oh, yes, of course. She'll be with us then. I think I won't say anything about her to you, as I'd rather you'd see her first with entirely unprejudiced eyes."

"So you, too, think Miss Lloyd is implicated?"

"I don't think anything about it, Mr. Burroughs. As coroner it is not my place to think along such lines."

"Well, everybody else thinks so," broke in Parmalee. "And why? Because there's no one else for suspicion to light on. No one else who by any possibility could have done the deed."

"Oh, come now, Mr. Parmalee," said I, "there must be others. They may not yet have come to our notice, but surely you must admit an intruder could have come into the room by way of those long, open windows."

"These speculations are useless, gentlemen," said Mr. Monroe, with his usual air of settling the matter. "Cease then, I beg, or at least postpone them. If you are walking down the avenue, Mr. Parmalee, perhaps you'll be good enough to conduct Mr. Burroughs to the Sedgwick Arms, where he doubtless can find comfortable accommodations."

I thanked Mr. Monroe for the suggestion, but said, straightforwardly enough, that I was not yet quite ready to leave the Crawford house, but that I would not detain Mr. Parmalee, for I could myself find my way to the inn, having noticed it on my drive from the train.

So Parmalee went away, and I was about to return to Mr. Crawford's office where I hoped to pursue a little uninterrupted investigation.

But Mr. Monroe detained me a moment, to present me to a tall, fine-looking man who had just come in.

He proved to be Philip Crawford, a brother of Joseph, and I at once observed a strong resemblance between their two faces.

"I am glad to meet you, Mr. Burroughs," he said. "Mr. Monroe tells me you are a clever and experienced detective, and I trust you can help us to avenge this dastardly crime. I am busy with some important matters just now, but later I shall be glad to confer with you, and be of any help I can in your investigation."

I looked at Mr. Philip Crawford curiously. Of course I didn't expect him to give way to emotional grief, but it jarred on me to hear him refer to his brother's tragic death in such cold tones, and with such a businesslike demeanor.

However, I realized I did not know the man at all, and this attitude might be due to his effort in concealing his real feelings.

He looked very like his brother Joseph, and I gathered from the appearance of both men, and the manner of Philip, that the Crawford nature was one of repression and self-control. Moreover, I knew nothing of the sentiments of the two brothers, and it might easily be that they were not entirely in sympathy.

I thanked him for his offer of help, and then as he volunteered no further observations, I excused myself and proceeded alone to the library.

As I entered the great room and closed the door behind me, I was again impressed by the beauty and luxury of the appointments. Surely Joseph Crawford must have been a man of fine calibre and refined tastes to enjoy working in such an atmosphere. But I had only two short hours before the inquest, and I had many things to do, so for the moment I set myself assiduously to work examining the room again. As in my first examination, I did no microscopic scrutinizing; but I looked over the papers on and in the desk, I noted conditions in the desk of Mr. Hall, the secretary, and I paid special attention to the position of the furniture and windows, my thoughts all directed to an intruder from outside on Mr. Crawford's midnight solitude.

I stepped through the long French window on to the veranda, and after a thorough examination of the veranda, I went on down the steps to the gravel walk. Against a small rosebush, just off the walk, I saw a small slip of pink paper. I picked it up, hardly daring to hope it might be a clue, and I saw it was a trolley transfer, whose punched holes indicated that it had been issued the evening before. It might or might not be important as evidence, but I put it carefully away in my note-book for later consideration.

Returning to the library I took the newspaper which I had earlier discovered from the drawer where I had hidden it, and after one more swift but careful glance round the room, I went away, confident that I had not done my work carelessly.

I left the Crawford house and walked along the beautiful avenue to the somewhat pretentious inn bearing the name of Sedgwick Arms.

Here, as I had been led to believe, I found pleasant, even luxurious accommodations. The landlord of the inn was smiling and pleasant, although landlord seems an old-fashioned term to apply to the very modern and up-to-date man who received me.

His name was Carstairs, and he had the genial, perceptive manner of a man about town.

"Dastardly shame!" he exclaimed, after he had assured himself of my identity. "Joseph Crawford was one of our best citizens, one of our finest men. He hadn't an enemy in the world, my dear Mr. Burroughs—not an enemy! generous, kindly nature, affable and friendly with all."

"But I understand he frowned on his ward's love affair, Mr. Carstairs."

"Yes; yes, indeed. And who wouldn't? Young Hall is no fit mate for Florence Lloyd. He's a fortune-hunter. I know the man, and his only ambition is the aggrandizement of his own precious self."

"Then you don't consider Miss Lloyd concerned in this crime?"

"Concerned in crime? Florence Lloyd! why, man, you must be crazy! The idea is unthinkable!"

I was sorry I had spoken, but I remembered too late that the suspicions which pointed toward Miss Lloyd were probably known only to those who had been in the Crawford house that morning. As for the townspeople in general, though they knew of the tragedy, they knew very little of its details.

I hastened to assure Mr. Carstairs that I had never seen Miss Lloyd, that I had formed no opinions whatever, and that I was merely repeating what were probably vague and erroneous suspicions of mistakenly-minded people.

At last, behind my locked door, I took from my pocket the newspaper I had brought from Mr. Crawford's office.

It seemed to me important, from the fact that it was an extra, published late the night before.

An Atlantic liner had met with a serious accident, and an extra had been hastily put forth by one of the most enterprising of our evening papers. I, myself, had bought one of these extras, about midnight; and the finding of a copy in the office of the murdered man might prove a clue to the criminal.

I then examined carefully the transfer slip I had picked up on the Crawford lawn. It had been issued after nine o'clock the evening before. This seemed to me to prove that the holder of that transfer must have been on the Crawford property and near the library veranda late last night, and it seemed to me that this was plain common-sense reasoning, and not mere intuition or divination. The transfer might have a simple and innocent explanation, but until I could learn of that, I should hold it carefully as a possible clue.

CHAPTER 4: THE INQUEST

Shortly before two o'clock I was back at the Crawford house and found the large library, where the inquest was to be held, already well filled with people. I took an inconspicuous seat, and turned my attention first to the group that comprised, without a doubt, the members of Mr. Crawford's household.

Miss Lloyd—for I knew at a glance the black-robed young woman must be she—was of a striking personality. Tall, large, handsome, she could have posed as a model for Judith, Zenobia, or any of the great and powerful feminine characters in history. I was impressed not so much by her beauty as by her effect of power and ability. I had absolutely no reason, save Parmalee's babblings, to suspect this woman of crime, but I could not rid myself of a conviction that she had every appearance of being capable of it.

Yet her face was full of contradictions. The dark eyes were haughty, even imperious; but the red, curved mouth had a tender expression, and the chin, though firm and decided-looking, yet gave an impression of gentleness.

On the whole, she fascinated me by the very mystery of her charm, and I found my eyes involuntarily returning again and again to that beautiful face.

She was dressed in a black, trailing gown of material which I think is called China crepe. It fell around her in soft waving folds and lay in little billows on the floor. Her dark hair was dressed high on her head, and seemed to form a sort of crown which well suited her regal type. She held her head high, and the uplift of her chin seemed to be a natural characteristic.

Good birth and breeding spoke in every phase of her personality, and in her every movement and gesture. I remembered Parmalee's hint of unworthy ancestors, and cast it aside as impossible of belief. She spoke seldom, but occasionally turned to the lady at her side with a few murmured words that were indubitably those of comfort or encouragement.

Her companion, a gray-haired, elderly lady, was, of course, Mrs. Pierce. She was trembling with the excitement of the occasion, and seemed to depend on Florence Lloyd's strong personality and affectionate sympathy to keep her from utter collapse.

Mrs. Pierce was of the old school of gentlewomen. Her quiet, black gown with its crepe trimmings, gave, even to my masculine eye an effect of correct and fashionable, yet quiet and unostentatious mourning garb.

She had what seemed to me a puzzling face. It did not suggest strength of character, for the soft old cheeks and quivering lips indicated no strong self-control, and yet from her sharp, dark eyes she now and again darted glances that were unmistakably those of a keen and positive personality.

I concluded that hers was a strong nature, but shaken to its foundation by the present tragedy. There was, without doubt, a great affection existing between her and Miss Lloyd, and yet I felt that they were not in each other's complete confidence.

Though, for that matter, I felt intuitively that few people possessed the complete confidence of Florence Lloyd. Surely she was a wonderful creature, and as I again allowed myself to gaze on her beautiful face I was equally convinced of the possibility of her committing a crime and the improbability of her doing so.

Near these two sat a young man who, I was told, was Gregory Hall, the secretary. He had been reached by telephone, and had come out from New York, arriving shortly after I had left the Crawford house.

Mr. Hall was what may be termed the average type of young American citizens. He was fairly good-looking, fairly well-groomed, and so far as I could judge from his demeanor, fairly well-bred. His dark hair was commonplace, and parted on the side, while his small, carefully arranged mustache was commonplace also. He looked exactly what he was, the trusted secretary of a financial magnate, and he seemed to me a man whose dress, manner, and speech would always be made appropriate to the occasion or situation. In fact, so thoroughly did he exhibit just such a demeanor as suited a confidential secretary at the inquest of his murdered employer, that I involuntarily thought what a fine undertaker he would have made. For, in my experience, no class of men so perfectly adapt themselves to varying atmospheres as undertakers.

Philip Crawford and his son, an athletic looking young chap, were also in this group. Young Crawford inherited to a degree the fine appearance of his father and uncle, and bade fair to become the same kind of a first-class American citizen as they.

Behind these people, the ones most nearly interested in the procedure, were gathered the several servants of the house.

Lambert, the butler, was first interviewed.

The man was a somewhat pompous, middle-aged Englishman, and though of stolid appearance, his face showed what might perhaps be described as an intelligent stupidity.

After a few formal questions as to his position in the household, the coroner asked him to tell his own story of the early morning.

In a more clear and concise way than I should have thought the man capable of, he detailed his discovery of his master's body.

"I came down-stairs at seven this morning," he said, "as I always do. I opened the house, I saw the cook a few moments about matters pertaining to breakfast, and I attended to my usual duties. At about half-past seven I went to Mr. Crawford's office, to set it in order for the day, and as I opened the door I saw him sitting in his chair. At first I thought he'd dropped asleep there, and been there all night, then in a moment I saw what had happened."

"Well, what did you do next?" asked the coroner, as the man paused.

"I went in search of Louis, Mr. Crawford's valet. He was just coming down the stairs. He looked surprised, for he said Mr. Crawford was not in his room, and his bed hadn't been slept in."

"Did he seem alarmed?"

"No, sir. Not knowing what I knew, he didn't seemed alarmed. But he seemed agitated, for of course it was most unusual not finding Mr. Crawford in his own room."

"How did Louis show his agitation?" broke in Mr. Orville.

"Well, sir, perhaps he wasn't to say agitated,—he looked more blank, yes, as you might say, blank."

"Was he trembling?" persisted Mr. Orville, "was he pale?" and the coroner frowned slightly at this juror's repeated inquisitiveness.

"Louis is always pale," returned the butler, seeming to make an effort to speak the exact truth.

"Then of course you couldn't judge of his knowledge of the matter," Mr. Orville said, with an air of one saying something of importance.

"He had no knowledge of the matter, if you mean Mr. Crawford's death," said Lambert, looking disturbed and a little bewildered.

"Tell your own story, Lambert," said Coroner Monroe, rather crisply. "We'll hear what Louis has to say later."

"Well, sir, then I took Louis to the office, and we both saw the—the accident, and we wondered what to do. I was for telephoning right off to Doctor Fairchild, but Louis said first we'd better tell Miss Florence about it."

"And did you?"

"We went out in the hall, and just then Elsa, Miss Lloyd's maid, was on the stairs. So we told her, and told her to tell Miss Lloyd, and ask her for orders. Well, her orders was for us to call up Doctor Fairchild, and so we did. He came as soon as he could, and he's been in charge ever since, sir."

"A straightforward story, clearly told," observed the coroner, and then he called upon Louis, the valet. This witness, a young Frenchman, was far more nervous and excited than the calm-mannered butler, but the gist of his story corroborated Lambert's.

Asked if he was not called upon to attend his master at bedtime, he replied,

"Non, M'sieu; when Monsieur Crawford sat late in his library, or his office, he dismiss me and say I may go to bed, or whatever I like. Almost alway he tell me that."

"And he told you this last night?"

"But yes. When I lay out his clothes for dinner, he then tell me so."

Although the man seemed sure enough of his statements he was evidently troubled in his mind. It might have been merely that his French nature was more excitable than the stolid indifference of the English butler. But at the same time I couldn't help feeling that the man had not told all he knew. This was merely surmise on my part, and I could not persuade myself that there was enough ground for it to call it even an intuition. So I concluded it best to ask no questions of the valet at present, but to look into his case later.

Parmalee, however, seemed to have concluded differently. He looked at Louis with an intent gaze as he said, "Had your master said or done anything recently to make you think he was despondent or troubled in any way?"

"No, sir," said the man; but the answer was not spontaneous, and Louis's eyes rolled around with an expression of fear. I was watching him closely myself, and I could not help seeing that against his will his glance sought always Florence Lloyd, and though he quickly averted it, he was unable to refrain from furtive, fleeting looks in her direction.

"Do you know anything more of this matter than you have told us?" inquired the coroner of the witness.

"No, sir," replied Louis, and this time he spoke as with more certainty. "After Lambert and I came out of Mr. Crawford's office, we did just exactly as Lambert has tell you."

"That's all, Louis.... But, Lambert, one other matter. Tell us all you know of Mr. Joseph Crawford's movements last evening."

"He was at dinner, as usual, sir," said the butler, in his monotonous drawl. "There were no guests, only the family. After dinner Mr. Crawford went out for a time. He returned about nine o'clock. I saw him come in, with his own key, and I saw him go to his office. Soon after Mr. Porter called."

"Mr. Lemuel Porter?" asked the coroner.

"Yes, sir," said the butler; and Mr. Porter, who was one of the jurors, gravely nodded his head in acquiescence.

"He stayed until about ten, I should say," went on the butler, and again Mr. Porter gave an affirmative nod. "I let him out myself," went on Lambert, "and soon after that I went to the library to see if Mr. Crawford had any orders for me. He told me of some household matters he wished me to attend to to-day, and then he said he would sit up for some time longer, and I might go to bed if I liked. A very kind and considerate man, sir, was Mr. Crawford."

"And did you then go to bed?"

"Yes, sir. I locked up all the house, except the office. Mr. Crawford always locks those windows himself, when he sits up late. The ladies had already gone to their rooms; Mr. Hall was away for the night, so I closed up the front of the house, and went to bed. That's all I know about the matter, sir—until I came down-stairs this morning."

"You heard no sound in the night—no revolver shot?"

"No, sir. But my room is on the third floor, and at the other end of the house, sir. I couldn't hear a shot fired in the office, I'm sure, sir."

"And you found no weapon of any sort in the office this morning?"

"No, sir; Louis and I both looked for that, but there was none in the room. Of that I'm sure, sir."

"That will do, Lambert."

"Yes, sir; thank you, sir."

"One moment," said I, wishing to know the exact condition of the house at midnight. "You say, Lambert, you closed up the front of the house. Does that mean there was a back door open?"

"It means I locked the front door, sir, and put the chain on. The library door opening on to the veranda I did not lock, for, as I said, Mr. Crawford always locks that and the windows in there when he is there late. The back door I left on the night latch, as Louis was spending the evening out."

"Oh, Louis was spending the evening out, was he?" exclaimed Mr. Orville. "I think that should be looked into, Mr. Coroner. Louis said nothing of this in his testimony."

Coroner Monroe turned again to Louis and asked him where he was the evening before.

The man was now decidedly agitated, but by an effort he controlled himself and answered steadily enough:

"I have tell you that Mr. Crawford say I may go wherever I like. And so, last evening I spend with a young lady."

"At what time did you go out?"

"At half after the eight, sir."

"And what time did you return?"

"I return about eleven."

"And did you then see a light in Mr. Crawford's office?"

Louis hesitated a moment. It could easily be seen that he was pausing only to enable himself to speak naturally and clearly, but it was only after one of those darting glances at Miss Lloyd that he replied:

"I could not see Mr. Crawford's office, because I go around the other side of the house. I make my entree by the back door; I go straight to my room, and I know nothing of my master until I go to his room this morning and find him not there."

"Then you didn't go to his room last night on your return?"

"As I pass his door, I see it open, and his light low, so I know he is still below stair."

"And you did not pass by the library on your way round the house?"

Louis's face turned a shade whiter than usual, but he said distinctly, though in a low voice, "No, sir."

An involuntary gasp as of amazement was heard, and though I looked quickly at Miss Lloyd, it was not she who had made the sound. It was one of the maidservants, a pretty German girl, who sat behind Miss Lloyd. No one else seemed to notice it, and I realized it was not surprising that the strain of the occasion should thus disturb the girl.

"You heard Louis come in, Lambert?" asked Mr. Monroe, who was conducting the whole inquiry in a conversational way, rather than as a formal inquest.

"Yes, sir; he came in about eleven, and went directly to his room."

The butler stood with folded hands, a sad expression in his eyes, but with an air of importance that seemed to be inseparable from him, in any circumstances.

Doctor Fairchild was called as the next witness.

He testified that he had been summoned that morning at about quarter before eight o'clock. He had gone immediately to Mr. Crawford's house, was admitted by the butler, and taken at once to the office. He found Mr. Crawford dead in his chair, shot through the left temple with a thirty-two calibre revolver.

"Excuse me," said Mr. Lemuel Porter, who, with the other jurors, was listening attentively to all the testimony. "If the weapon was not found, how do you know its calibre?"

"I extracted the bullet from the wound," returned Doctor Fairchild, "and those who know have pronounced it to be a ball fired from a small pistol of thirty-two calibre."

"But if Mr. Crawford had committed suicide, the pistol would have been there," said Mr. Porter; who seemed to be a more acute thinker than the other jurymen.

"Exactly," agreed the coroner. "That's why we must conclude that Mr. Crawford did not take his own life."

"Nor would he have done so," declared Doctor Fairchild. "I have known the deceased for many years. He had no reason for wishing to end his life, and, I am sure, no inclination to do so. He was shot by an alien hand, and the deed was probably committed at or near midnight."

"Thus we assume," the coroner went on, as the doctor finished his simple statement and resumed his seat, "that Mr. Crawford remained in his office, occupied with his business matters, until midnight or later, when some person or persons came into his room, murdered him, and went away again, without making sufficient noise or disturbance to arouse the sleeping household."

"Perhaps Mr. Crawford himself had fallen asleep in his chair," suggested one of the jurors,—the Mr. Orville, who was continually taking notes in his little book.

"It is possible," said the doctor, as the remark was practically addressed to him, "but not probable. The attitude in which the body was found indicates that the victim was awake, and in full possession of his faculties. Apparently he made no resistance of any sort."

"Which seems to show," said the coroner, "that his assailant was not a burglar or tramp, for in that case he would surely have risen and tried to put him out. The fact that Mr. Crawford was evidently shot by a person standing in front of him, seems to imply that that person's attitude was friendly, and that the victim had no suspicion of the danger that threatened him."

This was clear and logical reasoning, and I looked at the coroner in admiration, until I suddenly remembered Parmalee's hateful suspicion and wondered if Coroner Monroe was preparing for an attack upon Miss Lloyd.

Gregory Hall was summoned next.

He was self-possessed and even cool in his demeanor. There was a frank manner about him that pleased me, but there was also a something which repelled me.

I couldn't quite explain it to myself, but while he had an air of extreme straightforwardness, there was also an indefinable effect of reserve. I couldn't help feeling that if this man had anything to conceal, he would be quite capable of doing so under a mask of great outspokenness.

But, as it turned out, he had nothing either to conceal or reveal, for he had been away from West Sedgwick since six o'clock the night before, and knew nothing of the tragedy until he heard of it by telephone at Mr. Crawford's New York office that morning about half-past ten. This made him of no importance as a witness, but Mr. Monroe asked him a few questions.

"You left here last evening, you say?"

"On the six o'clock train to New York, yes."

"For what purpose?"

"On business for Mr. Crawford."

"Did that business occupy you last evening?"

Mr. Hall looked surprised at this question, but answered quietly

"No; I was to attend to the business to-day. But I often go to New York for several days at a time."

"And where were you last evening?" pursued the coroner.

This time Mr. Hall looked more surprised still, and said

"As it has no bearing on the matter in hand, I prefer not to answer that rather personal question."

Mr. Monroe looked surprised in his turn, and said: "I think I must insist upon an answer, Mr. Hall, for it is quite necessary that we learn the whereabouts of every member of this household last evening."

"I cannot agree with you, sir," said Gregory Hall, coolly; "my engagements for last evening were entirely personal matters, in no way connected with Mr. Crawford's business. As I was not in West Sedgwick at the time my late employer met his death, I cannot see that my private affairs need be called into question."

"Quite so, quite so," put in Mr. Orville; but Lemuel Porter interrupted him.

"Not at all so. I agree with Mr. Monroe, that Mr. Hall should frankly tell us where he spent last evening."

"And I refuse to do so," said Mr. Hall, speaking not angrily, but with great decision.

"Your refusal may tend to direct suspicion toward yourself, Mr. Hall," said the coroner.

Gregory Hall smiled slightly. "As I was out of town, your suggestion sounds a little absurd. However, I take that risk, and absolutely refuse to answer any questions save those which relate to the matter in hand."

Coroner Monroe looked rather helplessly at his jurors, but as none of them said anything further, he turned again to Gregory Hall.

"The telephone message you received this morning, then, was the first knowledge you had of Mr. Crawford's death?"

"It was."

"And you came out here at once?"

"Yes; on the first train I could catch."

"I am sorry you resent personal questions, Mr. Hall, for I must ask you some. Are you engaged to Mr. Crawford's niece, Miss Lloyd?"

"I am."

This answer was given in a low, quiet tone, apparently without emotion of any kind, but Miss Lloyd showed, a different attitude. At the words of Gregory

Hall, she blushed, dropped her eyes, fingered her handkerchief nervously, and evinced just such embarrassment as might be expected from any young woman, in the event of a public mention of her betrothal. And yet I had not looked for such an exhibition from Florence Lloyd. Her very evident strength of character would seem to preclude the actions of an inexperienced debutante.

"Did Mr. Crawford approve of your engagement to his niece?" pursued Mr. Monroe.

"With all due respect, Mr. Coroner," said Gregory Hall, in his subdued but firm way, "I cannot think these questions are relevant or pertinent. Unless you can assure me that they are, I prefer not to reply."

"They are both relevant and pertinent to the matter in hand, Mr. Hall; but I am now of the opinion that they would better be asked of another witness. You are excused. I now call Miss Florence Lloyd."

CHAPTER 5: FLORENCE LLOYD

A stir was perceptible all through the room as Miss Lloyd acknowledged by a bow of her beautiful head the summons of the coroner.

The jurors looked at her with evident sympathy and admiration, and I remembered that as they were fellow-townsmen and neighbors they probably knew the young woman well, and she was doubtless a friend of their own daughters.

It seemed as if such social acquaintance must prejudice them in her favor, and perhaps render them incapable of unbiased judgment, should her evidence be incriminating. But in my secret heart, I confess, I felt glad of this. I was glad of anything that would keep even a shadow of suspicion away from this girl to whose fascinating charm I had already fallen a victim.

Nor was I the only one in the room who dreaded the mere thought of Miss Lloyd's connection with this horrible matter.

Mr. Hamilton and Mr. Porter were, I could see, greatly concerned lest some mistaken suspicion should indicate any doubt of the girl. I could see by their kindly glances that she was a favorite, and was absolutely free from suspicion in their minds.

Mr. Orville had not quite the same attitude. Though he looked at Miss Lloyd admiringly, I felt sure he was alertly ready to pounce upon anything that might seem to connect her with a guilty knowledge of this crime.

Gregory Hall's attitude was inexplicable, and I concluded I had yet much to learn about that young man. He looked at Miss Lloyd critically, and though his glance could not be called quite unsympathetic, yet it showed no definite sympathy. He seemed to be coldly weighing her in his own mental balance, and he seemed to await whatever she might be about to say with the impartial air of a disinterested judge. Though a stranger myself, my heart ached for the young woman who was placed so suddenly in such a painful position, but Gregory Hall apparently lacked any personal interest in the case.

I felt sure this was not true, that he was not really so unconcerned as he appeared; but I could not guess why he chose to assume an impassive mask.

Miss Lloyd had not risen as it was not required of her, and she sat expectant, but with no sign of nervousness. Mrs. Pierce, her companion, was simply quivering with agitation. Now and again she would touch Miss Lloyd's shoulder or hand, or whisper a word of encouragement, or perhaps wring her own hands in futile despair.

Of course these demonstrations were of little avail, nor did it seem as if Florence Lloyd needed assistance or support.

She gave the impression not only of general capability in managing her own affairs, but of a special strength in an emergency.

And an emergency it was; for though the two before-mentioned jurors, who had been intimate friends of her uncle, were doubtless in sympathy with Miss Lloyd, and though the coroner was kindly disposed toward her, yet the other jurors took little pains to conceal their suspicious attitude, and as for Mr. Parmalee, he was fairly eager with anticipation of the revelations about to come.

"Your name?" said the corner briefly, as if conquering his own sympathy by an unnecessarily formal tone.

"Florence Lloyd," was the answer.

"Your position in this house?"

"I am the niece of Mrs. Joseph Crawford, who died many years ago. Since her death I have lived with Mr. Crawford, occupying in every respect the position of his daughter, though not legally adopted as such."

"Mr. Crawford was always kind to you?"

"More than kind. He was generous and indulgent, and, though not of an affectionate nature, he was always courteous and gentle."

"Will you tell us of the last time you saw him alive?"

Miss Lloyd hesitated. She showed no embarrassment, no trepidation; she merely seemed to be thinking.

Her gaze slowly wandered over the faces of the servants, Mrs. Pierce, Mr. Philip Crawford, the jurors, and, lastly, dwelt for a moment on the now anxious, worried countenance of Gregory Hall.

Then she said slowly, but in an even, unemotional voice: "It was last night at dinner. After dinner was over, my uncle went out, and before he returned I had gone to my room."

"Was there anything unusual about his appearance or demeanor at dinner-time?"

"No; I noticed nothing of the sort."

"Was he troubled or annoyed about any matter, that you know of?"

"He was annoyed about one matter that has been annoying him for some time: that is, my engagement to Mr. Hall."

Apparently this was the answer the coroner had expected, for he nodded his head in a satisfied way.

The jurors, too, exchanged intelligent glances, and I realized that the acquaintances of the Crawfords were well informed as to Miss Lloyd's romance.

"He did not approve of that engagement?" went on the coroner, though he seemed to be stating a fact, rather than asking a question.

"He did not," returned Miss Lloyd, and her color rose as she observed the intense interest manifest among her hearers.

"And the subject was discussed at the dinner table?"

"It was."

"What was the tenor of the conversation?"

"To the effect that I must break the engagement."

"Which you refused to do?"

"I did."

Her cheeks were scarlet now, but a determined note had crept into her voice, and she looked at her betrothed husband with an air of affectionate pride that, it seemed to me, ought to lift any man into the seventh heaven. But I noted Mr. Hall's expression with surprise. Instead of gazing adoringly at this girl who was thus publicly proving her devotion to him, he sat with eyes cast down, and frowning—positively frowning—while his fingers played nervously with his watch-chain.

Surely this case required my closest attention, for I place far more confidence in deductions from facial expression and tones of the voice, than from the discovery of small, inanimate objects.

And if I chose to deduce from facial expressions I had ample scope in the countenances of these two people.

I was particularly anxious not to jump at an unwarrantable conclusion, but the conviction was forced upon me then and there that these two people knew more about the crime than they expected to tell. I certainly did not suspect either of them to be touched with guilt, but I was equally sure that they were not ingenuous in their testimony.

While I knew that they were engaged, having heard it from both of them, I could not think that the course of their love affair was running smoothly. I found myself drifting into idle speculation as to whether this engagement was more desired by one than the other, and if so, by which.

But though I could not quite understand these two, it gave me no trouble to know which I admired more. At the moment, Miss Lloyd seemed to me to represent all that was beautiful, noble and charming in womanhood, while Gregory Hall gave me the impression of a man crafty, selfish and undependable. However, I fully realized that I was theorizing without sufficient data, and determinedly I brought my attention back to the coroner's catalogue of questions.

"Who else heard this conversation, besides yourself, Miss Lloyd?"

"Mrs. Pierce was at the table with us, and the butler was in the room much of the time."

The purport of the coroner's question was obvious. Plainly he meant that she might as well tell the truth in the matter, as her testimony could easily be overthrown or corroborated.

Miss Lloyd deliberately looked at the two persons mentioned. Mrs. Pierce was trembling as with nervous apprehension, but she looked steadily at Miss Lloyd, with eyes full of loyalty and devotion.

And yet Mrs. Pierce was a bit mysterious also. If I could read her face aright, it bore the expression of one who would stand by her friend whatever might come. If she herself had had doubts of Florence Lloyd's integrity, but was determined to suppress them and swear to a belief in her, she would look just as she did now.

On the other hand the butler, Lambert, who stood with folded arms, gazed straight ahead with an inscrutable countenance, but his set lips and square jaw betokened decision.

As I read it, Miss Lloyd knew, as she looked, that should she tell an untruth about that talk at the dinner-table, Mrs. Pierce would repeat and corroborate her story; but Lambert would refute her, and would state veraciously what his master had said. Clearly, it was useless to attempt a false report, and, with a little sigh, Miss Lloyd seemed to resign herself to her fate, and calmly awaited the coroner's further questions.

But though still calm, she had lost her poise to some degree. The lack of responsive glances from Gregory Hall's eyes seemed to perplex her. The eager interest of the six jurymen made her restless and embarrassed. The coroner's abrupt questions frightened her, and I feared her self-enforced calm must sooner or later give way.

And now I noticed that Louis, the valet, was again darting those uncontrollable glances toward her. And as the agitated Frenchman endeavored to control his own countenance, I chanced to observe that the pretty-faced maid I had noticed before, was staring fixedly at Louis. Surely there were wheels within wheels, and the complications of this matter were not to be solved by the simple questions of the coroner. But of course this preliminary examination was necessary, and it was from this that I must learn the main story, and endeavor to find out the secrets afterward.

"What was your uncle's response when you refused to break your engagement to Mr. Hall?" was the next inquiry.

Again Miss Lloyd was silent for a moment, while she directed her gaze successively at several individuals. This time she favored Mr. Randolph, who was Mr. Crawford's lawyer, and Philip Crawford, the dead man's brother. After looking in turn at these two, and glancing for a moment at Philip Crawford's son, who sat by his side, she said, in a lower voice than she had before used,

"He said he would change his will, and leave none of his fortune to me."

"His will, then, has been made in your favor?"

"Yes; he has always told me I was to be sole heiress to his estate, except for some comparatively small bequests."

"Did he ever threaten this proceeding before?"

"He had hinted it, but not so definitely."

"Did Mr. Hall know of Mr. Crawford's objection to his suit?"

"He did."

"Did he know of your uncle's hints of disinheritance?"

"He did."

"What was his attitude in the matter?"

Florence Lloyd looked proudly at her lover.

"The same as mine," she said. "We both regretted my uncle's protest, but we had no intention of letting it stand in the way of our happiness."

Still Gregory Hall did not look at his fiancee. He sat motionless, preoccupied, and seemingly lost in deep thought, oblivious to all that was going on.

Whether his absence from Sedgwick at the time of the murder made him feel that he was in no way implicated, and so the inquiry held no interest for him; or whether he was looking ahead and wondering whither these vital questions were leading Florence Lloyd, I had no means of knowing. Certainly, he was a man of most impassive demeanor and marvellous self-control.

"Then, in effect, you defied your uncle?"

"In effect, I suppose I did; but not in so many words. I always tried to urge him to see the matter in a different light."

"What was his objection to Mr. Hall as your husband?"

"Must I answer that?"

"Yes; I think so; as I must have a clear understanding of the whole affair."

"Well, then, he told me that he had no objection to Mr. Hall, personally. But he wished me to make what he called a more brilliant alliance. He wanted me to marry a man of greater wealth and social position."

The scorn in Miss Lloyd's voice for her uncle's ambitions was so unmistakable that it made her whole answer seem a compliment to Mr. Hall, rather than the reverse. It implied that the sterling worth of the young secretary was far more to be desired than the riches and rank advocated by her uncle. This time Gregory Hall looked at the speaker with a faint smile, that showed appreciation, if not adoration.

But I did not gather from his attitude that he did not adore his beautiful bride-to-be; I only concluded that he was not one to show his feelings in public.

However, I couldn't help feeling that I had learned which of the two was more anxious for the engagement to continue.

"In what way was your uncle more definite in his threat last night, than he had been heretofore?" the coroner continued.

Miss Lloyd gave a little gasp, as if the question she had been dreading had come at last. She looked at the inexorable face of the butler, she looked at Mr. Randolph, and then flashed a half-timid glance at Hall, as she answered,

"He said that unless I promised to give up Mr. Hall, he would go last night to Mr. Randolph's and have a new will drawn up."

"Did he do so?" exclaimed Gregory Hall, an expression almost of fear appearing on his commonplace face.

Miss Lloyd looked at him, and seemed startled. Apparently his sudden question had surprised her.

Mr. Monroe paid no attention to Mr. Hall's remark, but said to Miss Lloyd, "He had made such threats before, had he not?"

"Yes, but not with the same determination. He told me in so many words, I must choose between Mr. Hall or the inheritance of his fortune."

"And your answer to this?"

"I made no direct answer. I had told him many times that I had no intention of breaking my engagement, whatever course he might choose to pursue."

Mr. Orville was clearly delighted with the turn things were taking. He already scented a sensation, and he scribbled industriously in his rapidly filling note-book.

This habit of his disgusted me, for surely the jurors on this preliminary inquest could come to their conclusions without a detailed account of all these conversations.

I also resented the looks of admiration which Mr. Orville cast at the beautiful girl. It seemed to me that with the exception of Mr. Hamilton and Mr. Porter, who were family friends, the jurors should have maintained a formal and impersonal attitude.

Mr. Hamilton spoke directly to Miss Lloyd on the subject.

"I am greatly surprised," he said, "that Mr. Crawford should take such a stand. He has often spoken to me of you as his heiress, and to my knowledge, your engagement to Mr. Hall is not of immediately recent date."

"No," said Miss Lloyd, "but it is only recently that my uncle expressed his disapprobation so strongly; and last night at dinner was the first time he positively stated his intention in regard to his will."

At this Mr. Hamilton and Mr. Porter conversed together in indignant whispers, and it was quite evident that they did not approve of Mr. Crawford's treatment of his niece.

Mr. Philip Crawford looked astounded, and also dismayed, which surprised me, as I had understood that had it not been for Miss Lloyd, he himself would have been his brother's heir.

Mr. Randolph showed only a lawyer-like, noncommittal expression, and Gregory Hall, too, looked absolutely impassive.

The coroner grew more alert, as if he had discovered something of definite import, and asked eagerly,

"Did he do so? Did he go to his lawyer's and make another will?"

Miss Lloyd's cold calm had returned, and seemed to rebuke the coroner's excited interest.

"I do not know," she replied. "He went out after dinner, as I have told you, but I retired to my bedroom before he came home."

"And you did not come down-stairs again last night?"

"I did not."

The words were spoken in a clear, even tone; but something made me doubt their truth. It was not the voice or inflection; there was no hesitation or stammer, but a sudden and momentary droop of Miss Lloyd's eyelids seemed to me to give the lie to her words.

I wondered if Gregory Hall had the same thought, for he slowly raised his own eyes and looked at her steadily for the first time since her testimony began.

She did not look at him. Instead, she was staring at the butler. Either she had reason to fear his knowledge, or I was fanciful. With an endeavor to shake off these shadows of suspicion, I chanced to look at Parmalee. To my disgust, he was quite evidently gloating over the disclosures being made by the witness. I felt my anger rise, and I determined then and there that if suspicion of guilt or complicity should by any chance unjustly light on that brave and lovely girl, I would make the effort of my life to clear her from it.

"You did not come down again," the coroner went on pointedly, "to ask your uncle if he had changed his will?"

"No, I did not," she replied, with such a ring of truth in her scornful voice, that my confidence returned, and I truly believed her.

"Then you were not in your uncle's office last evening at all?"

"I was not."

"Nor through the day?"

She reflected a moment. "No, nor through the day. It chanced I had no occasion to go in there yesterday at all."

At these assertions of Miss Lloyd's, the Frenchman, Louis, looked greatly disturbed. He tried very hard to conceal his agitation, but it was not at all difficult to read on his face an endeavor to look undisturbed at what he heard.

I hadn't a doubt, myself, that the man either knew something that would incriminate Miss Lloyd, or that they two had a mutual knowledge of some fact as yet concealed.

I was surprised that no one else seemed to notice this, but the attention of every one in the room was concentrated on the coroner and the witness, and so Louis's behavior passed unnoticed.

At this juncture, Mr. Lemuel Porter spoke with some dignity.

"It would seem," he said, "that this concludes Miss Lloyd's evidence in the matter. She has carried the narrative up to the point where Mr. Joseph Crawford went out of his house after dinner. As she herself retired to her room before his return, and did not again leave her room until this morning, she can have nothing further to tell us bearing on the tragedy. And as it is doubtless a most painful experience for her, I trust, Mr. Coroner, that you will excuse her from further questioning."

"But wait a minute," Parmalee began, when Mr Hamilton interrupted him—"Mr. Porter is quite right," he said; "there is no reason why Miss Lloyd should be further troubled in this matter. I feel free to advise her dismissal from the witness stand, because of my acquaintance and friendship with this household. Our coroner and most of our jurors are strangers to Miss Lloyd, and perhaps cannot appreciate as I do the terrible strain this experience means to her."

"You're right Hamilton," said Mr. Philip Crawford; "I was remiss not to think of it myself. Mr. Monroe, this is not a formal inquest, and in the interest of kindness and humanity, I ask you to excuse Miss Lloyd from further questioning for the present."

I was surprised at the requests of these elderly gentlemen, for though it seemed to me that Miss Lloyd's testimony was complete, yet it also seemed as if Gregory Hall were the one to show anxiety that she be spared further annoyance.

However, Florence Lloyd spoke for herself.

"I am quite willing to answer any further questions," she said; "I have answered all you have asked, and I have told you frankly the truth. Though it is far from pleasant to have my individual affairs thus brought to notice, I am quite ready to do anything to forward the cause of justice or to aid in any way the discovery of my uncle's murderer."

"Thank you," said Mr. Monroe; "I quite appreciate the extreme unpleasantness of your position. But, Miss Lloyd, there are a few more questions I must ask you. Pardon me if I repeat myself, but I ask you once more if you did not come down to your uncle's office last evening after he had returned from his call on Mr. Randolph."

As I watched Florence Lloyd I saw that her eyes did not turn toward the coroner, or toward her fiance, or toward the jury, but she looked straight at Louis, the valet, as she replied in clear tones,

"I did not."

CHAPTER 6: THE GOLD BAG

"Is this yours?" asked Mr. Monroe, suddenly whisking into sight the gold-mesh bag.

Probably his intent had been to startle her, and thus catch her off her guard. If so, he succeeded, for the girl was certainly startled, if only at the suddenness of the query.

"N-no," she stammered; "it's—it's not mine."

"Are you sure?" the coroner went on, a little more gently, doubtless moved by her agitation.

"I'm—I'm quite sure. Where did you find it?"

"What size gloves do you wear, Miss Lloyd?"

"Number six." She said this mechanically, as if thinking of something else, and her face was white.

"These are number six," said the coroner, as he took a pair of gloves from the bag. "Think again, Miss Lloyd. Do you not own a gold-chain bag, such as this?"

"I have one something like that—or, rather, I did have one."

"Ah! And what did you do with it?"

"I gave it to my maid, Elsa, some days ago."

"Why did you do that?"

"Because I was tired of it, and as it was a trifle worn, I had ceased to care to carry it."

"Is it not a somewhat expensive trinket to turn over to your maid?"

"No; they are not real gold. At least, I mean mine was not. It was gilt over silver, and cost only about twelve or fourteen dollars when new."

"What did you usually carry in it?"

"What every woman carries in such a bag. Handkerchief, some small change, perhaps a vanity-box, gloves, tickets—whatever would be needed on an afternoon's calling or shopping tour."

"Miss Lloyd, you have enumerated almost exactly the articles in this bag."

"Then that is a coincidence, for it is not my bag."

The girl was entirely self-possessed again, and even a little aggressive.

I admit that I did not believe her statements. Of course I could not be sure she was telling untruths, but her sudden embarrassment at the first sight of the bag, and the way in which she regained her self-possession, made me doubt her clear conscience in the matter.

Parmalee, who had come over and sat beside me, whispered: "Striking coincidence, isn't it?"

Although his sarcasm voiced my own thoughts, yet it irritated me horribly to hear him say it.

"But ninety-nine women out of a hundred would experience the same coincidence," I returned.

"But the other ninety-eight weren't in the house last night, and she was."

At this moment Mrs. Pierce, whom I had suspected of feeling far deeper interest than she had so far shown, volunteered a remark.

"Of course that isn't Florence's bag," she said; "if Florence had gone to her uncle's office last evening, she would have been wearing her dinner gown, and certainly would not carry a street bag."

"Is this a street bag?" inquired Mr. Monroe, looking with a masculine helplessness at the gilt bauble.

"Of course it is," said Mrs. Pierce, who now that she had found her voice, seemed anxious to talk. "Nobody ever carries a bag like that in the house,—in the evening."

"But," began Parmalee, "such a thing might have occurred, if Miss Lloyd had had occasion to go to her uncle's office with, we will say, papers or notes."

Personally I thought this an absurd suggestion, but Mr. Monroe seemed to take it seriously.

"That might be," he said, and I could see that momentarily the suspicions against Florence Lloyd were growing in force and were taking definite shape.

As I noted the expressions, on the various faces, I observed that only Mr. Philip Crawford and the jurors Hamilton and Porter seemed entirely in sympathy with the girl. The coroner, Parmalee, and even the lawyer, Randolph, seemed to be willing, almost eager for her to incriminate herself.

Gregory Hall, who should have been the most sympathetic of all, seemed the most coldly indifferent, and as for Mrs. Pierce, her actions were so erratic and uncertain, no one could tell what she thought.

"You are quite positive it is not your bag?" repeated the coroner once more.

"I'm positive it is not mine," returned Miss Lloyd, without undue emphasis, but with an air of dismissing the subject.

"Is your maid present?" asked the coroner. "Let her be summoned."

Elsa came forward, the pretty, timid young girl, of German effects, whom I had already noticed.

"Have you ever seen this bag before?" asked the coroner, holding it up before her.

"Yes, sir."

"When?"

"This morning, sir. Lambert showed it to me, sir. He said he found it in Mr. Crawford's office."

The girl was very pale, and trembled pitiably. She seemed afraid of the coroner, of Lambert, of Miss Lloyd, and of the jury. It might have been merely the unreasonable fear of an ignorant mind, but it had the appearance of some more definite apprehension.

Especially did she seem afraid of the man, Louis. Though perhaps the distressed glances she cast at him were not so much those of fear as of anxiety.

The coroner spoke kindly to her, and really seemed to take more notice of her embarrassment, and make more effort to put her at her ease than he had done with Miss Lloyd.

"Is it Miss Lloyd's bag?"

"I don't think so, sir."

"Don't you know? As her personal maid, you must be acquainted with her belongings."

"Yes, sir. No, it isn't hers, sir."

But as this statement was made after a swift but noticeable glance of inquiry at her mistress, a slight distrust of Elsa formed in my own mind, and probably in the minds of others.

"She has one like this, has she not?"

"She—she did have, sir; but she—she gave it to me."

"Yes? Then go and get it and let us see it."

"I haven't it now, sir. I—I gave it away."

"Oh, you gave it away! To whom? Can you get it back?"

"No, sir; I gave it to my cousin, who sailed for Germany last week."

Miss Lloyd looked up in surprise, and that look of surprise told against her. I could see Parmalee's eyes gleam as he concluded in his own mind that the bag story was all false, was made up between mistress and maid, and that the part about the departing cousin was an artistic touch added by Elsa.

The coroner, too, seemed inclined to disbelieve the present witness, and he sat thoughtfully snapping the catch of the bag.

He turned again to Miss Lloyd. "Having given away your own bag," he said suavely, "you have perhaps provided yourself with another, have you not?"

"Why, no, I haven't," said Florence Lloyd. "I have been intending to do so, and shall get one shortly, but I haven't yet selected it."

"And in the meantime you have been getting along without any?"

"A gold-mesh bag is not an indispensable article; I have several bags of other styles, and I'm in no especial haste to purchase a new one."

Miss Lloyd's manner had taken on several degrees of hauteur, and her voice was incisive in its tone. Clearly she resented this discussion of her personal belongings, and as she entirely repudiated the ownership of the bag in the coroner's possession, she was annoyed at his questions.

Mr. Monroe looked at her steadily.

"If this is not your bag, Miss Lloyd," he said, with some asperity, "how did it get on Mr. Crawford's desk late last night? The butler has assured me it was not there when he looked in at a little after ten o'clock. Yet this morning it lay there, in plain sight on the desk. Whose bag is it?"

"I have not the slightest idea," said Miss Lloyd firmly; "but, I repeat, it is not mine."

"Easy enough to see the trend of Monroe's questions," said Parmalee in my ear. "If he can prove this bag to be Miss Lloyd's, it shows that she was in the office after ten o'clock last night, and this she has denied."

"Don't you believe her?" said I.

"Indeed I don't. Of course she was there, and of course it's her bag. She put that pretty maid of hers up to deny it, but any one could see the maid was lying, also."

"Oh, come now, Parmalee, that's too bad! You've no right to say such things!"

"Oh, pshaw! you think the same yourself, only you think it isn't chivalrous to put it into words."

Of course what annoyed me in Parmalee's speech was its inherent truth. I didn't believe Florence Lloyd. Much as I wanted to, I couldn't; for the appearance, manner and words of both women were not such as to inspire belief in their hearers.

If she and Elsa were in collusion to deny her ownership of the bag, it would be hard to prove the contrary, for the men-servants could not be supposed to know, and I had no doubt Mrs. Pierce would testify as Miss Lloyd did on any matter.

I was sorry not to put more confidence in the truth of the testimony I was hearing, but I am, perhaps, sceptical by nature. And, too, if Florence Lloyd were in any way implicated in the death of her uncle, I felt pretty sure she would not hesitate at untruth.

Her marvellous magnetism attracted me strongly, but it did not blind me to the strength of her nature. While I could not, as yet, believe her in any way implicated in the death of her uncle, I was fully convinced she knew more concerning it than she had told and I knew, unless forced to, she would not tell what she desired to keep secret.

My sympathy, of course, was with her, but my duty was plain. As a detective, I must investigate fairly, or give up the case.

At this juncture, I knew the point at issue was the presence of Miss Lloyd in the office last night, and the two yellow rose petals I had picked up on the floor might prove a clue.

At any rate it was my duty to investigate the point, so taking a card from my pocket I wrote upon it: "Find out if Miss Lloyd wore any flowers last evening, and what kind."

I passed this over to Mr. Monroe, and rather enjoyed seeing his mystification as he read it.

To my surprise he did not question Florence Lloyd immediately, but turned again to the maid.

"At what time did your mistress go to her room last evening?"

"At about ten o'clock, sir. I was waiting there for her, and so I am sure."

"Did she at once retire?"

"No, sir. She changed her evening gown for a teagown, and then said she would sit up for an hour or so and write letters, and I needn't wait."

"You left her then?"

"Yes, sir."

"Did Miss Lloyd wear any flowers at dinner last evening?"

"No, sir. There were no guests—only the family."

"Ah, quite so. But did she, by chance, pin on any flowers after she went to her room?"

"Why, yes, sir; she did. A box of roses had come for her by a messenger, and when she found them in her room, she pinned one on the lace of her teagown."

"Yes? And what time did the flowers arrive?"

"While Miss Lloyd was at dinner, sir. I took them from the box and put them in water, sir."

"And what sort of flowers were they?"

"Yellow roses, sir."

"That will do, Elsa. You are excused."

The girl looked bewildered, and a little embarrassed as she returned to her place among the other servants, and Miss Lloyd looked a little bewildered also.

But then, for that matter, no body understood the reason for the questions about the flowers, and though most of the jury merely looked preternaturally wise on the subject, Mr. Orville scribbled it all down in his little book. I was now glad to see the man keep up his indefatigable note-taking. If the reporters or stenographers missed any points, I could surely get them from him.

But from the industry with which he wrote, I began to think he must be composing an elaborate thesis on yellow roses and their habits.

Mr. Porter, looking greatly puzzled, observed to the coroner, "I have listened to your inquiries with interest; and I would like to know what, if any, special importance is attached to this subject of yellow roses."

"I'm not able to tell you," replied Mr. Monroe. "I asked these questions at the instigation of another, who doubtless has some good reason for them, which he will explain in due time."

Mr. Porter seemed satisfied with this, and I nodded my head at the coroner, as if bidding him to proceed.

But if I had been surprised before at the all but spoken intelligence which passed between the two servants, Elsa and Louis, I was more amazed now. They shot rapid glances at each other, which were evidently full of meaning to themselves. Elsa was deathly white, her lips trembled, and she looked at the Frenchman as if in terror of her life. But though he glanced at her meaningly, now and then, Louis's anxiety seemed to me to be more for Florence Lloyd than for her maid.

But now the coroner was talking very gravely to Miss Lloyd.

"Do you corroborate," he was saying, "the statements of your maid about the flowers that were sent you last evening?"

"I do," she replied.

"From whom did they come?"

"From Mr. Hall."

"Mr. Hall," said, the coroner, turning toward the young man, "how could you send flowers to Miss Lloyd last evening if you were in New York City?"

"Easily," was the cool reply. "I left Sedgwick on the six o'clock train. On my way to the station I stopped at a florist's and ordered some roses sent to Miss Lloyd. If they did not arrive until she was at dinner, they were not sent immediately, as the florist promised."

"When did you receive them, Miss Lloyd?"

"They were in my room when I went up there at about ten o'clock last evening," she replied, and her face showed her wonderment at these explicit questions.

The coroner's face showed almost as much wonderment, and I said: "Perhaps, Mr. Monroe, I may ask a few questions right here."

"Certainly," he replied.

And thus it was, for the first time in my life, I directly addressed Florence Lloyd.

"When you went up to your room at ten o'clock, the flowers were there?" I asked, and I felt a most uncomfortable pounding at my heart because of the trap I was deliberately laying for her. But it had to be done, and even as I spoke, I experienced a glad realization, that if she were innocent, my questions could do her no harm.

"Yes," she repeated, and for the first time favored me with a look of interest. I doubt if she knew my name or scarcely knew why I was there.

"And you pinned one on your gown?"

"I tucked it in among the laces at my throat, yes."

"Miss Lloyd, do you still persist in saying you did not go down-stairs again, to your uncle's office?"

"I did not," she repeated, but she turned white, and her voice was scarce more than a whisper.

"Then," said I, "how did two petals of a yellow rose happen to be on the floor in the office this morning?"

CHAPTER 7: YELLOW ROSES

If any one expected to see Miss Lloyd faint or collapse at this crisis he must have been disappointed, and as I had confidently expected such a scene, I was completely surprised at her quick recovery of self-possession.

For an instant she had seemed stunned by my question, and her eyes had wandered vaguely round the room, as if in a vain search for help.

Her glance returned to me, and in that instant I gave her an answering look, which, quite involuntarily on my part, meant a grave and serious offer of my best and bravest efforts in her behalf. Disingenuous she might be, untruthful she might be, yes, even a criminal she might be, but in any case I was her sworn ally forever. Not that I meant to defeat the ends of justice, but I was ready to fight for her or with her, until justice should defeat us. Of course she didn't know all this, though I couldn't help hoping she read a little of it as my eyes looked into hers. If so, she recognized it only by a swift withdrawal of her own glance. Again she looked round at her various friends.

Then her eyes rested on Gregory Hall, and, though he gave her no responsive glance, for some reason her poise returned like a flash. It was as if she had been invigorated by a cold douche.

Determination fairly shone in her dark eyes, and her mouth showed a more decided line than I had yet seen in its red curves, as with a cold, almost hard voice she replied,

"I have no idea. We have many flowers in the house, always."

"But I have learned from the servants that there were no other yellow roses in the house yesterday."

Miss Lloyd was not hesitant now. She replied quickly, and it was with an almost eager haste that she said,

"Then I can only imagine that my uncle had some lady visitor in his office late last evening."

The girl's mood had changed utterly; her tone was almost flippant, and more than one of the jurors looked at her in wonderment.

Mr. Porter, especially, cast an her a glance of fatherly solicitude, and I was sure that he felt, as I did, that the strain was becoming too much for her.

"I don't think you quite mean that, Florence," he said; "you and I knew your uncle too well to say such things."

But the girl made no reply, and her beautiful mouth took on a hard line.

"It is not an impossible conjecture," said Philip Crawford thoughtfully. "If the bag does not belong to Florence, what more probable than that it was left by its feminine owner? The same lady might have worn or carried yellow roses."

Perhaps it was because of my own desire to help her that these other men had joined their efforts to mine to ease the way as much as possible.

The coroner looked a little uncomfortable, for he began to note the tide of sympathy turning toward the troubled girl.

"Yellow roses do not necessarily imply a lady visitor," he said, rather more kindly. "A man in evening dress might have worn one."

To his evident surprise, as well as to my own, this remark, intended to be soothing, had quite the opposite effect.

"That is not at all probable," said Miss Lloyd quite angrily. "Mr. Porter was in the office last evening; if he was wearing a yellow rose at the time, let him say so."

"I was not," said Mr. Porter quietly, but looking amazed at the sudden outburst of the girl.

"Of course you weren't!" Miss Lloyd went on, still in the same excited way. "Men don't wear roses nowadays, except perhaps at a ball; and, anyway, the gold bag surely implies that a woman was there!"

"It seems to," said Mr. Monroe; and then, unable longer to keep up her brave resistance, Florence Lloyd fainted.

Mrs. Pierce wrung her hands and moaned in a helpless fashion. Elsa started forward to attend her young mistress, but it was the two neighbors who were jurors, Mr. Hamilton and Mr. Porter, who carried the unconscious girl from the room.

Gregory Hall looked concerned, but made no movement to aid, and I marvelled afresh at such strange actions in a man betrothed to a particularly beautiful woman.

Several women in the audience hurried from the room, and in a few moments the two jurors returned.

"Miss Lloyd will soon be all right, I think," said Mr. Porter to the coroner. "My wife is with her, and one or two other ladies. I think we may proceed with our work here."

There was something about Mr. Lemuel Porter that made men accept his dictum, and without further remark Mr. Monroe called the next witness, Mr. Roswell Randolph, and a tall man, with an intellectual face, came forward.

While the coroner was putting the formal and preliminary questions to Mr. Randolph, Parmalee quietly drew my attention to a whispered conversation going on between Elsa and Louis.

If this girl had fainted instead of Miss Lloyd, I should not have been surprised for she seemed on the very verge of nervous collapse. She seemed, too, to be accusing the man of something, which he vigorously denied. The girl interested me far more than the Frenchman. Though of the simple, rosy-cheeked type of German, she had an air of canniness and subtlety that was at variance with her naive effect. I soon concluded she was far more clever than most people thought, and Parmalee's whispered words showed that he thought so too.

"Something doing in the case of Dutch Elsa, eh?" he said; "she and Johnny Frenchy have cooked up something between them."

"Nothing of any importance, I fancy," I returned, for Miss Lloyd's swoon seemed to me a surrender, and I had little hope now of any other direction in which to look.

But I resumed my attention to the coroner's inquiries of Mr. Randolph.

In answer to a few formal questions, he stated that he had been Mr. Crawford's legal adviser for many years, and had entire charge of all such matters as required legal attention.

"Did you draw up the late Mr. Crawford's will?" asked the coroner.

"Yes; after the death of his wife—about twelve years ago."

"And what were the terms of that will?"

"Except for some minor bequests, the bulk of his fortune was bequeathed to Miss Florence Lloyd."

"Have you changed that will in any way, or drawn a later one?"

"No."

It was by the merest chance that I was looking at Gregory Hall, as the lawyer gave this answer.

It required no fine perception to understand the look of relief and delight that fairly flooded his countenance. To be sure, it was quickly suppressed, and his former mask of indifference and preoccupation assumed, but I knew as well as if he had put it into words, that he had trembled lest Miss Lloyd had been disinherited before her uncle had met his death in the night.

This gave me many new thoughts, but before I could formulate them, I heard the coroner going an with his questions.

"Did Mr. Crawford visit you last evening?"

"Yes; he was at my house for perhaps half an hour or more between eight and nine o'clock."

"Did he refer to the subject of changing his will?"

"He did. That was his errand. He distinctly stated his intention of making a new will, and asked me to come to his office this morning and draw up the instrument."

"But as that cannot now be done, the will in favor of Miss Lloyd still stands?"

"It does," said Mr. Randolph, "and I am glad of it. Miss Lloyd has been brought up to look upon this inheritance as her own, and while I would have used no undue emphasis, I should have tried to dissuade Mr. Crawford from changing his will."

"But before we consider the fortune or the will, we must proceed with our task of bringing to light the murderer, and avenging Mr. Crawford's death."

"I trust you will do so, Mr. Coroner, and that speedily. But I may say, if allowable, that you are on the wrong track when you allow your suspicions to tend towards Florence Lloyd."

"As your opinion, Mr. Randolph, of course that sentiment has some weight, but as a man of law, yourself, you must know that such an opinion must be proved before it can be really conclusive."

"Yes, of course," said Mr. Randolph, with a deep sigh. "But let me beg of you to look further in search of other indications before you press too hard upon Miss Lloyd with the seeming clues you now have."

I liked Mr. Randolph very much. Indeed it seemed to me that the men of West Sedgwick were of a fine class as to both intellect and judgment, and though Coroner Monroe was not a brilliant man, I began to realize that he had some sterling qualities and was distinctly just and fair in his decisions.

As for Gregory Hall, he seemed like a man free from a great anxiety. Though still calm and reserved in appearance, he was less nervous, and quietly awaited further developments. His attitude was not hard to understand. Mr. Crawford had objected to his secretary's engagement to his niece, and now Mr. Crawford's objections could no longer matter. Again, it was not surprising that Mr. Hall should be glad to learn that his fiancee was the heiress she had supposed herself to he. Even though he were marrying the girl simply for love of her, a large fortune in addition was by no means to be despised. At any rate, I concluded that Gregory Hall thought so.

As often happened, Parmalee read my thoughts. "A fortune-hunter," he murmured, with a meaning glance at Hall.

I remembered that Mr. Carstairs, at the inn had said the same thing, and I thoroughly believed it myself.

"Has he any means of his own?"

"No," said Parmalee, "except his salary, which was a good one from Mr. Crawford, but of course he's lost that now."

"I don't feel drawn toward him. I suppose one would call him a gentleman and yet he isn't manly."

"He's a cad," declared Parmalee; "any fortune hunter is a cad, and I despise him."

Although I tried to hold my mind impartially open regarding Mr. Hall, I was conscious of an inclination to despise him myself. But I was also honest enough to realize that my principal reason for despising him was because he had won the hand of Florence Lloyd.

I heard Coroner Monroe draw a long sigh.

Clearly, the man was becoming more and more apprehensive, and really dreaded to go on with the proceedings, because he was fearful of what might be disclosed thereby.

The gold bag still lay on the table before him; the yellow rose petals were not yet satisfactorily accounted for; Miss Lloyd's agitation and sudden loss of consciousness, though not surprising in the circumstances, were a point in her disfavor. And now the revelation that Mr. Crawford was actually on the point of disinheriting his niece made it impossible to ignore the obvious connection between that fact and the event of the night.

But no one had put the thought into words, and none seemed inclined to.

Mechanically, Mr. Monroe called the next witness on his list, and Mrs. Pierce answered.

For some reason she chose to stand during her interview, and as she rose, I realized that she was a prim little personage, but of such a decided nature that she might have been stigmatized by the term stubborn. I had seen such women before; of a certain soft, outward effect, apparently pliable and amenable, but in reality, deep, shrewd and clever.

And yet she was not strong, for the situation in which she found herself made her trembling and unstrung.

When asked by the coroner to tell her own story of the events of the evening before, she begged that he would question her instead.

Desirous of making it as easy for her as possible, Mr. Monroe acceded to her wishes, and put his questions in a kindly and conversational tone.

"You were at dinner last night, with Miss Lloyd and Mr. Crawford?"

"Yes," was the almost inaudible reply, and Mrs. Pierce seemed about to break down at the sad recollection.

"You heard the argument between Mr. Crawford and his niece at the dinner table?"

"Yes."

"This resulted in high words on both sides?"

"Well, I don't know exactly what you mean by high words. Mr. Crawford rarely lost his temper and Florence never."

"What then did Mr. Crawford say in regard to disinheriting Miss Lloyd?"

"Mr. Crawford said clearly, but without recourse to what may be called high words, that unless Florence would consent to break her engagement he would cut her off with a shilling."

"Did he use that expression?"

"He did at first, when he was speaking more lightly; then when Florence refused to do as he wished he said he would go that very evening to Mr. Randolph's and have a new will made which should disinherit Florence, except for a small annuity."

"And what did Miss Lloyd reply to this threat?" asked the coroner.

"She said," replied Mrs. Pierce, in her plaintive tones, "that her uncle might do as he chose about that; but she would never give up Mr. Hall."

At this moment Gregory Hall looked more manly than I had yet seen him.

Though he modestly dropped his eyes at this tacit tribute to his worthiness, yet he squared his shoulders, and showed a justifiable pride in the love thus evinced for him.

"Was the subject discussed further?" pursued the coroner.

"No; nothing more was said about it after that."

"Will the making of a new will by Mr. Crawfard affect yourself in any way, Mrs. Pierce?"

"No," she replied, "Mr. Crawford left me a small bequest in his earlier will and I had reason to think he would do the same in a later will, even though he changed his intentions regarding Florence."

"Miss Lloyd thoroughly believed that he intended to carry out his threat last evening?"

"She didn't say so to me, but Mr. Crawford spoke so decidedly on the matter, that I think both she and I believed he was really going to carry out his threat at last."

"When Mr. Crawford left the house, did you and Miss Lloyd know where he was going?"

"We knew no more than he had said at the table. He said nothing when he went away."

"How did you and Miss Lloyd spend the remainder of the evening?"

"It was but a short evening. We sat in the music-room for a time, but at about ten o'clock we both went up to our rooms."

"Had Mr. Crawford returned then?"

"Yes, he came in perhaps an hour earlier. We heard him come in at the front door, and go at once to his office."

"You did not see him, or speak to him?"

"We did not. He had a caller during the evening. It was Mr. Porter, I have since learned."

"Did Miss Lloyd express no interest as to whether he had changed his will or not?"

"Miss Lloyd didn't mention the will, or her engagement, to me at all. We talked entirely of other matters."

"Was Miss Lloyd in her usual mood or spirits?"

"She seemed a little quiet, but not at all what you might call worried."

"Was not this strange when she was fully expecting to be deprived of her entire fortune?"

"It was not strange for Miss Lloyd. She rarely talks of her own affairs. We spent an evening similar in all respects to our usual evening when we do not have guests."

"And you both went upstairs at ten. Was that unusually early for you?"

"Well, unless we have guests, we often go at ten or half-past ten."

"And did you see Miss Lloyd again that night?"

"Yes; about half an hour later, I went to her room for a book I wanted."

"Miss Lloyd had not retired?"

"No; she asked me to sit down for awhile and chat."

"Did you do so?"

"Only for a few moments. I was interested in the book I had come for, and I wanted to take it away to my own room to read."

"And Miss Lloyd, then, did not seem dispirited or in any way in an unusual mood?"

"Not that I noticed. I wasn't quizzing her or looking into her eyes to see what her thoughts were, for it didn't occur to me to do so. I knew her uncle had dealt her a severe blow, but as she didn't open the subject, of course I couldn't discuss it with her. But I did think perhaps she wanted to be by herself to consider the matter, and that was one reason why I didn't stay and chat as she had asked me to."

"Perhaps she really wanted to discuss the matter with you."

"Perhaps she did; but in that case she should have said so. Florence knows well enough that I am always ready to discuss or sympathize with her in any matter, but I never obtrude my opinions. So as she said nothing to lead me to think she wanted to talk to me especially, I said good-night to her."

CHAPTER 8: FURTHER INQUIRY

"Did you happen to notice, Mrs. Pierce, whether Miss Lloyd was wearing a yellow rose when you saw her in her room?"

Mrs. Pierce hesitated. She looked decidedly embarrassed, and seemed disinclined to answer. But she might have known that to hesitate and show embarrassment was almost equivalent to an affirmative answer to the coroner's question. At last she replied,

"I don't know; I didn't notice."

This might have been a true statement, but I think no one in the room believed it. The coroner tried again.

"Try to think, Mrs. Pierce. It is important that we should know if Miss Lloyd was wearing a yellow rose."

"Yes," flared out Mrs. Pierce angrily, "so that you can prove she went down to her uncle's office later and dropped a piece of her rose there! But I tell you I don't remember whether she was wearing a rose or not, and it wouldn't matter if she had on forty roses! If Florence Lloyd says she didn't go down-stairs, she didn't."

"I think we all believe in Miss Lloyd's veracity," said Mr. Monroe, "but it is necessary to discover where those rose petals in the library came from. You saw the flowers in her room, Mrs. Pierce?"

"Yes, I believe I did. But I paid no attention to them, as Florence nearly always has flowers in her room."

"Would you have heard Miss Lloyd if she had gone down-stairs after you left her?"

"I don't know," said Mrs. Pierce, doubtfully.

"Is your room next to hers?"

"No, not next."

"Is it on the same corridor?"

"No."

"Around a corner?"

"Yes."

"And at some distance?"

"Yes." Mrs. Pierce's answers became more hesitating as she saw the drift of Mr. Monroe's questions. Clearly, she was trying to shield Florence, if necessary, at the expense of actual truthfulness.

"Then," went on Mr. Monroe, inexorably, "I understand you to say that you think you would have heard Miss Lloyd, had she gone down-stairs, although your room is at a distance and around a corner and the hall and stairs are thickly carpeted. Unless you were listening especially, Mrs. Pierce, I think you would scarcely have heard her descend."

"Well, as she didn't go down, of course I didn't hear her," snapped Mrs. Pierce, with the feminine way of settling an argument by an unprovable statement.

Mr. Monroe began on another tack.

"When you went to Miss Lloyd's room," he said, "was the maid, Elsa, there?"

"Miss Lloyd had just dismissed her for the night."

"What was Miss Lloyd doing when you went to her room?"

"She was looking over some gowns that she proposed sending to the cleaner's."

The coroner fairly jumped. He remembered the newspaper clipping of a cleaner's advertisement, which was even now in the gold bag before him. Though all the jurors had seen it, it had not been referred to in the presence of the women.

Recovering himself at once, he said quietly "Was not that rather work for Miss Lloyd's maid?"

"Oh, Elsa would pack and send them, of course," said Mrs. Pierce carelessly. "Miss Lloyd was merely deciding which ones needed cleaning."

"Do you know where they were to be sent?"

Mrs. Pierce looked a little surprised at this question.

"Miss Lloyd always sends her things to Carter & Brown's," she said.

Now, Carter & Brown was the firm name on the advertisement, and it was evident at once that the coroner considered this a damaging admission.

He sat looking greatly troubled, but before he spoke again, Mr. Parmalee made an observation that decidedly raised that young man in my estimation.

"Well," he said, "that's pretty good proof that the gold bag doesn't belong to Miss Lloyd."

"How so?" asked the coroner, who had thought quite the contrary.

"Why, if Miss Lloyd always sends her goods to be cleaned to Carter & Brown, why would she need to cut their address from a newspaper and save it?"

At first I thought the young man's deduction distinctly clever, but on second thought I wasn't so sure. Miss Lloyd might have wanted that address for a dozen good reasons. To my mind, it proved neither her ownership of the gold bag, nor the contrary.

In fact, I thought the most important indication that the bag might be hers lay in the story Elsa told about the cousin who sailed to Germany. Somehow that sounded untrue to me, but I was more than willing to believe it if I could.

I longed for Fleming Stone, who, I felt sure, could learn from the bag and its contents the whole truth about the crime and the criminal.

But I had been called to take charge of the case, and my pride forbade me to call on any one for help.

I had scorned deductions from inanimate objects, but I resolved to study that bag again, and study it more minutely. Perhaps there were some threads or shreds caught in its meshes that might point to its owner. I remembered a detective story I read once, in which the whole discovery of the criminal depended on identifying a few dark blue woollen threads which were found in a small pool of candle grease on a veranda roof. As it turned

out, they were from the trouser knee of a man who had
knelt there to open a window. The patent absurdity of
leaving threads from one's trouser knee, amused me very
much, but the accommodating criminals in fiction almost
always leave threads or shreds behind them. And surely a
gold-mesh bag, with its thousands of links would be a fine
trap to catch some threads of evidence, however minute
they might be.

Furthermore I decided to probe further into that
yellow rose business. I was not at all sure that those
petals I found on the floor had anything to do with Miss
Lloyd's roses, but it must be a question possible of
settlement, if I went about it in the right way. At any
rate, though I had definite work ahead of me, my duty
just now was to listen to the forthcoming evidence,
though I could not help thinking I could have put
questions more to the point than Mr. Monroe did.

Of course the coroner's inquest was not formally
conducted as a trial by jury would be, and so any one
spoke, if he chose, and the coroner seemed really glad
when suggestions were offered him.

At this point Philip Crawford rose.

"It is impossible," he said, "not to see whither these
questions are tending. But you are on the wrong tack, Mr.
Coroner. No matter how evidence may seem to point
toward Florence Lloyd's association with this crime, it is
only seeming. That gold bag might have been hers and it
might not. But if she says it isn't, why, then it isn't!
Notwithstanding the state of affairs between my brother
and his niece, there is not the shadow of a possibility that
the young woman is implicated in the slightest degree,
and the sooner you leave her name out of consideration,
and turn your search into other channels, the sooner you
will find the real criminal."

It was not so much the words of Philip Crawford, as
the sincere way in which they were spoken, that
impressed me. Surely he was right; surely this beautiful
girl was neither principal nor accessory in the awful

crime which, by a strange coincidence, gave to her her fortune and her lover.

"Mr. Crawford's right," said Lemuel Porter. "If this jury allows itself to be misled by a gold purse and two petals of a yellow rose, we are unworthy to sit on this case. Why, Mr. Coroner, the long French windows in the office were open, or, at least, unfastened all through the night. We have that from the butler's testimony. He didn't lock them last night; they were found unlocked this morning. Therefore, I hold that an intruder, either man or woman, may have come in during the night, accomplished the fatal deed, and departed without any one being the wiser. That this intruder was a woman, is evidenced by the bag she left behind her. For, as Mr. Crawford has said, if Miss Lloyd denies the ownership of that bag, it is not hers."

After all, these declarations were proof, of a sort. If Mr. Porter and Mr. Philip Crawford, who had known Florence Lloyd for years, spoke thus positively of her innocence, it could not be doubted.

And then the voice of Parmalee again sounded in my ears.

"Of course Mr. Porter and Mr. Crawford would stand up for Miss Lloyd; it would be strange if they didn't. And of course, Mrs. Pierce will do all she can to divert suspicion. But the evidences are against her."

"They only seem to be," I corrected. "Until we prove the gold bag and the yellow rose to be hers; there is no evidence against her at all."

"She also had motive and opportunity. Those two points are of quite as much importance as evidence."

"She had motive and opportunity," I agreed, "but they were not exclusive. As Mr. Porter pointed out, the open windows gave opportunity that was world wide; and as to motive, how are we to know who had or who hadn't it."

"You're right, I suppose. Perhaps I am too positive of Miss Lloyd's implication in the matter, but I'm quite willing to be convinced to the contrary."

The remarks of Mr. Parmalee were of course not audible to any one save myself. But the speeches which had been made by Mr. Crawford and Mr. Porter, and which, strange to say, amounted to an arraignment and a vindication almost in the same breath, had a decided effect upon the assembly.

Mrs. Pierce began to weep silently. Gregory Hall looked startled, as if the mere idea of Miss Lloyd's implication was a new thought to him. Lawyer Randolph looked considerably disturbed, and I at once suspected that his legal mind would not allow him to place too much dependence on the statements of the girl's sympathetic friends.

Mr. Hamilton, another of the jurors whom I liked, seemed to be thoughtfully weighing the evidence. He was not so well acquainted with Miss Lloyd as the two men who had just spoken in her behalf, and he made a remark somewhat diffidently.

"I agree," he said, "with the sentiments just expressed; but I also think that we should endeavor to find some further clues or evidence. Had Mr. Crawford any enemies who would come at night to kill him? Or are there any valuables missing? Could robbery have been the motive?"

"It does not seem so," replied the coroner. "Nothing is known to be missing. Mr. Crawford's watch and pocket money were not disturbed."

"The absence of the weapon is a strange factor in the case," put in Mr. Orville, apparently desirous of having his voice heard as well as those of the other jurors.

"Yes," agreed Mr. Monroe; "and yet it is not strange that the criminal carried away with him what might have been a proof of his identity."

"Does Miss Lloyd own a pistol?" blurted out Mr. Parmalee.

Gregory Hall gave him an indignant look, but Coroner Monroe seemed rather glad to have the question raised— probably so that it could be settle at once in the negative.

And it was.

"No," replied Mrs. Pierce, when the query was put to her. "Both Florence and I are desperately afraid of firearms. We wouldn't dream of owning a pistol—either of us."

Of course, this was significant, but in no way decisive. Granting that Miss Lloyd could have been the criminal, it would have been possible for her secretly to procure a revolver, and secretly to dispose of it afterward. Then, too, a small revolver had been used. To be sure, this did not necessarily imply that a woman had used it, but, taken in connection with the bag and the rose petals, it gave food for thought.

But the coroner seemed to think Mrs. Pierce's assertions greatly in Miss Lloyd's favor, and, being at the end of his list of witnesses, he inquired if any one else in the room knew of anything that could throw light on the matter.

No one responded to this invitation, and the coroner then directed the jury to retire to find a verdict. The six men passed into another room, and I think no one who awaited their return apprehended any other result than the somewhat unsatisfactory one of "person or persons unknown."

And this was what the foreman announced when the jury returned after their short collocation.

Then, as a jury, they were dismissed, but from that moment the mystery of Joseph Crawford's death became the absorbing thought of all West Sedgwick.

"The murderer of my brother shall be found and brought to justice!" declared Philip Crawford, and all present seemed to echo his vow.

Then and there, Mr. Crawford retained Lawyer Randolph to help him in running down the villain, and, turning to me, asked to engage my services also.

To this, I readily agreed, for I greatly desired to go on with the matter, and cared little whether I worked for an individual or for the State.

Of course Mr. Crawford's determination to find the murderer proved anew his conviction that Florence Lloyd was above all suspicion, but in the face of certain details of the evidence so far, I could not feel so absolutely certain of this.

However, it was my business to follow up every clue, or apparent clue, and every bit of evidence, and this I made up my mind to do, regardless of consequences.

I confess it was difficult for me to feel regardless of consequences, for I had a haunting fear that the future was going to look dark for Florence Lloyd. And if it should be proved that she was in any way responsible for or accessory to this crime, I knew I should wish I had had nothing to do with discovering that fact. But back of this was an undefined but insistent conviction that the girl was innocent, and that I could prove it. This may have been an inordinate faith in my own powers, or it may have been a hope born of my admiration for the young woman herself. For there is no doubt, that for the first time in my life I was taking a serious interest in a woman's personality. Heretofore I had been a general admirer of womankind, and I had naturally treated them all with chivalry and respect. But now I had met one whom I desired to treat in a far tenderer way, and to my chagrin I realized that I had no right to entertain such thoughts toward a girl already betrothed.

So I concluded to try my best to leave Florence Lloyd's personality out of the question, to leave my feelings toward her out of the question, and to devote my energies to real work on the case and prove by intelligent effort that I could learn facts from evidence without resorting to the microscopic methods of Fleming Stone. I purposely ignored the fact that I would have been only too glad to use these methods had I the power to do so!

CHAPTER 9: THE TWELFTH ROSE

For the next day or two the Crawford house presented the appearance usual in any home during the days immediately preceding a funeral.

By tacit consent, all reference to the violence of Mr. Crawford's death was avoided, and a rigorous formality was the keynote of all the ceremonies. The servants were garbed in correct mourning, the ladies of the house refused to see anybody, and all personal callers were met by Philip Crawford or his wife, while business acquaintances were received by Gregory Hall.

As private secretary, of course Mr. Hall was in full charge of Mr. Crawford's papers and personal effects. But, in addition to this, as the prospective husband of the heiress, he was practically the head of the house.

He showed no elation or ostentation at this state of affairs, but carried himself with an air of quiet dignity, tinged with a suggestion of sadness, which, if merely conventional, seemed none the less sincere.

I soon learned that the whole social atmosphere of West Sedgwick was one of extreme formality, and everything was done in accordance with the most approved conventions. Therefore, I found I could get no chance for a personal conversation with Miss Lloyd until after the funeral.

I had, however, more or less talk with Gregory Hall, and as I became acquainted with him, I liked him less.

He was of a cold and calculating disposition, and when we were alone, he did not hesitate to gloat openly over his bright prospects.

"Terrible thing, to be put out of existence like that," he said, as we sat in Mr. Crawford's office, looking over some papers; "but it solved a big problem for Florence and me. However, we'll be married as soon as we decently can, and then we'll go abroad, and forget the tragic part of it all."

"I suppose you haven't a glimmer of a suspicion as to who did it," I ventured.

"No, I haven't. Not the faintest notion. But I wish you could find out. Of course, nobody holds up that bag business as against Florence, but—it's uncomfortable all the same. I wish I'd been here that night. I'm 'most sure I'd have heard a shot, or something."

"Where were you?" I said, in a careless tone.

Hall drew himself up stiffly. "Excuse me," he said. "I declined to answer that question before. Since I was not in West Sedgwick, it can matter to no one where I was."

"Oh, that's all right," I returned affably, for I had no desire to get his ill will. "But of course we detectives have to ask questions. By the way, where did you buy Miss Lloyd's yellow roses?"

"See here," said Gregory Hall, with a petulant expression, "I don't want to be questioned. I'm not on the witness-stand, and, as I've told you, I'm uncomfortable already about these so-called `clues' that seem to implicate Miss Lloyd. So, if you please, I'll say nothing."

"All right," I responded, "just as you like."

I went away from the house, thinking how foolish people could be. I could easily discover where he bought the roses, as there were only three florists' shops in West Sedgwick and I resolved to go at once to hunt up the florist who sold them.

Assuming he would naturally go to the shop nearest the railroad station, and which was also on the way from the Crawford house, I went there first, and found my assumption correct.

The florist was more than willing to talk on the subject.

"Yes, sir," he said; "I sold those roses to Mr. Hall— sold 'em to him myself. He wanted something extra nice, and I had just a dozen of those big yellow beauties. No, I don't raise my own flowers. I get 'em from the city. And so I had just that dozen, and I sent 'em right up. Well, there was some delay, for two of my boys were out to supper, and I waited for one to get back."

"And you had no other roses just like these in stock?"

"No, sir. Hadn't had for a week or more. Haven't any now. May not get any more at all. They're a scarce sort, at best, and specially so this year."

"And you sent Miss Lloyd the whole dozen?"

"Yes, sir; twelve. I like to put in an extra one or two when I can, but that time I couldn't. There wasn't another rose like them short of New York City."

I thanked the florist, and, guessing that he was not above it, I gave him a more material token of my gratitude for his information, and then walked slowly back to my room at the inn.

Since there were no other roses of that sort in West Sedgwick that evening, it seemed to me as if Florence Lloyd must have gone down to her uncle's office after having pinned the blossom on her bodice. The only other possibility was that some intruder had entered by way of the French window wearing or carrying a similar flower, and that this intruder had come from New York, or at least from some place other than West Sedgwick. It was too absurd. Murderers don't go about decked with flowers, and yet at midnight a man in evening dress was not impossible, and evening dress might easily imply a boutonniere.

Well, this well-dressed man I had conjured up in my mind must have come from out of town, or else whence the flower, after all?

And then I bethought myself of that late newspaper. An extra, printed probably as late as eleven o'clock at night, must have been brought out to West Sedgwick by a traveller on some late train. Why not Gregory Hall, himself? I let my imagination run riot for a minute. Mr. Hall refused to say where he was on the night of the murder. Why not assume that he had come out from New

York, in evening dress, at or about midnight? This would account for the newspaper and the yellow rose petals, for, if he bought a boutonniere in the city, how probable he would select the same flower he had just sent his fiancee.

I rather fancied the idea of Gregory Hall as the criminal. He had the same motive as Miss Lloyd. He knew of her uncle's objection to their union, and his threat of disinheritance. How easy for him to come out late from New York, on a night when he was not expected, and remove forever the obstacle to his future happiness!

I drew myself up with a start. This was not detective work. This was mere idle speculation. I must shake it off, and set about collecting some real evidence.

But the thought still clung to me; mere speculation it might be, but it was founded on the same facts that already threw suspicion on Florence Lloyd. With the exception of the gold bag—and that she disclaimed—such evidence as I knew of pointed toward Mr. Hall as well as toward Miss Lloyd.

However at present I was on the trail of those roses, and I determined to follow that trail to a definite end. I went back to the Crawford house and as I did not like to ask for Miss Lloyd, I asked for Mrs. Pierce.

She came down to the drawing room, and greeted me rather more cordially than I had dared to hope. I had a feeling that both ladies resented my presence there, for so many women have a prejudice against detectives.

But though nervous and agitated, Mrs. Pierce spoke to me kindly.

"Did you want to see me for anything in particular, Mr. Burroughs?" she asked.

"Yes, I do, Mrs. Pierce," I replied; "I may as well tell you frankly that I want to find out all I can about those yellow roses."

"Oh, those roses! Shall I never hear the last of them? I assure you, Mr. Burroughs, they're of no importance whatever."

"That is not for you to decide," I said quietly, and I began to see that perhaps a dictatorial attitude might be the best way to manage this lady. "Are the rest of those flowers still in Miss Lloyd's room? If so I wish to see them."

"I don't know whether they are or not; but I will find out, and if so I'll bring them down."

"No," I said, "I will go with you to see them."

"But Florence may be in her room."

"So much the better. She can tell me anything I wish to know."

"Oh, please don't interview her! I'm sure she wouldn't want to talk with you."

"Very well, then ask her to vacate the room, and I will go there with you now."

Mrs. Pierce went away, and I began to wonder if I had gone too far or had overstepped my authority. But it was surely my duty to learn all I could about Florence Lloyd, and what so promising of suggestions as her own room?

Mrs. Pierce returned in a few moments, and affably enough she asked me to accompany her to Miss Lloyd's room.

I did so, and after entering devoted my whole attention to the bunch of yellow roses, which in a glass vase stood on the window seat. Although somewhat wilted, they were still beautiful, and without the slightest doubt were the kind of rose from which the two tell-tale petals had fallen.

Acting upon a sudden thought, I counted them. There were nine, each one seemingly with its full complement of petals, though of this I could not be perfectly certain.

"Now, Mrs.—Pierce," I said, turning to her with an air of authority which was becoming difficult to maintain, "where are the roses which Miss Lloyd admits having pinned to her gown?"

"Mercy! I don't know," exclaimed Mrs. Pierce, looking bewildered. "I suppose she threw them away."

"I suppose she did," I returned; "would she not be likely to throw them in the waste basket?"

"She might," returned Mrs. Pierce, turning toward an ornate affair of wicker-work and pink ribbons.

Sure enough, in the basket, among a few scraps of paper, were two exceedingly withered yellow roses. I picked them out and examined them, but in their present state it was impossible to tell whether they had lost any petals or not, so I threw them back in the basket.

Mrs. Pierce seemed to care nothing for evidence or deduction in the matter, but began to lament the carelessness of the chambermaid who had not emptied the waste basket the day before.

But I secretly blessed the delinquent servant, and began pondering on this new development of the rose question. The nine roses in the vase and the two in the basket made but eleven, and the florist had told me that he had sent a dozen. Where was the twelfth?

The thought occurred to me that Miss Lloyd might have put away one as a sentimental souvenir, but to my mind she did not seem the kind of a girl to do that. I knew my reasoning was absurd, for what man can predicate what a woman will do? but at the same time I could not seem to imagine the statuesque, imperial Miss Lloyd tenderly preserving a rose that her lover had given her.

But might not Gregory Hall have taken one of the dozen for himself before sending the rest? This was merely surmise, but it was a possibility, and at any rate the twelfth rose was not in Miss Lloyd's room.

Therefore the twelfth rose was a factor to be reckoned with, a bit of evidence to be found; and I determined to find it.

I asked Mrs. Pierce to arrange for me an interview with Miss Lloyd, but the elder lady seemed doubtful.

"I'm quite sure she won't see you," she said, "for she has declared she will see no one until after the funeral. But if you want me to ask her anything for you, I will do so."

"Very well," I said, surprised at her willingness; "please ask Miss Lloyd if she knows what became of the twelfth yellow rose; and beg her to appreciate the fact that it is a vital point in the case."

Mrs. Pierce agreed to do this, and as I went down the stairs she promised to join me in the library a few moments later.

She kept her promise, and I waited eagerly her report.

"Miss Lloyd bids me tell you," she said, "that she knows nothing of what you call the twelfth rose. She did not count the roses, she merely took two of them to pin on her dress, and when she retired, she carelessly threw those two in the waste basket. She thinks it probable there were only eleven in the box when it arrived. But at any rate she knows nothing more of the matter."

I thanked Mrs. Pierce for her courtesy and patience, and feeling that I now had a real problem to consider, I started back to the inn.

It could not be that this rose matter was of no importance. For the florist had assured me he had sold exactly twelve flowers to Mr. Gregory Hall, and of these, I could account for only eleven. The twelfth rose must have been separated from the others, either by Mr. Hall, at the time of purchase, or by some one else later. If the petals found on the floor fell from that twelfth rose, and if Florence Lloyd spoke the truth when she declared she knew nothing of it, then she was free from suspicion in that direction.

But until I could make some further effort to find out about the missing rose I concluded to say nothing of it to anybody. I was not bound to tell Parmalee any points I might discover, for though colleagues, we were working independently of each other.

But as I was anxious to gather any side lights possible, I determined to go for a short conference with the district attorney, in whose hands the case had been put after the coroner's inquest.

He was a man named Goodrich, a quiet mannered, untalkative person, and as might be expected he had made little or no progress as yet.

He said nothing could be done until after the funeral and the reading of the will, which ceremonies would occur the next afternoon.

I talked but little to Mr. Goodrich, yet I soon discovered that he strongly suspected Miss Lloyd of the crime, either as principal or accessory.

"But I can't believe it," I objected. "A girl, delicately brought up, in refined and luxurious surroundings, does not deliberately commit an atrocious crime."

"A woman thwarted in her love affair will do almost anything," declared Mr. Goodrich. "I have had more experience than you, my boy, and I advise you not to bank too much on the refined and luxurious surroundings. Sometimes such things foster crime instead of preventing it. But the truth will come out, and soon, I think. The evidence that seems to point to Miss Lloyd can be easily proved or disproved, once we get at the work in earnest. That coroner's jury was made up of men who were friends and neighbors of Mr. Crawford. They were so prejudiced by sympathy for Miss Lloyd, and indignation at the unknown criminal, that they couldn't give unbiased judgment. But we will yet see justice done. If Miss Lloyd is innocent, we can prove it. But remember the provocation she was under. Remember the opportunity she had, to visit her uncle alone in his office, after every one else in the house was asleep. Remember that she had a motive—a strong motive—and no one else had."

"Except Mr. Gregory Hall," I said meaningly.

"Yes; I grant he had the same motive. But he is known to have left town at six that evening, and did not return until nearly noon the next day. That lets him out."

"Yes, unless he came back at midnight, and then went back to the city again."

"Nonsense!" said Mr. Goodrich. "That's fanciful. Why, the latest train—the theatre train, as we call it—gets in at one o'clock, and it's always full of our society people returning from gayeties in New York. He would have been seen had he come on that train, and there is no later one."

I didn't stay to discuss the matter further. Indeed, Mr. Goodrich had made me feel that my theories were fanciful.

But whatever my theories might be there were still facts to be investigated.

Remembering my determination to examine that gold bag more thoroughly I asked Mr. Goodrich to let me see it, for of course, as district attorney, it was now in his possession.

He gave it to me with an approving nod. "That's the way to work," he said. "That bag is your evidence. Now from that, you detectives must go ahead and learn the truth."

"Whose bag is it?" I said, with the intention of drawing him out.

"It's Miss Lloyd's bag," he said gravely. "Any woman in the world would deny its ownership, in the existing circumstances, and I am not surprised that she did so. Nor do I blame her for doing so. Self preservation is a mighty strong impulse in the human heart, and we've all got a right to obey it."

As I took the gold bag from his hand, I didn't in the least believe that Florence Lloyd was the owner of it, and I resolved anew to prove this to the satisfaction of everybody concerned.

Mr. Goodrich turned away and busied himself about other matters, and I devoted myself to deep study.

The contents of the bag proved as blank and unsuggestive as ever. The most exhaustive examination of its chain, its clasp and its thousands of links gave me not the tiniest thread or shred of any sort.

But as I poked and pried around in its lining I found a card, which had slipped between the main lining and an inside pocket.

I drew it out as carefully as I could, and it proved to be a small plain visiting card bearing the engraved name, "Mrs. Egerton Purvis."

I sat staring at it, and then furtively glanced at Mr. Goodrich. He was not observing me, and I instinctively felt that I did not wish him to know of the card until I myself had given the matter further thought.

I returned the card to its hiding place and returned the bag to Mr. Goodrich, after which I went away.

I had not copied the name, for it was indelibly photographed upon my brain. As I walked along the street I tried to construct the personality of Mrs. Egerton Purvis from her card. But I was able to make no rational deductions, except that the name sounded aristocratic, and was quite in keeping with the general effect of the bag and its contents.

To be sure I might have deduced that she was a lady of average height and size, because she wore a number six glove; that she was careful of her personal appearance, because she possessed a vanity case; that she was of tidy habits, because she evidently expected to send her gowns to be cleaned. But all these things seemed to me puerile and even ridiculous, as such characteristics would apply to thousands of woman all over the country.

Instead of this, I went straight to the telegraph office and wired to headquarters in a cipher code. I instructed them to learn the identity and whereabouts of Mrs. Egerton Purvis, and advise me as soon as possible.

Then I returned to the Sedgwick Arms, feeling decidedly well satisfied with my morning's work, and content to wait until after Mr. Crawford's funeral to do any further real work in the matter.

CHAPTER 10: THE WILL

I went to the Crawford house on the day of the funeral; but as I reached there somewhat earlier than the hour appointed, I went into the office with the idea of looking about for further clues.

In the office I found Gregory Hall; looking decidedly disturbed.

"I can't find Mr. Crawford's will," he said, as he successively looked through one drawer after another.

"What!" I responded. "Hasn't that been located already?"

"No; it's this way: I didn't see it here in this office, or in the New York office, so I assumed Mr. Randolph had it in his possession. But it seems he thought it was here, all the time. Only this morning we discovered our mutual error, and Mr. Randolph concluded it must be in Mr. Crawford's safety deposit box at the bank in New York. So Mr. Philip Crawford hurried through his administration papers—he is to be executor of the estate—and went in to get it from the bank. But he has just returned with the word that it wasn't there. So we've no idea where it is."

"Oh, well," said I, "since he hadn't yet made the new will he had in mind, everything belongs to Miss Lloyd."

"That's just the point," said Hall, his face taking on a despairing look. "If we don't find that will, she gets nothing!"

"How's that?" I said.

"Why, she's really not related to the Crawfords. She's a niece of Joseph Crawford's wife. So in the absence of a will his property will all go to his brother Philip, who is his legal heir."

"Oho!" I exclaimed. "This is a new development. But the will will turn up."

"Oh, yes, I'm sure of it," returned Hall, but his anxious face showed anything but confidence in his own words.

"But," I went on, "didn't Philip Crawford object to his brother's giving all his fortune to Miss Lloyd?"

"It didn't matter if he did. Nobody could move Joseph Crawford's determination. And I fancy Philip didn't make any great disturbance about it. Of course, Mr. Joseph had a right to do as he chose with his own, and the will gave Philip a nice little sum, any way. Not much, compared to the whole fortune, but, still, a generous bequest."

"What does Mr. Randolph say?"

"He's completely baffled. He doesn't know what to think."

"Can it have been stolen?"

"Why, no; who would steal it? I only fear he may have destroyed it because he expected to make a different one. In that case, Florence is penniless, save for such bounty as Philip Crawford chooses to bestow on her."

I didn't like the tone in which Hall said this. It was distinctly aggrieved, and gave the impression that Florence Lloyd, penniless, was of far less importance than Miss Lloyd, the heiress of her uncle's millions.

"But he would doubtless provide properly for her," I said.

"Oh, yes, properly. But she would find herself in a very different position, dependent on his generosity, from what she would be as sole heir to her uncle's fortune."

I looked steadily at the man. Although not well acquainted with him, I couldn't resist giving expression to my thought.

"But since you are to marry her," I said, "she need not long be dependent upon her uncle's charity."

"Philip Crawford isn't really her uncle, and no one can say what he will do in the matter."

Gregory Hall was evidently greatly disturbed at the new situation brought about by the disappearance of Mr. Crawford's will. But apparently the main reason for his disturbance was the impending poverty of his fiancee. There was no doubt that Mr. Carstairs and others who had called this man a fortune-hunter had judged him rightly.

However, without further words on the subject, I waited while Hall locked the door of the office, and then we went together to the great drawing-room, where the funeral services were about to take place.

I purposely selected a position from which I could see the faces of the group of people most nearly connected with the dead man. I had a strange feeling, as I looked at them, that one of them might be the instrument of the crime which had brought about this funeral occasion.

During the services I looked closely and in turn at each face, but beyond the natural emotions of grief which might be expected, I could read nothing more.

The brother, Philip Crawford, the near neighbors, Mr. Porter and Mr. Hamilton, the lawyer, Mr. Randolph, all sat looking grave and solemn as they heard the last words spoken above their dead friend. The ladies of the household, quietly controlling their emotions, sat near me, and next to Florence Lloyd Gregory Hall had seated himself.

All of these people I watched closely, half hoping that some inadvertent sign might tell me of someone's knowledge of the secret. But when the clergyman referred to the retribution that would sooner or later overtake the criminal. I could see an expression of fear or apprehension on no face save that of Florence Lloyd. She turned even whiter than before, her pale lips compressed in a straight line, and her small black gloved hand softly crept into that of Gregory Hall. The movement was not generally noticeable, but it seemed to me pathetic above all things. Whatever her position in the matter, she was surely appealing to him for help and protection.

Without directly repulsing her, Hall was far from responsive. He allowed her hand to rest in his own but gave her no answering pressure, and looked distinctly relieved when, after a moment, she withdrew it.

I saw that Parmalee also had observed this, and I could see that to him it was an indication of the girl's perturbed spirit. To me it seemed that it might equally well mean many other things. For instance it might mean her apprehension for Gregory Hall, who, I couldn't help thinking was far more likely to be a wrongdoer than the girl herself.

With a little sigh I gave up trying to glean much information from the present opportunity, and contented myself with the melancholy pleasure it gave me simply to look at the sad sweet face of the girl who was already enshrined in my heart.

After the solemn and rather elaborate obsequies were over, a little assembly gathered in the library to hear the reading of the will.

As, until then, no one had known of the disappearance of the will, except the lawyer and the secretary, it came as a thunderbolt.

"I have no explanation to offer," said Mr. Randolph, looking greatly concerned, but free of all personal responsibility. "Mr. Crawford always kept the will in his own possession. When he came to see me, the last evening he was alive, in regard to making a new will, he did not bring the old one with him. We arranged to meet in his office the next morning to draw up the new instrument, when he doubtless expected to destroy the old one.

"He may have destroyed it on his return home that evening. I do not know. But so far it has not been found among his papers in either of his offices or in the bank. Of course it may appear, as the search, though thorough, has not yet been exhaustive. We will, therefore, hold the matter in abeyance a few days, hoping to find the missing document."

His hearers were variously affected by this news. Florence Lloyd was simply dazed. She could not seem to grasp a situation which so suddenly changed her prospects. For she well knew that in the event of no will being found, Joseph Crawford's brother would be his rightful heir, and she would be legally entitled to nothing at all.

Philip Crawford sat with an utterly expressionless face. Quite able to control his emotion, if he felt any, he made no sign that he welcomed this possibility of a great fortune unexpectedly coming to him.

Lemuel Porter, who, with his wife, had remained because of their close friendship with the family, spoke out rather abruptly,

"Find it! Of course it must be found! It's absurd to think the man destroyed one will before the other was drawn."

"I agree with you," said Philip Crawford.

"Joseph was very methodical in his habits, and, besides, I doubt if he would really have changed his will. I think he merely threatened it, to see if Florence persisted in keeping her engagement."

This was a generous speech on the part of Philip Crawford. To be sure, generosity of speech couldn't affect the disposal of the estate. If no will were found, it must by law go to the brother, but none the less the hearty, whole-souled way in which he spoke of Miss Lloyd was greatly to his credit as a man.

"I think so, too," agreed Mr. Porter. "As you know, I called on Mr. Joseph Crawford during the—the last evening of his life."

The speaker paused, and indeed it must have been a sad remembrance that pictured itself to his mind.

"Did he then refer to the matter of the will?" asked Mr. Randolph, in gentle tones.

"He did. Little was said on the subject, but he told me that unless Florence consented to his wishes in the matter of her engagement to Mr. Hall, he would make a new will, leaving her only a small bequest."

"In what manner did you respond, Mr. Porter?"

"I didn't presume to advise him definitely, but I urged him not to be too hard on the girl, and, at any rate, not to make a new will until he had thought it over more deliberately."

"What did he then say?"

"Nothing of any definite import. He began talking of other matters, and the will was not again referred to. But I can't help thinking he had not destroyed it."

At this, Miss Lloyd seemed about to speak, but, glancing at Gregory Hall, she gave a little sigh, and remained silent.

"You know of nothing that can throw any light on the matter of the will, Mr. Hall?" asked Mr. Randolph.

"No, sir. Of course this whole situation is very embarrassing for me. I can only say that I have known for a long time the terms of Mr. Crawford's existing will; I have known of his threats of changing it; I have known of his attitude toward my engagement to his niece. But I never spoke to him on any of these subjects, nor he to me, though several times I have thought he was on the point of doing so. I have had access to most of his private papers, but of two or three small boxes he always retained the keys. I had no curiosity concerning the contents of these boxes, but I naturally assumed his will was in one of them. I have, however, opened these boxes since Mr. Crawford's death, in company with Mr. Randolph, and we found no will. Nor could we discover any in the New York office or in the bank. That is all I know of the matter."

Gregory Hall's demeanor was dignified and calm, his voice even and, indeed, cold. He was like a bystander, with no vital interest in the subject he talked about.

Knowing, as I did, that his interest was vital, I came to the conclusion that he was a man of unusual self-control, and an ability to mask his real feelings completely. Feeling that nothing more could be learned at present, I left the group in the library discussing the loss of the will, and went down to the district attorney's office.

He was, of course, surprised at my news, and agreed with me that it gave us new fields for conjecture.

"Now, we see," he said eagerly, "that the motive for the murder was the theft of the will."

"Not necessarily," I replied. "Mr. Crawford may have destroyed the will before he met his death."

"But that would leave no motive. No, the will supplies the motive. Now, you see, this frees Miss Lloyd from suspicion. She would have no reason to kill her uncle and then destroy or suppress a will in her own favor."

"That reasoning also frees Mr. Hall from suspicion," said I, reverting to my former theories.

"Yes, it does. We must look for the one who has benefited by the removal of the will. That, of course, would be the brother, Mr. Philip Crawford."

I looked at the attorney a moment, and then burst into laughter.

"My dear Mr. Goodrich," I said, "don't be absurd! A man would hardly shoot his own brother, but aside from that, why should Philip Crawford kill Joseph just at the moment he is about to make a new will in Philip's favor? Either the destruction of the old will or the drawing of the new would result in Philip's falling heir to the fortune. So he would hardly precipitate matters by a criminal act. And, too, if he had been keen about the money, he could have urged his brother to disinherit Florence Lloyd, and Joseph would have willingly done so. He was on the very point of doing so, any way."

"That's true," said Mr. Goodrich, looking chagrined but unconvinced. "However, it frees Miss Lloyd from all doubts, by removing her motive. As you say, she wouldn't suppress a will in her favor, and thereby turn the fortune over to Philip. And, as you also said, this lets Gregory Hall out, too, though I never suspected him for a moment.

But, of course, his interests and Miss Lloyd's are identical."

"Wait a moment," I said, for new thoughts were rapidly following one another through my brain. "Not so fast, Mr. District Attorney. The disappearance of the will does not remove motive from the possibility of Miss Lloyd's complicity in this crime—or Mr. Hall's either."

"How so?"

"Because, if Florence Lloyd thought her uncle was in possession of that will, her motive was identically the same as if he had possessed it. Now, she certainly thought he had it, for her surprise at the news of its loss was as unfeigned as my own. And of course Hall thought the will was among Mr. Crawford's effects, for he has been searching constantly since the question was raised."

"But I thought that yesterday you were so sure of Miss Lloyd's innocence," objected Mr. Goodrich.

"I was," I said slowly, "and I think I am still. But in the light of absolute evidence I am only declaring that the non-appearance of that will in no way interferes with the motive Miss Lloyd must have had if she is in any way guilty. She knew, or thought she knew, that the will was there, in her favor. She knew her uncle intended to revoke it and make another in her disfavor. I do not accuse her—I'm not sure I suspect her—I only say she had motive and opportunity."

As I walked away from Mr. Goodrich's office, those words rang in my mind, motive and opportunity. Truly they applied to Mr. Hall as well as to Miss Lloyd, although of course it would mean Hall's coming out from the city and returning during the night. And though this might have been a difficult thing to do secretly, it was by no means impossible. He might not have come all the way to West Sedgwick Station, but might have dropped off the train earlier and taken the trolley. The trolley! that thought reminded me of the transfer I had picked up on the grass plot near the office veranda. Was it possible that slip of paper was a clue, and pointing toward Hall?

Without definite hope of seeing Gregory Hall, but hopeful of learning something about him, I strolled back to the Crawford house. I went directly to the office, and by good luck found Gregory Hall there alone. He was still searching among the papers of Mr. Crawford's desk.

"Ah, Mr. Burroughs," he said, as I entered, "I'm glad to see you. If detectives detect, you have a fine chance here to do a bit of good work. I wouldn't mind offering you an honorarium myself, if you could unearth the will that has so mysteriously disappeared."

Hall's whole manner had changed. He had laid aside entirely the grave demeanor which he had shown at the funeral, and was again the alert business man. He was more than this. He was eager,—offensively so,—in his search for the will. It needed no detective instinct to see that the fortune of Joseph Crawford and its bestowment were matters of vital interest to him.

But though his personal feelings on the subject might be distasteful to me, it was certainly part of my duty to aid in the search, and so with him I looked through the various drawers and filing cabinets. The papers representing or connected with the financial interests of the late millionaire were neatly filed and labelled; but in some parts of the desk we found the hodge-podge of personal odds and ends which accumulates with nearly everybody.

Hall seemed little interested in those, but to my mind they showed a possibility of casting some light on Mr. Crawford's personal affairs.

But among old letters, photographs, programs, newspaper clippings, and such things, there was nothing that seemed of the slightest interest, until at last I chanced upon a photograph that arrested my attention.

"Do you know who this is?" I inquired.

"No," returned Hall, with a careless glance at it; "a friend of Mr. Crawford's, I suppose."

"More than a friend, I should judge," and I turned the back of the picture toward him. Across it was written, "with loving Christmas greetings, from M.S.P."; and it was dated as recently as the Christmas previous.

"Well," said Hall, "Mr. Crawford may have had a lady friend who cared enough about him to send an affectionate greeting, but I never heard of her before, and I doubt if she is in any way responsible for the disappearance of this will."

He went on searching through the desks, giving no serious heed to the photograph. But to me it seemed important. I alone knew of the visiting card in the gold bag. I alone knew that that bag belonged to a lady named Purvis. And here was a photograph initialed by a lady whose surname began with P, and who was unmistakably on affectionate terms with Mr. Crawford. To my mind the links began to form a chain; the lady who had sent her photograph at Christmas, and who had left her gold bag in Mr. Crawford's office the night he was killed, surely was a lady to be questioned.

But I had not yet had a reply to my telegram to headquarters, so I said nothing to Hall on this subject, and putting the photograph in my pocket continued to assist him to look for the will, but without success. However, the discovery of the photograph had in a measure diverted my suspicions from Gregory Hall; and though I endeavored to draw him into general conversation, I did not ask him any definite questions about himself.

But the more I talked with him, the more I disliked him: He not only showed a mercenary, fortune-hunting spirit, but he showed himself in many ways devoid of the finer feelings and chivalrous nature that ought to belong to the man about to marry such a perfect flower of womanhood as Florence Lloyd.

CHAPTER 11: LOUIS'S STORY

After spending an evening in thinking over the situation and piecing together my clues, I decided that the next thing to be done was to trace up that transfer. If I could fasten that upon Gregory Hall, it would indeed be a starting point to work from. Although this seemed to eliminate Mrs. Purvis, who had already become a living entity in my mind, I still had haunting suspicions of Hall; and then, too, there was a possibility of collusion between these two. It might be fanciful, but if Hall and the Purvis woman were both implicated, Hall was quite enough a clever villain to treat the photograph lightly as he had done.

And so the next morning, I started for the office of the trolley car company.

I learned without difficulty that the transfer I had found, must have been given to some passenger the night of Mr. Crawford's death, but was not used. It had been issued after nine o'clock in the evening, somewhere on the line between New York and West Sedgwick. It was a transfer which entitled a passenger on that line to a trip on the branch line running through West Sedgwick, and the fact that it had not been used, implied either a negligent conductor or a decision on the part of the passenger not to take his intended ride.

All this was plausible, though a far from definite indication that Hall might have come out from New York by trolley, or part way by trolley, and though accepting a transfer on the West Sedgwick branch, had concluded not to use it. But the whole theory pointed equally as well to Mrs. Purvis, or indeed to the unknown intruder insisted upon by so many. I endeavored to learn something from certain conductors who brought their cars into West

Sedgwick late at night, but it seemed they carried a great many passengers and of course could not identify a transfer, of which scores of duplicates had been issued.

Without much hope I interviewed the conductors of the West Sedgwick Branch Line. Though I could learn nothing definite, I fell into conversation with one of them, a young Irishman, who was interested because of my connection with the mystery.

"No, sir," he said, "I can't tell you anythin' about a stray transfer. But one thing I can tell you. That 'ere murder was committed of a Toosday night, wasn't it?"

"Yes," I returned.

"Well, that 'ere parlyvoo vally of Mr. Crawford's, he's rid, on my car 'most every Toosday night fer weeks and weeks. It's his night off. And last Toosday night he didn't ride with me. Now I don't know's that means anything, but agin it might."

It didn't seem to me that it meant much, for certainly Louis was not under the slightest suspicion. And yet as I came to think about it, if that had been Louis's transfer and if he had dropped it near the office veranda, he had lied when he said that he went round the other side of the house to reach the back entrance.

It was all very vague, but it narrowed itself down to the point that if that were Louis's transfer it could be proved; and if not it must be investigated further. For a trolley transfer, issued at a definite hour, and dropped just outside the scene of the crime was certainly a clue of importance.

I proceeded to the Crawford house, and though I intended to have a talk with Louis later, I asked first for Miss Lloyd. Surely, if I were to carry on my investigation of the case, in her interests, I must have a talk with her. I had not intruded before, but now that the funeral was over, the real work of tracking the criminal must be commenced, and as one of the principal characters in the sad drama, Miss Lloyd must play her part.

Until I found myself in her presence I had not actually realized how much I wanted this interview.

I was sure that what she said, her manner and her facial expression, must either blot out or strengthen whatever shreds of suspicion I held against her.

"Miss Lloyd," I began, "I am, as you know, a detective; and I am here in Sedgwick for the purpose of discovering the cowardly assassin of your uncle. I assume that you wish to aid me in any way you can. Am I right in this?"

Instead of the unhesitating affirmative I had expected, the girl spoke irresolutely. "Yes," she said, "but I fear I cannot help you, as I know nothing about it."

The fact that this reply did not sound to me as a rebuff, for which it was doubtless intended, I can only account for by my growing appreciation of her wonderful beauty.

Instead of funereal black, Miss Lloyd was clad all in white, and her simple wool gown gave her a statuesque appearance; which, however, was contradicted by the pathetic weariness in her face and the sad droop of her lovely mouth. Her helplessness appealed to me, and, though she assumed an air of composure, I well knew it was only assumed, and that with some difficulty.

Resolving to make it as easy as possible for her, I did not ask her to repeat the main facts, which I already knew.

"Then, Miss Lloyd," I said, in response to her disclaimer, "if you cannot help me, perhaps I can help you. I have reason to think that possibly Louis, your late uncle's valet, did not tell the truth in his testimony at the coroner's inquest. I have reason to think that instead of going around the house to the back entrance as he described, he went around the other side, thus passing your uncle's office."

To my surprise this information affected Miss Lloyd much more seriously than I supposed it would.

"What?" she said, and her voice was a frightened whisper. "What time did he come home?"

"I don't know," I replied; "but you surely don't suspect Louis of anything wrong. I was merely hoping, that if he did pass the office he might have looked in, and so could tell us of your uncle's well-being at that time."

"At what time?"

"At whatever time he returned home. Presumably rather late. But since you are interested in the matter, will you not call Louis and let us question him together?"

The girl fairly shuddered at this suggestion. She hesitated, and for a moment was unable to speak. Of course this behavior on her part filled my soul with awful apprehension. Could it be possible that she and Louis were in collusion, and that she dreaded the Frenchman's disclosures? I remembered the strange looks he had cast at her while being questioned by the coroner. I remembered his vehement denial of having passed the office that evening,—too vehement, it now seemed to me. However, if I were to learn anything damaging to Florence Lloyd's integrity, I would rather learn it now, in her presence, than elsewhere. So I again asked her to send for the valet.

With a despairing look, as of one forced to meet an impending fate, she rose, crossed the room and rang a bell. Then she returned to her seat and said quietly, "You may ask the man such questions as you wish, Mr. Burroughs, but I beg you will not include me in the conversation."

"Not unless it should be necessary," I replied coldly, for I did not at all like her making this stipulation. To me it savored of a sort of cowardice, or at least a presumption on my own chivalry.

When the man appeared, I saw at a glance he was quite as much agitated as Miss Lloyd. There was no longer a possibility of a doubt that these two knew something, had some secret in common, which bore directly on the case, and which must be exposed. A sudden hope flashed into my mind that it might be only some trifling secret, which seemed of importance to them, but which was merely a side issue of the great question.

I considered myself justified in taking advantage of the man's perturbation, and without preliminary speech I drew the transfer from my pocket and fairly flashed it in his face.

"Louis," I said sternly, "you dropped this transfer when you came home the night of Mr. Crawford's death."

The suddenness of my remark had the effect I desired, and fairly frightened the truth out of the man.

"Y-yes, sir," he stammered, and then with a frightened glance at Miss Lloyd, he stood nervously interlacing his fingers.

I glanced at Miss Lloyd myself, but she had regained entire self-possession, and sat looking straight before her with an air that seemed to say, "Go on, I'm prepared for the worst."

As I paused myself to contemplate the attitudes of the two, I lost my ground of vantage, for when I again spoke to the man, he too was more composed and ready to reply with caution. Doubtless he was influenced by Miss Lloyd's demeanor, for he imitatively assumed a receptive air.

"Where did you get the transfer?" I went on.

"On the trolley, sir; the main line."

"To be used on the Branch Line through West Sedgwick?"

"Yes, sir."

"Why did you not use it?"

"As I tell you, sir, and as I tell monsieur, the coroner, I have spend that evening with a young lady. We went for a trolley ride, and as we returned I take a transfer for myself, but not for her, as she live near where we alight."

"Oh, you left the main line and took the young lady home, intending then yourself to come by trolley through West Sedgwick?"

"Yes, sir; it was just that way."

At this point Louis seemed to forget his embarrassment, his gaze strayed away, and a happy expression came into his eyes. I felt sure I was reading his volatile French nature aright, when I assumed his mind had turned back to the pleasant evening he had spent with his young lady acquaintance. Somehow this went far to convince me of the fellow's innocence for it was quite evident the murder and its mystery were not uppermost in his thoughts at that moment. But my next question brought him beck to realization of the present situation.

"And why didn't you use your transfer?"

"Only that the night, he was so pleasant, I desired to walk."

"And so you walked through the village, holding, perhaps, the transfer in your hand?"

"I think, yes; but I do not remember the transfer in my hand, though he may have been there."

And now the man's unquiet had returned. His lips twitched and his dark eyes rolled about, as he endeavored in vain to look anywhere but at Miss Lloyd. She, too, was controlling herself by a visible effort.

Anxious to bring the matter to a crisis, I said at once, and directly:

"And then you entered the gates of this place, you walked to the house, you walked around the house to the back by way of the path which leads around by the library veranda, and you accidentally dropped your transfer near the veranda step."

I spoke quietly enough, but Louis immediately burst into voluble denial.

"No, no!" he exclaimed; "I do not go round by the office, I go the other side of the house. I have tell you so many times."

"But I myself picked up your transfer near the office veranda."

"Then he blow there. The wind blow that night, oh, something fearful! He blow the paper around the house, I think."

"I don't think so," I retorted; "I think you went around the house that way, I think you paused at the office window—"

Just here I made a dramatic pause myself, hoping thus to appeal to the emotional nature of my victim. And I succeeded. Louis almost shrieked as he pressed his hands against his eyes, and cried out: "No! no! I tell you I did not go round that way! I go round the other way, and the wind—the wind, he blow my transfer all about!"

I tried a more quiet manner, I tried persuasive arguments, I finally resorted to severity and even threats, but no admission could I get from Louis, except that he had not gone round the house by way of the office. I was positive the man was lying, and I was equally positive that Miss Lloyd knew he was lying, and that she knew why, but the matter seemed to me at a deadlock. I could have questioned her, but I preferred to do that when Louis was not present. If she must suffer ignominy it need not be before a servant. So I dismissed Louis, perhaps rather curtly, and turning to Miss Lloyd, I asked her if she believed his assertion that he did not pass by the office that night.

"I don't know what I believe," she answered, wearily drawing her hand across her brow. "And I can't see that it matters anyway. Supposing he did go by the office, you certainly don't suspect him of my uncle's murder, do you?"

"It is my duty, Miss Lloyd," I said gently, for the girl was pitiably nervous, "to get the testimony of any one who was in or near the office that night. But of course testimony is useless unless it is true."

I looked her straight in the eyes as I said this, for I was thoroughly convinced that her own testimony at the inquest had not been entirely true.

I think she understood my glance, for she arose at once, and said with extreme dignity: "I cannot see any necessity for prolonging this interview, Mr. Burroughs. It is of course your work to discover the truth or falsity of Louis's story, but I cannot see that it in any way implicates or even interests me."

The girl was superb. Her beauty was enhanced by the sudden spirit she showed, and her flashing dark eyes suggested a baited animal at bay. Apparently she had reached the limit of her endurance, and was unwilling to be questioned further or drawn into further admissions. And yet, some inexplicable idea came to me that she was angry, not with me, but with the tangle in which I had remorselessly enmeshed her. Of a high order of intelligence, she knew perfectly well that I was conscious of the fact that there was a secret of some sort between her and the valet. Her haughty disdain, I felt sure, was to convey the impression that though there might be a secret between them, it was no collusion or working together, and that though her understanding with the man was mysterious, it was in no way beneath her dignity. Her imperious air as she quietly left the room thrilled me anew, and I began to think that a woman who could assume the haughty demeanor of an empress might have chosen, as empresses had done before her, to commit crime.

However, she went away, and the dark and stately library seemed to have lost its only spot of light and charm. I sat for a few minutes pondering over it all, when I saw passing through the hall, the maid, Elsa. It suddenly occurred to me, that having failed with the mistress of the house, I might succeed better with her maid, so I called the girl in.

She came willingly enough, and though she seemed timid, she was not embarrassed or afraid.

"I'm in authority here," I said, "and I'm going to ask you some questions, which you must answer truthfully."

"Yes, sir," she said, without any show of interest.

"Have you been with Miss Lloyd long?"

"Yes, sir; about four years, sir."

"Is she a kind mistress?"

"Indeed she is, sir. She is the loveliest lady I ever worked for. I'd do anything for Miss Lloyd, that I would."

"Well, perhaps you can best serve her by telling all you know about the events of Tuesday night."

"But I don't know anything, sir," and Elsa's eyes opened wide in absolutely unfeigned wonderment.

"Nothing about the actual murder; no, of course not. But I just want you to tell me a few things about some minor matters. Did you take the yellow flowers from the box that was sent to Miss Lloyd?"

"Yes, sir; I always untie her parcels. And as she was at dinner, I arranged the flowers in a vase of water."

"How many flowers were there?"

For some reason this simple query disturbed the girl greatly. She flushed scarlet, and then she turned pale. She twisted the corner of her apron in her nervous fingers, and then said, only half audibly, "I don't know, sir."

"Oh, yes, you do, Elsa," I said in kindly tones, being anxious not to frighten her; "tell me how many there were. Were there not a dozen?"

"I don't know, sir; truly I don't. I didn't count them at all."

It was impossible to disbelieve her; she was plainly telling the truth. And, too, why should she count the roses? The natural thing would be not to count them, but merely to put them in the vase as she had said. And yet, there was something about those flowers that Elsa knew and wouldn't tell. Could it be that I was on the track of that missing twelfth rose? I knew, though perhaps Elsa did not, how many roses the florist had sent in that box. And unless Gregory Hall had abstracted one at the time of his purchase, the twelfth rose had been taken by some one else after the flowers reached the Crawford House. Could it have been Elsa, and was her perturbation only because of a guilty conscience over a petty theft of a flower? But I realized I must question her adroitly if I would find out these things.

"Is Miss Lloyd fond of flowers?" I asked, casually.

"Oh, yes, sir, she always has some by her."

"And do you love flowers too, Elsa?"

"Yes, sir." But the quietly spoken answer, accompanied by a natural and straightforward look promised little for my new theory.

"Does Miss Lloyd sometimes give you some of her flowers?"

"Oh, yes, sir, quite often."

"That is, if she's there when they arrive. But if she isn't there, and you open the box yourself, she wouldn't mind if you took one or two blossoms, would she?"

"Oh, no, sir, she wouldn't mind. Miss Lloyd's awful kind about such things. But I wouldn't often do it, sir."

"No; of course not. But you did happen to take one of those yellow roses, didn't you, though?"

I breathlessly awaited the answer, but to my surprise, instead of embarrassment the girl's eyes flashed with anger, though she answered quietly enough, "Well, yes, I did, sir."

Ah, at last I was on the trail of that twelfth rose! But from the frank way in which the girl admitted having taken the flower, I greatly feared that the trail would lead to a commonplace ending.

"What did you do with it?" I said quietly, endeavoring to make the question sound of little importance.

"I don't want to tell you;" and the pout on her scarlet lips seemed more like that of a wilful child than of one guarding a guilty secret.

"Oh, yes, tell me, Elsa;" and I even descended to a coaxing tone, to win the girl's confidence.

"Well, I gave it to that Louis."

"To Louis? and why do you call him that Louis?"

"Oh, because. I gave him the flower to wear because I thought he was going to take me out that evening. He had promised he would, at least he had sort of promised, and then,—and then—"

"And then he took another young lady," I finished for her in tones of such sympathy and indignation that she seemed to think she had found a friend.

"Yes," she said, "he went and took another girl riding on the trolley, after he had said he would take me."

"Elsa," I said suddenly, and I fear she thought I had lost interest in her broken heart, "did Louis wear that rose you gave him that night?"

"Yes, the horrid man! I saw it in his coat when he went away."

"And did he wear it home again?"

"How should I know?" Elsa tossed her head with what was meant to be a haughty air, but which was belied by the blush that mantled her cheek at her own prevarication.

"But you do know," I insisted, gently; "did he wear it when he came home?"

"Yes, he did."

"How do you know?"

"Because I looked in his room the next day, and I saw it there all withered. He had thrown it on the floor!"

The tragedy in Elsa's eyes at this awful relation of the cruelty of the sterner sex called for a spoken sympathy, and I said at once, and heartily: "That was horrid of him! If I were you I'd never give him another flower."

In accordance with the natural impulses of her sex, Elsa seemed pleased at my disapproval of Louis's behavior, but she by no means looked as if she would never again bestow her favor upon him. She smiled and tossed her head, and seemed willing enough for further conversation, but for the moment I felt that I had enough food for thought. So I dismissed Elsa, having first admonished her not to repeat our conversation to any one. In order to make sure that I should be obeyed in this matter, I threatened her with some unknown terrors which the law would bring upon her if she disobeyed me.

When I felt sure she was thoroughly frightened into secrecy concerning our interview, I sent her away and began to cogitate on what she had told me.

If Louis came to the house late that night, as by his own admission he did; if he went around the house on the side of the office, as the straying transfer seemed to me to prove; and if, at the time, he was wearing in his coat a yellow rose with petals similar to those found on the office floor the next morning, was not one justified in looking more deeply into the record of Louis the valet?

CHAPTER 12: LOUIS'S CONFESSION

Elsa had been gone but a few moments when Florence Lloyd returned to the library. I arose to greet her and marvelled at the change which had come over her. Surely here was a girl of a thousand moods. She had left me with an effect of hauteur and disdain; she returned, gentle and charming, almost humble. I could not understand it, and remained standing after she had seated herself, awaiting developments.

"Sit down, Mr. Burroughs," she said, and her low, sweet voice seemed full of cordial invitation. "I'm afraid I was rude to you, when I went away just now; and I want to say that if I can tell you anything you wish to know, I should be glad to do so."

I drew up a chair and seated myself near her. My heart was pounding with excitement at this new phase of the girl's nature. For an instant it seemed as if she must have a personal kindly feeling toward me, and then my reason returned, and with a suddenly falling heart and slowing pulses, I realized that I was a fool, and that after thinking over the disclosures Louis had made, Miss Lloyd had shrewdly concluded it was to her best advantage to curry favor with the detective. This knowledge came to me instinctively, and so I distrusted her gentle voice and winning smile, and hardening my heart against her, I resolved to turn this new mood of hers to my own advantage, and learn what I could while she was willing to converse:

"I'm glad of this opportunity, Miss Lloyd," I said, "for there are some phases of this affair that I want to discuss with you alone. Let us talk the matter over quietly. It is as well that you should know that there are some doubts felt as to the entire truth of the story you told at the inquest. I do not say this to frighten you," I added, as the poor girl clasped her hands and gave me a look of dumb alarm; "but, since it is so, I want to do all I can to set the matter right. Do you remember exactly all that took place, to your knowledge, on the night of your uncle's death?"

"Yes," she replied, looking more frightened still. It was evident that she knew more than she had yet revealed, but I almost forgot my inquiry, so absorbed was I in watching her lovely face. It was even more exquisite in its terrified pallor than when the fleeting pink showed in her cheeks.

"Then," I said, "let us go over it. You heard your uncle go out at about eight o'clock and return about nine?"

"Yes, I heard the front door open and close both times."

"You and Mrs. Pierce being in the music-room, of course. Then, later, you heard a visitor enter, and again you heard him leave?"

"Yes—Mr. Porter."

"Did you know it was Mr. Porter, at the time he was here?"

"No; I think not. I didn't think at all who it might be. Uncle Joseph often had men to call in the evening."

"About what time did Mr. Porter leave?"

"A few minutes before ten. I heard Lambert say, `Good-night, sir,' as he closed the door after him."

"And soon after, you and Mrs. Pierce went upstairs?"

"Yes; only a few minutes after."

"And, later, Mrs. Pierce came to your room?"

"Yes; about half-past ten, I should say; she came to get a book. She didn't stay two minutes."

"And after that, you went down-stairs again to speak to your uncle?" For the merest instant Miss Lloyd's eyes closed and she swayed as if about to faint, but she regained her composure at once, and answered with some asperity,

"I did not. I have told you that I did not leave my room again that night."

Her dark eyes blazed, her cheeks flushed, and though her full lower lip quivered it was with anger now, not fear.

As I watched her, I wondered how I could have thought her more beautiful when pale. Surely with this glowing color she was at her glorious best.

"Then when did you drop the two rose petals there?" I went on, calmly enough, though my own heart was beating fast.

"I did not drop them. They were left there by some intruder."

"But, Miss Lloyd," and I observed her closely, "the petals were from a rose such as those Mr. Hall sent you that evening. The florist assures me there were no more such blossoms in West Sedgwick at that time. The fallen petals, then, were from one of your own roses, or—"

"Or?" asked Miss Lloyd, her hands pressed against the laces at her throbbing bosom. "Or?"

"Or," I went on, "from a rose worn by some one who had come out from New York on a late train."

For the moment I chose to ignore Louis's rose for I wanted to learn anything Miss Lloyd could tell me. And, too, the yellow petals might have fallen from a flower in Hall's coat after all. I thought it possible by suggesting this idea, to surprise from her some hint as to whether she had any suspicion of him.

She gave a gasp, and, leaning back in her chair, she closed her eyes, as if spent with a useless struggle.

"Wait a moment," she said, putting out her hand with an imploring gesture. "Wait a moment. Let me think. I will tell you all, but—wait—"

With her eyes still closed, she lay back against the satin chair cushion, and I gazed at her, fascinated.

I knew it! Then and there the knowledge came to me! Not her guilt, not her innocence. The crime seemed far away then, but I knew like a flash not only that I loved this girl, this Florence Lloyd, but that I should never love any one else. It mattered not that she was betrothed to another man; the love that had suddenly sprung to life in my heart was such pure devotion that it asked no return. Guilty or innocent, I loved her. Guilty or innocent, I would clear her; and if the desire of her heart were toward another, she should ever know or suspect my adoration for her.

I gazed at her lovely face, knowing that when her eyes opened I must discreetly turn my glance aside, but blessing every instant of opportunity thus given me.

Her countenance, though troubled and drawn with anxiety, was so pure and sweet that I felt sure of her innocence. But it should be my work to prove that to the world.

Suddenly her eyes flashed open; again her mood had changed.

"Mr. Burroughs," she said, and there was almost a challenge in her tone, "why do you ask me these things? You are a detective, you are here to find out for yourself, not to ask others to find out. I am innocent of my uncle's death, of course, but when you cast suspicion on the man to whom I am betrothed, you cannot expect me to help you confirm that suspicion. You have made me think by your remark about a man on a late train that you refer to Mr. Hall. Do you?"

This was a change of base, indeed. I was being questioned instead of doing the catechising myself. Very well; if it were my lady's will to challenge me, I would meet her on her own ground.

"You took the hint very quickly," I said. "Had you thought of such a possibility before?"

"No, nor do I now. I will not." Again she was the offended queen. "But since you have breathed the suggestion, you may not count on any help from me."

"Could you have helped me otherwise?" I said, detaining her as she swept by.

To this she made no answer, but again her face wore a troubled expression, and as she went slowly from the room, she left me with a strong conviction that she knew far more about Gregory Hall's connection with the matter than she had told me.

I sat alone for a few moments wondering what I had better do next.

I had about decided to go in search of Parmalee, and talk things over with him, but I thought it would be better to see Louis first, and settle up the matter of his rose more definitely. Accordingly I rang the bell, and when the parlor maid answered it, I asked her to send both Louis and Elsa to me in the library.

I could see at once that these two were not friendly toward each other, and I hoped this fact would aid me in learning the truth from them.

"Now, Louis," I began, "you may as well tell me the truth about your home coming last Tuesday night. In the first place, you must admit that you were wearing in your coat one of the yellow roses which had been sent to Miss Lloyd."

"No, no, indeed!" declared Louis, giving Elsa a threatening glance, as if forbidding her to contradict him.

"Nonsense, man," I said; "don't stand there and tell useless lies. It will not help you. The best thing you can do for yourself and for all concerned is to tell the truth. And, moreover, if you don't tell it to me now, you will have to tell it to Mr. Goodrich, later. Elsa gave you a yellow rose and you wore it away that evening when you went to see your young lady. Now what became of that rose?"

"I—I lost it, sir."

"No, you didn't lose it. You wore it home again, and when you retired, you threw it on the floor, in your own room."

"No, sir. You make mistake. I look for him next day in my room, but cannot find him."

I almost laughed at the man's ingenuousness. He contradicted his own story so unconsciously, that I began to think he was more of a simpleton than a villain.

"Of course you couldn't find it," I informed him, "for it was taken from your room next day; and of course you didn't look for it until after you had heard yellow roses discussed at the inquest."

Louis's easily read face proved my statement correct, but he glowered at Elsa, as he said: "Who take him away? who take my rose from my room."

"But you denied having a rose, Louis. Now you're asking who took it away. Once again, let me advise you to tell the truth. You're not at all successful in telling falsehoods. Now answer me this: When you came home Tuesday night, did you or did you not walk around the house past the office window?"

"No, sir. I walked around the other side. I—"

"Stop, Louis! You're not telling the truth. You did walk around by the office, and you dropped your transfer there. It never blew all around the house, as you have said it did."

A look of dogged obstinacy came into the man's eyes, but he did not look at me. He shifted his gaze uneasily, as he repeated almost in a singsong way, "go round the other side of the house."

It was a sort of deadlock. Without a witness to the fact, I could not prove that he had gone by the office windows, though I was sure he had.

But help came from an unexpected quarter.

Elsa had been very quiet during the foregoing conversation, but now she spoke up suddenly, and said: "He did go round by the office, Mr. Burroughs, and I saw him."

I half expected to see Louis turn on the girl in a rage, but the effect of her speech on him was quite the reverse. He almost collapsed; he trembled and turned white, and though he tried to speak, he made no sound. Surely this man was too cowardly for a criminal; but I must learn the secret of his knowledge.

"Tell me about it, Elsa," I said, quietly.

"I was looking out at my window, sir, at the back of the house; and I saw Louis come around the house, and he came around by the office side."

"You're positive of this, Elsa? you would swear to it? Remember, you are making an important assertion."

"I am telling the truth, sir. I saw him plainly as he came around and entered at the back door."

"You hear, Louis?" I said sternly. "I believe Elsa's statement rather than yours, for she tells a straight story, while you are rattled and agitated, and have all the appearance of concealing something."

Louis looked helpless. He didn't dare deny Elsa's story, but he would not confirm it. At last he said, with a glance of hatred at the girl, "Elsa, she tell that story to make the trouble for me."

There was something in this. Elsa, I knew, was jealous, and her pride had been hurt because Louis had taken the rose she gave him, and then had gone to call on another girl. But I had no reason to doubt Elsa's statement, and I had every reason to doubt Louis's. I tried to imagine what Louis's experience had really been, and it suddenly occurred to me, that though innocent himself of real wrong, he had seen something in the office, or through the office windows that he wished to keep secret. I did not for a moment believe that the man had killed his master, so I concluded he was endeavoring to shield someone else.

"Louis," I said, suddenly, "I'll tell you what you did. You went around by the office, you saw a light there late at night, and you naturally looked in. You saw Mr. Crawford there, and he was perhaps already killed. You stepped inside and discovered this, and then you came away, and said nothing about it, lest you yourself be suspected of the crime. Incidentally you dropped two petals from the rose Elsa had given you."

Louis's answer to this accusation was a perfect storm of denials, expressed in voluble French and broken English, but all to the effect that it was not true, and that if he had seen his master dead, he would have raised an alarm.

I saw that I had not yet struck the right idea, so I tried again. "Then, Louis, you must have passed the office before Mr. Crawford was killed, which is really more probable. Then as you passed the window, you saw something or someone in the office, and you're not willing to tell about it. Is this it?"

This again brought forth only incoherent denial, and I could see that the man was becoming so rattled, it was difficult for him to speak clearly, had he desired to do so.

"Elsa," I said, suddenly, "you took that rose from Louis's room. What did you do with it?"

"I kept,—I mean, I don't know what I did with it," stammered the girl, blushing rosy red, and looking shyly at Louis.

I felt sorry to disclose the poor girl's little romance, for it was easy enough to see that she was in love with the fickle Frenchman, who evidently did not reciprocate her interest. He looked at her disdainfully, and she presented a pathetic picture of embarrassment.

But the situation was too serious for me to consider Elsa's sentiments, and I said, rather sternly: "You do know where it is. You preserved that rose as a souvenir. Go at once and fetch it."

It was a chance shot, for I was not at all certain that she had kept the withered flower, but dominated by my superior will she went away at once. She returned in a moment with the flower.

Although withered, it was still in fairly good condition; quite enough so for me to see at a glance that no petals had been detached from it. The green calyx leaves clung around the bud in such a manner as to prove positively that the unfolding flower had lost no petal. This settled the twelfth rose. Wherever those tell-tale petals had come from, they were not from Louis's rose. I gave the flower back to Elsa, and I said, "take your flower, my girl, and go away now. I don't want to question you any more for the present."

A little bewildered at her sudden dismissal, Elsa went away, and I turned my attention to the Frenchman.

"Louis," I began, "this must be settled here and now between us. Either you must tell me what I want to know, or you must be taken before the district attorney, and be made to tell him. I have proved to my own satisfaction that the rose petals in the office were not from the flower you wore. Therefore I conclude that you did not go into the office that night, but as you passed the window you did see someone in there with Mr. Crawford. The hour was later than Mr. Porter's visit, for he had already gone home, and Lambert had locked the front door and gone to bed. You came in later, and what you saw, or whom you saw through the office window so surprised you, or interested you, that you paused to look in, and there you dropped your transfer."

Though Louis didn't speak, I could see at once that I was on the right track at last. The man was shielding somebody. He was unwilling to tell what he had seen, lest it inculpate someone. Could it be Gregory Hall? If Hall had come out on a late train, and Louis had seen him there, he might, perhaps under Hall's coercion, be keeping the fact secret. Again, if a strange woman with the gold bag had been in the office, that also would have attracted Louis's attention. Again, and here my heart almost stopped beating, could he have seen Florence Lloyd in there? But a second thought put me at ease again. Surely to have seen Florence in there would have been so usual and natural a sight that it could not have caused him anxiety. And yet, again, for him to have seen Florence in her uncle's office, would have proved to him that the story she told at the inquest was false. I must get out of him the knowledge he possessed, if I had to resort to a sort of third degree. But I might manage it by adroit questioning.

"I quite understand, Louis, that you are shielding some person. But let me tell you that it is useless. It is much wiser for you to tell me all you know, and then I can go to work intelligently to find the man who murdered Mr. Crawford. You want me to find him, do you not?"

Louis seemed to have found his voice again. "Yes, sir, of course he must be found. Of course I want him found,— the miscreant, the villain! but, Mr. Burroughs, sir, what I have see in the office makes nothing to your search. I simply see Mr. Crawford alive and well. And I pass by. That fool girl Elsa, she tell you that I pass by, so I may say so. But I see nothing in the office to alarm me, and if I drop my transfer there, it is but because I think of him as no consequence, and I let him go."

"Louis," and I looked him straight in the eye, "all that sounds straightforward and true. But, if you saw nothing in the office to surprise or alarm you, why did you at first deny having passed by the office at all?"

The man had no answer for this. He was not ingenious in inventing falsehood, and he stood looking helpless and despairing. I perceived I should have to go on with my questioning.

"Was it a man or a woman you saw in there with Mr. Crawford?"

"I see nobody, sir, nobody but my master."

That wouldn't do, then. As long as I asked him direct questions he could answer falsely. I must trip him up in some roundabout way.

"Yes," I said pleasantly, "I understand that. And what was Mr. Crawford doing?"

"He sat at his desk;" and Louis spoke slowly, and picked his words with care.

"Was he writing?"

"No; that is, yes, sir, he was writing."

I now knew he was not writing, for the truth had slipped out before the man could frame up his lie. I believed I was going to learn something at last, if I could make the man tell. Surely the testimony of one who saw Joseph Crawford late that night was of value, and though that testimony was difficult to obtain, it was well worth the effort.

"And was Mr. Hall at his desk also?"

Louis stared at me. "Mr. Hall, he was in New York that night." This was said so simply and unpremeditatedly, that I was absolutely certain it was not Hall whom Louis had seen there.

"Oh, yes, of course, so he was," I said lightly; "and Mr. Crawford was writing, was he?"

"Yes, sir," spoken with the dogged scowl which I was beginning to learn always accompanied Louis's untruthful statements.

And now I decided to put my worst fear to the test and have it over with. It must be done, and I felt sure I could do it, but oh, how I dreaded it!

"Did Mr. Crawford look up or see you?"

"No, sir."

"And didn't Miss Florence see you, either?"

"No, sir."

It was out. The mere fact that Louis answered that question so calmly and unconsciously proved he was telling the truth. But what a truth! for it told me at the same time that Florence Lloyd was in the office with her uncle, that Louis had seen her, but that she had not seen him. I had learned the truth from my reading of the man's expression and demeanor, and though it made my heart sink, I didn't for a moment doubt that it was the truth.

Of course Louis realized the next instant what he had done, and again he began his stammering denials. "Of course, Miss Lloyd do not see me for she is not there. How can she see me, then? I tell you my master was alone!"

Had I been the least uncertain, this would have convinced me that I was right. For Louis's voice rose almost to a shriek, so angry was he with himself for having made the slip.

"Give it up, Louis," I said; "you have let out the truth, now be quiet. You couldn't help it, man, you were bound to trip yourself up sooner or later. You put up a good fight for Miss Florence, and now that I understand why you told your falsehoods, I can't help admiring your chivalry. You saw Miss Lloyd there that evening, you heard her next day at the inquest deny having been in the office in the evening. So, in a way, it was very commendable on your part to avoid contradicting her testimonies, with your own. But you are not clever enough, Louis, to carry out that deceit to the end. And now that you have admitted that you saw Miss Lloyd there, you can best help her cause, and best help me to help her cause, by telling me all about it. For rest assured, Louis, that I am quite as anxious to prove Miss Lloyd's innocence as you can possibly be, and the only way to accomplish that end, is to learn as much of the truth as I possibly can. Now, tell me what she was doing."

"Only talking to her uncle, sir." Louis had the air of a defeated man. He had tried to shield Miss Lloyd's name and had failed. Now he spoke sullenly, and as if his whole cause were lost.

"And Mr. Crawford was talking to her?"

"Yes, sir."

"He was not writing, then?"

"No, sir."

"Did they seem to be having an amicable conversation?"

Louis hesitated, and his hesitation was sufficient answer.

"Never mind," I said, "you need not tell me more. In fact, I would prefer to get the rest of the story from Miss Lloyd, herself."

Louis looked startled. "Don't tell Miss Lloyd I told you this," he begged; "I have try very hard not to tell you."

"I know you tried hard, Louis, not to tell me, and it was not your fault that I wrung the truth from you. I will not tell Miss Lloyd that you told me, unless it should become necessary, and I do not think it will. Go away now, Louis, and do not discuss this matter with anybody at all. And, also, do not think for a moment that you have been disloyal in telling me that you saw Miss Lloyd. As I say, you couldn't help it. I should simply have kept at you until I made you tell, so you need not blame yourself in the matter at all."

Louis went away, and though I could see that he believed what I said, he had a dejected air, and I couldn't help feeling sorry for the man who had so inadvertently given me the knowledge that must be used against the beautiful girl who had herself given untrue testimony.

Chapter 13: Miss Lloyd's Confidence

After Louis left me, I felt as if a dead weight had fallen on my heart. Florence Lloyd had gone down to her uncle's office late that night, and yet at the inquest she had testified that she had not done so. And even to me, when talking quietly and alone, she had repeated her false assertion. This much I knew, but why she had done if, I did not know. Not until I was forced to do so, would I believe that even her falsehood in the matter meant that she herself was guilty. There must be some other reason for her mendacity.

Well, I would find out this reason, and if it were not a creditable one to her, I would still endeavor to do all I could for her. I longed to see her, and try if perhaps kind and gentle urging might not elicit the truth. But she had left me with such an air of haughty disdain, I hesitated to send for her again just now. And as it was nearly dinner time, I resolved to go back to my hotel.

On the way, I came to the conclusion that it would do no harm to have a talk with Parmalee.

I had not much confidence in his detective ability, but he knew the people better than I did, and might be able to give me information of some sort.

After I reached the Sedgwick Arms I telephoned Parmalee to come over and dine with me, and he readily consented.

During dinner I told him all that I had learned from Elsa and Louis. Of course I had no right to keep this knowledge to myself, and, too, I wanted Parmalee's opinion on the situation as it stood at present.

"It doesn't really surprise me," he said, "for I thought all along, Miss Lloyd was not telling the truth. I'm not yet ready to say that I think she killed her uncle, although I must say it seems extremely probable. But if she didn't commit the deed, she knows perfectly well who did."

"Meaning Hall?"

"No, I don't mean Hall. In fact I don't mean any one in particular. I think Miss Lloyd was the instigator of the crime, and practically carried out its commission, but she may have had an assisting agent for the actual deed."

"Oh, how you talk! It quite gives me the shivers even to think of a beautiful young woman being capable of such thoughts or deeds."

"But, you see, Burroughs, that's because you are prejudiced in favor of Miss Lloyd. Women are capable of crime as well as men, and sometimes they're even more clever in the perpetration of it. And you must admit if ever a woman were capable of crime, Miss Lloyd is of that type."

"I have to agree to that, Parmalee," I admitted; "she certainly shows great strength of character."

"She shows more than that; she has indomitable will, unflinching courage, and lots of pluck. If, for any reason, she made up her mind to kill a man, she'd find a way to do it."

This talk made me cringe all over, but I couldn't deny it, for so far as I knew Florence Lloyd, Parmalee's words were quite true.

"All right," I said, "I'll grant her capability, but that doesn't prove a thing. I don't believe that girl is guilty, and I hope to prove her innocence."

"But look at the evidence, man! She denied her presence in the room, yet we now know she was there. She denied the ownership of the gold bag, yet probably she was also untruthful in that matter. She is a woman of a complex nature, and though I admire her in many ways, I shouldn't care to have much to do with her."

"Let us leave out the personal note, Parmalee," I said, for I was angry at his attitude toward Florence.

"All right. Don't you think for a moment that I don't see where you stand with regard to the haughty beauty, but that's neither here nor there."

"Indeed it isn't," I returned; "and whatever may be my personal feeling toward Miss Lloyd, I can assure you it in no way influences my work on this case."

"I believe you, old man; and so I'm sure you will agree with me that we must follow up the inquiry as to Miss Lloyd's presence in the office that night. She must be made to talk, and perhaps it would be best to tell Goodrich all about it, and let him push the matter."

"Oh, no," I cried involuntarily. "Don't set him on the track of the poor girl. That is, Parmalee, let me talk to her again, first. Now that I know she was down there that night, I think I can question her in a little different manner, and persuade her to own the truth. And, Parmalee, perhaps she was down there because Hall was there."

"Hall! He was in New York."

"So he says, but why should he speak the truth any more than Miss Lloyd?"

"You, mean they may both be implicated?"

"Yes; or he may have used her as a tool."

"Not Florence Lloyd. She's nobody's tool."

"Any woman might be a tool at the command of the man she loves. But," I went on, with an air of conviction which was not entirely genuine, "Miss Lloyd doesn't love Mr. Hall."

"I don't know about that," returned Parmalee; "you can't tell about a woman like Florence Lloyd. If she doesn't love him, she's at least putting up a bluff of doing so."

"I believe it is a bluff, though I'm sure I don't know why she should do that."

"On the other hand, why shouldn't she? For some reason she's dead set on marrying him, ready to give up her fortune to do so, if necessary. He must have some sort of a pretty strong hold on her."

"I admit all that, and yet I can't believe she loves him. He's such a commonplace man."

"Commonplace doesn't quite describe him. And yet Gregory Hall, with all the money in the world, could never make himself distinguished or worth while in any way."

"No; and what would Miss Florence Lloyd see in a man like that, to make her so determined to marry him?"

"I don't think she is determined, except that Hall has some sort of hold over her,—a promise or something,— that she can't escape."

My heart rejoiced at the idea that Florence was not in love with Hall, but I did not allow myself to dwell on that point, for I was determined to go on with the work, irrespective of my feelings toward her.

"You see," Parmalee went on, "you suspect Hall, only because you're prejudiced against him."

"Good gracious!" I exclaimed; "that's an awful thing to say, Parmalee. The idea of a detective suspecting a man, merely because he doesn't admire his personality! And besides, it isn't true. If I suspect Hall, it's because I think he had a strong motive, a possible opportunity, and more than all, because he refuses to tell where he was Tuesday night."

"But that's just the point, Burroughs. A man who'll commit murder would fix up his alibi first of all. He would know that his refusal to tell his whereabouts would be extremely suspicious. No, to my mind it's Hall's refusal to tell that stamps him as innocent."

"Then, in that case, it's the cleverest kind of an alibi he could invent, for it stamps him innocent at once."

"Oh, come, now, that's going pretty far; but I will say, Burroughs, that you haven't the least shred of proof against Hall, and you know it. Prejudice and unfounded suspicion and even a strong desire that he should be the villain, are all very well. But they won't go far as evidence in a court of law."

I was forced to admit that Parmalee was right, and that so far I had no proof whatever that Gregory Hall was at all implicated in Mr. Crawford's death. To be sure he might have worn a yellow rose, and he might have brought the late newspaper, but there was no evidence to connect him with those clues, and too, there was the gold bag. It was highly improbable that that should have been brought to the office and left there by a man.

However, I persuaded Parmalee to agree not to carry the matter to Mr. Goodrich until I had had one more interview with Miss Lloyd, and I promised to undertake that the next morning.

After Parmalee had gone, I indulged in some very gloomy reflections. Everything seemed to point one way. Every proof, every suspicion and every hint more or less implicated Miss Lloyd.

But the more I realized this, the more I determined to do all I could for her, and as to do this, I must gain her confidence, and even liking, I resolved to approach the subject the next day with the utmost tactfulness and kindliness, hoping by this means to induce the truth from her.

The next morning I started on my mission with renewed hopefulness. Reaching the Crawford house, I asked for Miss Lloyd, and I was shown into a small parlor to wait for her. It was a sort of morning room, a pretty little apartment that I had not been in before; and it was so much more cheerful and pleasant than the stately library, I couldn't help hoping that Miss Lloyd, too, would prove more amenable than she had yet been.

She soon came in, and though I was beginning to get accustomed to the fact that she was a creature of variable moods, I was unprepared for this one. Her hauteur had disappeared; she was apparently in a sweet and gentle frame of mind. Her large dark eyes were soft and gentle, and though her red lips quivered, it was not with anger or disdain as they had done the day before. She wore a plain white morning gown, and a long black necklace of small beads. The simplicity of this costume suited her well, and threw into relief her own rich coloring and striking beauty.

She greeted me more pleasantly than she had ever done before, and I couldn't help feeling that the cheerful sunny little room had a better effect on her moods than the darker furnishings of the library.

"I wish," I began, "that we had not to talk of anything unpleasant this morning. I wish there were no such thing as untruth or crime in the world, and that I were calling on you, as an acquaintance, as a friend might call."

"I wish so, too," she responded, and as she flashed a glance at me, I had a glimpse of what it might mean to be friends with Florence Lloyd without the ugly shadow between us that now was spoiling our tete-a-tete.

Just that fleeting glance held in it the promise of all that was attractive, charming and delightful in femininity. It was as if the veil of the great, gloomy sorrow had been lifted for a moment, and she was again an untroubled, merry girl. It seemed too, as if she wished that we could be together under pleasanter circumstances and could converse on subjects of less dreadful import. However, all these thoughts that tumultuously raced through my mind must be thrust aside in favor of the business in hand.

So though I hated to, I began at once.

"I am sorry, Miss Lloyd, to doubt your word, but I want to tell you myself rather than to have you learn it from others that I have a witness who has testified to your presence in your uncle's office that fateful Tuesday night, although you have said you didn't go down there."

As I had feared, the girl turned white and shivered as if with a dreadful apprehension.

"Who is the witness?" she said.

I seemed to read her mind, and I felt at once that to her, the importance of what I had said depended largely on my answer to this question, and I paused a moment to think what this could mean. And then it flashed across me that she was afraid I would say the witness was Gregory Hall. I became more and more convinced that she was shielding Hall, and I felt sure that when she learned it was not he, she would feel relieved. However, I had promised Louis not to let her know that he had told me of seeing her, unless it should be necessary.

"I think I won't tell you that; but since you were seen in the office at about eleven o'clock, will you not tell me,— I assure you it is for your own best interests,—what you were doing there, and why you denied being there?"

"First tell me the name of your informer;" and so great was her agitation that she scarcely breathed the words.

"I prefer not to do so, but I may say it is a reliable witness and one who gave his evidence most unwillingly."

"Well, if you will not tell me who he was, will you answer just one question about him? Was it Mr. Hall?"

"No; it was not Mr. Hall."

As I had anticipated, she showed distinctly her relief at my answer. Evidently she dreaded to hear Hall's name brought into the conversation.

"And now, Miss Lloyd, I ask you earnestly and with the best intent, please to tell me the details of your visit to Mr. Crawford that night in his office."

She sat silent for a moment, her eyes cast down, the long dark lashes lying on her pale cheeks. I waited patiently, for I knew she was struggling with a strong emotion of some sort, and I feared if I hurried her, her gentle mood would disappear, and she might again become angry or haughty of demeanor.

At last she spoke. The dark lashes slowly raised, and she seemed even more gentle than at first.

"I must tell you," she said. "I see I must. But don't repeat it, unless it is necessary. Detectives have to know things, but they don't have to tell them, do they?"

"We never repeat confidences, Miss Lloyd," I replied, "except when necessary to further the cause of right and justice."

"Truly? Is that so?"

She brightened up so much that I began to hope she had only some trifling matter to tell of.

"Well, then," she went on, "I will tell you, for I know it need not be repeated in the furtherance of justice. I did go down to my uncle's office that night, after Mrs. Pierce had been to my room; and it was I—it must have been I—who dropped those rose petals."

"And left the bag," I suggested.

"No," she said, and her face looked perplexed, but not confused. "No, the bag is not mine, and I did not leave it there. I know nothing of it, absolutely nothing. But I did go to the office at about eleven o'clock. I had a talk with my uncle, and I left him there a half-hour later—alive and well as when I went in."

"Was your conversation about your engagement?"

"Yes."

"Was it amicable?"

"No, it was not! Uncle Joseph was more angry than I had ever before seen him. He declared he intended to make a new will the next morning, which would provide only a small income for me. He said this was not revenge or punishment for my loyalty to Mr. Hall, but—but—"

"But what?" I urged gently.

"It scarcely seems loyal to Mr. Hall for me to say it," she returned, and the tears were in her eyes. "But this is all confidential. Well, Uncle Joseph said that Gregory only wanted to marry me for my fortune, and that the new will would prove this. Of course I denied that Mr. Hall was so mercenary, and then we had a good deal of an altercation. But it was not very different from many discussions we had had on the same subject, only Uncle was more decided, and said he had asked Mr. Randolph to come the next morning and draw up the new will. I left him still angry—he wouldn't even say good-night to me— and now I blame myself for not being more gentle, and trying harder to make peace. But it annoyed me to have him call Gregory mercenary—"

"Because you knew it was true," I said quietly.

She turned white to the very lips. "You are unnecessarily impertinent," she said.

"I am," I agreed. "I beg your pardon." But I had discovered that she did realize her lover's true nature.

"And then you went to your room, and stayed there?" I went on, with a meaning emphasis on the last clause.

"Yes," she said; "and so, you see, what I have told you casts no light on the mystery. I only told you so as to explain the bits of the yellow rose. I feared, from what you said, that Mr. Hall's name might possibly be brought into discussion."

"Why, he was not in West Sedgwick that night," I said.

"Where was he?" she countered quickly.

"I don't know. He refuses to tell. Of course you must see that his absolute refusal to tell where he was that night is, to say the least, an unwise proceeding."

"He won't even tell me where he was," she said, sighing. "But it doesn't matter. He wasn't here."

"That's just it," I rejoined. "If he was not here, it would be far better for him to tell where he really was. For the refusal to tell raises a question that will not be downed, except by an alibi. I don't want to be cruel, Miss Lloyd, but I must make you see that as the inquiry proceeds, the actions of both Mr. Hall and yourself will be subjected to very close scrutiny, and though perhaps undue attention will be paid to trifles, yet the trifles must be explained."

I was so sorry for the girl, that, in my effort not to divulge my too great sympathy, I probably used a sterner tone than I realized.

At any rate, I had wakened her at last to a sense of the danger that threatened her and her lover, and now, if she would let me, I would do all in my power to save them both. But I must know all she could tell me.

"When did Mr. Hall leave you?" I asked.

"You mean the day—last Tuesday?"

"Yes?"

"He left here about half-past five. He had been in the office with Uncle Joseph all the afternoon, and at five o'clock he came in here for a cup of tea with me. He almost always comes in at tea-time. Then he left about half-past five, saying he was going to New York on the six o'clock train."

"For what purpose?"

"I never ask him questions like that. I knew he was to attend to some business for Uncle the next day, but I never ask him what he does evenings when he is in the city, or at any time when he is not with me."

"But surely one might ask such questions of the man to whom she is betrothed."

Miss Lloyd again put on that little air of hauteur which always effectually stopped my "impertinence."

"It is not my habit," she said. "What Gregory wishes me to know he tells me of his own accord."

CHAPTER 14: MR. PORTER'S VIEWS

I began on a new tack.

"Miss Lloyd, why did you tell an untruth, and say you did not come down-stairs again, after going up at ten o'clock?"

Her hauteur disappeared. A frightened, appealing look came into her eyes, and she looked to me like a lovely child afraid of unseen dangers.

"I was afraid," she confessed. "Yes, truly, I was afraid that they would think I had something to do with the—with Uncle Joseph's death. And as I didn't think it could do any good to tell of my little visit to him, I just said I didn't come down. Oh, I know it was a lie—I know it was wicked—but I was so frightened, and it was such an easy way out of it, just to deny it."

"And why have you confessed it to me now?"

Her eyes opened wide in astonishment.

"I told you why," she said: "so you would know where the rose leaves came from, and not suspect Gregory."

"Do you suspect him?"

"N-no, of course not. But others might."

It is impossible to describe the dismay that smote my heart at the hesitation of this answer. It was more than hesitation. It was a conflict of unspoken impulses, and the words, when they were uttered, seemed to carry hidden meanings, and to my mind they carried the worst and most sinister meaning conceivable.

To me, it seemed to point unmistakably to collusion between Florence Lloyd, whom I already loved, and Gregory Hall, whom I already distrusted and disliked. Guilty collusion between these two would explain everything. Theirs the motive, theirs the opportunity, theirs the denials and false witnessing. The gold bag, as yet, remained unexplained, but the yellow rose petals and the late newspaper could be accounted for if Hall had come out on the midnight train, and Florence had helped him to enter and leave the house unseen.

Bah! it was impossible. And, any way, the gold bag remained as proof against this horrid theory. I would pin my faith to the gold bag, and through its presence in the room, I would defy suspicions of the two people I had resolved to protect.

"What do you think about the gold bag?" I asked.

"I don't know what to think. I hate to accuse Uncle Joseph of such a thing, but it seems as if some woman friend of his must have come to the office after I left. The long French windows were open—it was a warm night, you know—and any one could have come and gone unseen."

"The bag wasn't there when you were there?"

"I'm sure it was not! That is, not in sight, and Uncle Joseph was not the sort of man to have such a thing put away in his desk as a souvenir, or for any other reason."

"Forgive the insinuation, but of course you could not know positively that Mr. Crawford would not have a feminine souvenir in his desk."

She looked up surprised. "Of course I could not be positive," she said, "but it is difficult to imagine anything sentimental connected with Uncle Joseph."

She almost smiled as she said this, for apparently the mere idea was amusing, and I had a flashing glimpse of what it must be to see Florence Lloyd smile! Well it should not be my fault, or due to my lack of exertion, if the day did not come when she should smile again, and I promised myself I should be there to see it. But stifling these thoughts, I brought my mind back to duty. Drawing from my pocket the photograph I had found in Mr. Crawford's desk, I showed it to her.

"In Uncle's desk!" she exclaimed. "This does surprise me. I had no idea Uncle Joseph had received a photograph from a lady with an affectionate message, too. Are you quite sure it belonged to him?"

"I only know that we found it in his desk, hidden beneath some old letters and papers."

"Were the letters from this lady?"

"No; in no case could we find a signature that agreed with these initials."

"Here's your chance, Mr. Burroughs," and again Florence Lloyd's dimples nearly escaped the bondage which held them during these sad days. "If you're a detective, you ought to gather at once from this photograph and signature all the details about this lady; who she is, and what she had to do with Uncle Joseph."

"I wish I could do so," I replied, "but you see, I'm not that kind of detective. I have a friend, Mr. Stone, who could do it, and would tell you, as you say, everything about that lady, merely by looking at her picture."

As a case in point, I told her then and there the story of Fleming Stone's wonderful deductions from the pair of muddy shoes we had seen in a hotel one morning.

"But you never proved that it was true?" she asked, her dark eyes sparkling with interest, and her face alight with animation.

"No, but it wasn't necessary. Stone's deductions are always right, and if not, you know it is the exception that proves the rule."

"Well, let us try to deduce a little from this picture. I don't believe for a moment, that Uncle Joseph had a romantic attachment for any lady, though these words on the back of the picture do seem to indicate it."

"Well, go on," said I, so carried away by the fascination of the girl, when she had for a moment seemed to forget her troubles, that I wanted to prolong the moment. "Go ahead, and see what inferences you can draw from the photograph."

"I think she is about fifty years old," Florence began, "or perhaps fifty-five. What do you think?"

"I wouldn't presume to guess a lady's age," I returned, "and beside, I want you to try your powers on this. You may be better at deductions than I am. I have already confessed to you my inability in that direction."

"Well," she went on, "I think this lady is rather good-looking, and I think she appreciates the fact."

"The first is evident on the face of it, and the second is a universal truth, so you haven't really deduced much as yet."

"No, that's so," and she pouted a little. "But at any rate, I can deduce more about her dress than you can. The picture was taken, or at least that costume was made, about a year ago, for that is the style that was worn then."

"Marvellous, Holmes, marvellous!"

She flashed me a glance of understanding and appreciation, but undaunted, went on: "The gown also was not made by a competent modiste, but was made by a dressmaker in the house, who came in by the day. The lady is of an economical turn of mind, because the lace yoke of the gown is an old one, and has even been darned to make it presentable to use in the new gown."

"Now that is deduction," I said admiringly; "the only trouble is, that it doesn't do us much good. Somehow I can't seem to fancy this good-looking, economical, middle-aged lady, who has her dressmaking done at home, coming here in the middle of the night and killing Mr. Crawford."

"No, I can't, either," said Florence gravely; "but then, I can't imagine any one else doing that, either. It seems like a horrible dream, and I can't realize that it really happened to Uncle Joseph."

"But it did happen, and we must find the guilty person. I think with you, that this photograph is of little value as a clue, and yet it may turn out to be. And yet I do think the gold bag is a clue. You are quite sure it isn't yours?"

Perhaps it was a mean way to put the question, but the look of indignation she gave me helped to convince me that the bag was not hers.

"I told you it was not," she said, "but," and her eyes fell, "since I have confessed to one falsehood, of course you cannot believe my statement."

"But I do believe it," I said, and I did, thoroughly.

"At any rate, it is a sort of proof," she said, smiling sadly, "that any one who knows anything about women's fashions can tell you that it is not customary to carry a bag of that sort when one is in the house and in evening dress. Or rather, in a negligee costume, for I had taken off my evening gown and wore a tea-gown. I should not think of going anywhere in a tea-gown, and carrying a gold bag."

The girl had seemingly grown almost lighthearted. Her speech was punctuated by little smiles, and her half sad, half gay demeanor bewitched me. I felt sure that what little suggestion of lightheartedness had come into her mood had come because she had at last confessed the falsehood she had told, and her freed conscience gave her a little buoyancy of heart.

But there were still important questions to be asked, so, though unwillingly, I returned to the old subject.

"Did you see your uncle's will while you were there?"

"No; he talked about it, but did not show it to me."

"Did he talk about it as if it were still in his possession?"

"Why, yes; I think so. That is, he said he would make a new one unless I gave up Gregory. That implied that the old one was still in existence, though he didn't exactly say so."

"Miss Lloyd, this is important evidence. I must tell you that I shall be obliged to repeat much of it to the district attorney. It seems to me to prove that your uncle did not himself destroy the will."

"He might have done so after I left him."

"I can't think it, for it is not in scraps in the waste-basket, nor are there any paper-ashes in the grate."

"Well, then," she rejoined, "if he didn't destroy it, it may yet be found."

"You wish that very much?" I said, almost involuntarily.

"Oh, I do!" she exclaimed, clasping her hands. "Not so much for myself as—"

She paused, and I finished the sentence for her "For Mr. Hall."

She looked angry again, but said nothing.

"Well, Miss Lloyd," I said, as I rose to go, "I am going to do everything in my power in your behalf and in behalf of Mr. Hall. But I tell you frankly, unless you will both tell me the truth, and the whole truth, you will only defeat my efforts, and work your own undoing."

I had to look away from her as I said this, for I could not look on that sweet face and say anything even seemingly harsh or dictatorial.

Her lip quivered. "I will do my best," she said tremblingly. "I will try to make Mr. Hall tell where he was that night. I will see you again after I have talked with him."

More collusion! I said good-by rather curtly, I fear, and went quickly away from that perilous presence.

Truly, a nice detective, I! Bowled over by a fair face, I was unable to think clearly, to judge logically, or to work honestly!

Well, I would go home and think it out by myself. Away from her influence I surely would regain my cool-headed methods of thought.

When I reached the inn, I found Mr. Lemuel Porter there waiting for me.

"How do you do, Mr. Burroughs?" he said pleasantly. "Have you time for a half-hour's chat?"

It was just what I wanted. A talk with this clear-thinking man would help me, indeed, and I determined to get his opinions, even as I was ready to give him mine.

"Well, what do you think about it all?" I inquired, after we were comfortably settled at a small table on the shaded veranda, which was a popular gathering-place at this hour. But in our corner we were in no danger from listening ears, and I awaited his reply with interest.

His eyes smiled a little, as he said,

"You know the old story of the man who said he wouldn't hire a dog and then do his own barking. Well, though I haven't 'hired' you, I would be quite ready to pay your honorarium if you can ferret out our West Sedgwick mystery. And so, as you are the detective in charge of the case, I ask you, what do you think about it all?"

But I was pretty thoroughly on my guard now.

"I think," I began, "that much hinges on the ownership of that gold bag."

"And you do not think it is Miss Lloyd's?"

"I do not."

"It need not incriminate her, if it were hers," said Mr. Porter, meditatively knocking the ash from said his cigar. "She might have left it in the office at any time previous to the day of the crime. Women are always leaving such things about. I confess it does not seem to me important."

"Was it on Mr. Crawford's desk when you were there?" I asked suddenly.

He looked up at me quickly, and again that half-smile came into his eyes.

"Am I to be questioned?" he said. "Well, I've no objections, I'm sure. No, I do not think it was there when I called on Mr. Crawford that evening. But I couldn't swear to this, for I am not an observant man, and the thing might have lain there in front of me and never caught my eye. If I had noticed it, of course I should have thought it was Florence's."

"But you don't think so now, do you?"

"No; I can't say I think so. And yet I can imagine a girl untruthfully denying ownership under such circumstances."

I started at this. For hadn't Miss Lloyd untruthfully denied coming down-stairs to talk to her uncle?

"But," went on Mr. Porter, "if the bag is not Florence's, then I can think of but one explanation for its presence there."

"A lady visitor, late at night," I said slowly.

"Yes," was the grave reply; "and though such an occurrence might have been an innocent one, yet, taken in connection with the crime, there is a dreadful possibility."

"Granting this," I suggested, "we ought to be able to trace the owner of the bag."

"Not likely. If the owner of that bag—a woman, presumably—is the slayer of Joseph Crawford, and made her escape from the scene undiscovered, she is not likely to stay around where she may be found. And the bag itself, and its contents, are hopelessly unindividual."

"They are that," I agreed. "Not a thing in it that mightn't be in any woman's bag in this country. To me, that cleaner's advertisement means nothing in connection with Miss Lloyd."

"I am glad to hear you say that, Mr. Burroughs. I confess I have had a half-fear that your suspicions had a trend in Florence's direction, and I assure you, sir, that girl is incapable of the slightest impulse toward crime."

"I'm sure of that," I said heartily, my blood bounding in my veins at an opportunity to speak in defense of the woman I loved. "But how if her impulses were directed, or even coerced, by another?"

"Just what do you mean by that?"

"Oh, nothing. But sometimes the best and sweetest women will act against their own good impulses for those they love."

"I cannot pretend to misunderstand you," said Mr. Porter. "But you are wrong. If the one you have in mind— I will say no name—was in any way guiltily implicated, it was without the knowledge or connivance of Florence

Lloyd. But, man, the idea is absurd. The individual in question has a perfect alibi."

"He refuses to give it."

"Refuses the details, perhaps. And he has a right to, since they concern no one but himself. No, my friend, you know the French rule; well, follow that, and search for the lady with the gold-mesh bag."

"The lady without it, at present," I said, with an apologetic smile for my rather grim jest.

"Yes; and that's the difficulty. As she hasn't the bag, we can't discover her. So as a clue it is worthless."

"It seems to be," I agreed.

I thought best not to tell Mr. Porter of the card I had found in the bag, for I hoped soon to hear from headquarters concerning the lady whose name it bore. But I told him about the photograph I had found in Mr. Crawford's desk, and showed it to him. He did not recognize it as being a portrait of any one he had ever seen. Nor did he take it very seriously as a clue.

"I'm quite sure," he said, "that Joseph Crawford has not been interested in any woman since the death of his wife. He has always seemed devoted to her memory, and as one of his nearest friends, I think I would have known if he had formed any other attachment. Of course, in a matter like this, a man may well have a secret from his nearest friends, but I cannot think this mild and gentle-looking lady is at all concerned in the tragedy."

As a matter of fact, I agreed with Mr. Porter, for nothing I had discovered among the late Mr. Crawford's effects led me to think he had any secret romance.

After Mr. Porter's departure I studied long over my puzzles, and I came to the conclusion that I could do little more until I should hear from headquarters.

CHAPTER 15: THE PHOTOGRAPH EXPLAINED

That evening I went to see Philip Crawford. As one of the executors of his late brother's estate, and as probable heir to the same, he was an important personage just now.

He seemed glad to see me, and glad to discuss ways and means of running down the assassin. Like Mr. Porter, he attached little importance to the gold bag.

"I can't help thinking it belongs to Florence," he said. "I know the girl so well, and I know that her horrified fear of being in any way connected with the tragedy might easily lead her to, disown her own property, thinking the occasion justified the untruth. That girl has no more guilty knowledge of Joseph's death than I have, and that is absolutely none. I tell you frankly, Mr. Burroughs, I haven't even a glimmer of a suspicion of any one. I can't think of an enemy my brother had; he was the most easy-going of men. I never knew him to quarrel with anybody. So I trust that you, with your detective talent, can at least find a clue to lead us in the right direction."

"You don't admit the gold bag as a clue, then?" I asked.

"Nonsense! No! If that were a clue, it would point to some woman who came secretly at night to visit Joseph. My brother was not that sort of man, sir. He had no feminine acquaintances that were unknown to his relatives."

"That is, you suppose so."

"I know it! We have been brothers for sixty years or more, and whatever Joseph's faults, they did not lie in that direction. No, sir; if that bag is not Florence's, then there is some other rational and commonplace explanation of its presence there."

"I'm glad to hear you speak so positively, Mr. Crawford, as to your brother's feminine acquaintances. And in connection with the subject, I would like to show you this photograph which I found in his desk."

I handed the card to Mr. Crawford, whose features broke into a smile as he looked at it.

"Oh, that," he said; "that is a picture, of Mrs. Patton." He looked at the picture with a glance that seemed to be of admiring reminiscence, and he studied the gentle face of the photograph a moment without speaking.

Then he said, "She was beautiful as a girl. She used to be a school friend of both Joseph and myself."

"She wrote rather an affectionate message on the back," I observed.

Mr. Crawford turned the picture over.

"Oh, she didn't send this picture to Joseph. She sent it to my wife last Christmas. I took it over to show it to Joseph some months ago, and left it there without thinking much about it. He probably laid it in his desk without thinking much about it, either. No, no, Burroughs, there is no romance there, and you can't connect Mrs. Patton with any of your detective investigations."

"I rather thought that, Mr. Crawford; for this is evidently a sweet, simple-minded lady, and more over nothing has turned up to indicate that Mr. Crawford had a romantic interest of any kind."

"No, he didn't. I knew Joseph as I know myself. No; whoever killed my brother, was a man; some villain who had a motive that I know nothing about."

"But you were intimately acquainted with your brother's affairs?"

"Yes, that is what proves to me that whoever this assassin was, it was some one of whose motive I know nothing. The fact that my brother was murdered, proves to me that my brother had an enemy, but I had never suspected it before."

"Do you know a Mrs. Egerton Purvis?"

I flung the question at him, suddenly, hoping to catch him unawares. But he only looked at me with the blank expression of one who hears a name for the first time.

"No," he answered, "I never heard of her. Who is she?"

"Well, when I was hunting through that gold-mesh bag, I discovered a lady's visiting card with that name on it. It had slipped between the linings, and so had not been noticed before."

To my surprise, this piece of information seemed to annoy Mr. Crawford greatly.

"No!" he exclaimed. "In the bag? Then some one has put it there! for I looked over all the bag's contents myself."

"It was between the pocket and the lining," said I; "it is there still, for as I felt sure no one else would discover it, I left it there. Mr. Goodrich has the bag."

"Oh, I don't want to see it," he exclaimed angrily. "And I tell you anyway, Mr. Burroughs, that bag is worthless as a clue. Take my advice, and pay no further attention to it."

I couldn't understand Mr. Crawford's decided attitude against the bag as a clue, but I dropped the subject, for I didn't wish to tell him I had made plans to trace up that visiting card.

"It is difficult to find anything that is a real clue," I said.

"Yes, indeed. The whole affair is mysterious, and, for my part, I cannot form even a conjecture as to who the villain might have been. He certainly left no trace."

"Where is the revolver?" I said, picturing the scene in imagination.

Philip Crawford started as if caught unawares.

"How do I know?" he cried, almost angrily. "I tell you, I have no suspicions. I wish I had! I desire, above all things, to bring my brother's murderer to justice. But I don't know where to look. If the weapon were not missing, I should think it a suicide."

"The doctor declares it could not have been suicide, even if the weapon had been found near him. This they learned from the position of his arms and head."

"Yes, yes; I know it. It was, without doubt, murder. But who—who would have a motive?"

"They say," I observed, "motives for murder are usually love, revenge, or money."

"There is no question of love or revenge in this instance. And as for money, as I am the one who has profited financially, suspicion should rest on me."

"Absurd!" I said.

"Yes, it is absurd," he went on, "for had I desired Joseph's fortune, I need not have killed him to acquire it. He told me the day before he died that he intended to disinherit Florence, and make me his heir, unless she broke with that secretary of his. I tried to dissuade him from this step, for we are not a mercenary lot, we Crawfords, and I thought I had made him reconsider his decision. Now, as it turns out, he persisted in his resolve, and was only prevented from carrying it out by this midnight assassin. We must find that villain, Mr. Burroughs! Do not consider expense; do anything you can to track him down."

"Then, Mr. Crawford," said I, "if you do not mind the outlay, I advise that we send for Fleming Stone. He is a detective of extraordinary powers, and I am quite willing to surrender the case to him."

Philip Crawford eyed me keenly.

"You give up easily, young man," he said banteringly.

"I know it seems so," I replied, "but I have my reasons. One is, that Fleming Stone makes important deductions from seemingly unimportant clues; and he holds that unless these clues are followed immediately, they are lost sight of and great opportunities are gone."

"H'm," mused Philip Crawford, stroking his strong, square chin. "I don't care much for these spectacular detectives. Your man, I suppose, would glance at the gold bag, and at once announce the age, sex, and previous condition of servitude of its owner."

"Just what I have thought, Mr. Crawford. I'm sure he could do just that."

"And that's all the good it would do! That bag doesn't belong to the criminal."

"How do you know?"

"By common-sense. No woman came to the house in the dead of night and shot my brother, and then departed, taking her revolver with her. And again, granting a woman did have nerve and strength enough to do that, such a woman is not going off leaving her gold bag behind her as evidence!"

This speech didn't affect me much. It was pure conjecture. Women are uncertain creatures, at best; and a woman capable of murder would be equally capable of losing her head afterward, and leaving circumstantial evidence behind her.

I was sorry Mr. Crawford didn't seem to take to the notion of sending for Stone. I wasn't weakening in the case so far as my confidence in my own ability was concerned; but I could see no direction to look except toward Florence Lloyd or Gregory Hall, or both. And so I was ready to give up.

"What do you think of Gregory Hall?" I said suddenly.

"As a man or as a suspect?" inquired Mr. Crawford.

"Both."

"Well, as a man, I think he's about the average, ordinary young American, of the secretary type. He has little real ambition, but he has had a good berth with Joseph, and he has worked fairly hard to keep it. As a suspect, the notion is absurd. He wasn't even in West Sedgwick."

"How do you know?"

"Because he went away at six that evening, and was in New York until nearly noon the next day."

"How do you know?"

Philip Crawford stared at me.

"He says so," I went on; "but no one can prove his statement. He refuses to say where he was in New York, or what he did. Now, merely as a supposition, why couldn't he have come out here—say on the midnight train—called on Mr. Joseph Crawford, and returned to New York before daylight?"

"Absurd! Why, he had no motive for killing Joseph."

"He had the same motive Florence would have. He knew of Mr. Crawford's objection to their union, and he knew of his threat to change his will. Mr. Hall is not blind to the advantages of a fortune."

"Right you are, there! In fact, I always felt he was marrying Florence for her money. I had no real reason to think this, but somehow he gave me that impression."

"Me, too. Moreover, I found a late extra of a New York paper in Mr. Crawford's office. This wasn't on sale until about half past eleven that night, so whoever left it there must have come out from the city on that midnight train, or later."

A change came over Philip Crawford's face. Apparently he was brought to see the whole matter in a new light.

"What? What's that?" he cried excitedly, grasping his chair-arms and half rising. "A late newspaper! An extra!"

"Yes; the liner accident, you know."

"But—but—Gregory Hall! Why man, you're crazy! Hall is a good fellow. Not remarkably clever, perhaps, and a fortune-hunter, maybe, but not—surely not a murderer!"

"Don't take it so hard, Mr. Crawford," I broke in. "Probably. Mr. Hall is innocent. But the late paper must have been left there by some one, after, say, one o'clock."

"This is awful! This is terrible!" groaned the poor man, and I couldn't help wondering if he had some other evidence against Hall that this seemed to corroborate.

Then, by an effort, he recovered himself, and began to talk in more normal tones.

"Now, don't let this new idea run away with you, Mr. Burroughs," he said. "If Hall had an interview with my brother that night, he would have learned from him that he intended to make a new will, but hadn't yet done so."

"Exactly; and that would constitute a motive for putting Mr. Crawford out of the way before he could accomplish his purpose."

"But Joseph had already destroyed the will that favored Florence."

"We don't know that," I responded gravely. "And, anyway, if he had done so, Mr. Hall didn't know it. This leaves his motive unchanged."

"But the gold bag," said Mr. Crawford, apparently to get away—from the subject of Gregory Hall.

"If, as you say," I began, "that is Florence's bag—"

I couldn't go on. A strange sense of duty had forced those words from me, but I could say no more.

Fleming Stone might take the case if they wanted him to; or they might get some one else. But I could not go on, when the only clues discoverable pointed in a way I dared not look.

Philip Crawford was ghastly now. His face was working and he breathed quickly.

"Nonsense, Dad!" cried a strong, young voice, and his son, Philip, Jr., bounded into the room and grasped his father's hands. "I overheard a few of your last words, and you two are on the wrong track. Florrie's no more mixed up in that horrible business than I am. Neither is Hall. He's a fool chap, but no villain. I heard what you said about the late newspaper, but lots of people come out on that midnight train. You may as well suspect some peaceable citizen coming home from the theatre, as to pick out poor Hall, without a scrap of evidence to point to him."

I was relieved beyond all words at the hearty assurance of the boy, and I plucked up new courage. Apprehension had made me faint-hearted, but if he could show such flawless confidence in Florence and her betrothed, surely I could do as much.

"Good for you, young man!" I cried, shaking his hand. "You've cheered me up a lot. I'll take a fresh start, and surely we'll find out something. But I'd like to send for Stone."

"Wait a bit, wait a bit," said Mr. Crawford. "Phil's right; there's no possibility of Florrie or Hall in the matter. Leave the gold bag, the newspapers, and the yellow posies out of consideration, and go to work in some sensible way."

"How about Mr. Joseph's finances?" I asked. "Are they in satisfactory shape?"

"Never finer," said Philip Crawford. "Joseph was a very rich man, and all due to his own clever and careful investments. A bit of a speculator, but always on the right side of the market. Why, he fairly had a corner in X.Y. stock. Just that deal—and it will go through in a few days—means a fortune in itself. I shall settle that on Florence."

"Then you think the will will never be found?" I said.

Mr. Crawford looked a little ashamed, as well he might, but he only said,

"If it is, no one will be more glad than I to see Florrie reinstated in her own right. If no will turns up, Joe's estate is legally mine, but I shall see that Florence is amply provided for."

He spoke with a proud dignity, and I was rather sorry I had caught him up so sharply.

I went back to the inn, and, after vainly racking my brain over it all for a time, I turned in, but to a miserably broken night's rest.

CHAPTER 16: A CALL ON MRS. PURVIS

The next morning I received information from headquarters. It was a long-code telegram, and I eagerly deciphered it, to learn that Mrs. Egerton Purvis was an English lady who was spending a few months in New York City. She was staying at the Albion Hotel, and seemed to be in every way above suspicion of any sort.

Of course I started off at once to see Mrs. Purvis.

Parmalee came just as I was leaving the inn, and was of course anxious and inquisitive to know where I was going, and what I was going to do.

At first I thought I would take him into my confidence, and I even thought of taking him with me. But I felt sure I could do better work alone. It might be that Mrs. Egerton Purvis should turn out to be an important factor in the case, and I suppose it was really an instinct of vanity that made me prefer to look her up without Parmalee by my side.

So I told him that I was going to New York on a matter in connection with the case, but that I preferred to go alone, but I would tell him the entire result of my mission as soon as I returned. I think he was a little disappointed, but he was a good-natured chap, and bade me a cheerful goodby, saying he would meet me on my return.

I went to New York and went straight to the Albion Hotel.

Learning at the desk that the lady was really there, I sent my card up to her with a request for an immediate audience, and very soon I was summoned to her apartment.

She greeted me with that air of frigid reserve typical of an English woman. Though not unattractive to look at, she possessed the high cheekbones and prominent teeth which are almost universal in the women of her nation. She was perhaps between thirty and forty years old, and had the air of a grande dame.

"Mr. Burroughs?" she said, looking through her lorgnon at my card, which she held in her hand.

"Yes," I assented, and judging from her appearance that she was a woman of a decided and straightforward nature I came at once to the point.

"I'm a detective, madam," I began, and the remark startled her out of her calm.

"A detective!" she cried out, with much the same tone as if I had said a rattlesnake.

"Do not be alarmed, I merely state my profession to explain my errand."

"Not be alarmed! when a detective comes to see me! How can I help it? Why, I've never had such an experience before. It is shocking! I've met many queer people in the States, but not a detective! Reporters are bad enough!"

"Don't let it disturb you so, Mrs. Purvis. I assure you there is nothing to trouble you in the fact of my presence here, unless it is trouble of your own making."

"Trouble of my own making!" she almost shrieked. "Tell me at once what you mean, or I shall ring the bell and have you dismissed."

Her fear and excitement made me think that perhaps I was on the track of new developments, and lest she should carry out her threat of ringing the bell, I plunged at once into the subject.

"Mrs. Purvis, have you lost a gold-mesh bag?" I said bluntly.

"No, I haven't," she snapped, "and if I had, I should take means to recover it, and not wait for a detective to come and ask me about it."

I was terribly disappointed. To be sure she might be telling a falsehood about the bag, but I didn't think so. She was angry, annoyed, and a little frightened at my intrusion, but she was not at all embarrassed at my question.

"Are you quite sure you have not lost a gold-link bag?" I insisted, as if in idiotic endeavor to persuade her to have done so.

"Of course I'm sure," she replied, half laughing now; "I suppose I should know it if I had done so."

"It's a rather valuable bag," I went on, "with a gold frame-work and gold chain."

"Well, if it's worth a whole fortune, it isn't my bag," she declared; "for I never owned such a one."

"Well," I said, in desperation, "your visiting card is in it."

"My visiting card!" she said, with an expression of blank wonderment. "Well, even if that is true, it doesn't make it my bag. I frequently give my cards to other people."

This seemed to promise light at last. Somehow I couldn't doubt her assertion that it was not her bag, and yet the thought suddenly occurred to me if she were clever enough to be implicated in the Crawford tragedy, and if she had left her bag there, she would be expecting this inquiry, and would probably be clever enough to have a story prepared.

"Mrs. Purvis, since you say it is not your bag, I'm going to ask you, in the interests of justice, to help me all you can."

"I'm quite willing to do so, sir. What is it you wish to know?"

"A crime has been committed in a small town in New Jersey. A gold-link bag was afterward discovered at the scene of the crime, and though none of its other contents betokened its owner, a visiting card with your name on it was in the bag."

Becoming interested in the story, Mrs. Purvis seemed to get over her fright, and was exceedingly sensible for a woman.

"It certainly is not my bag, Mr. Burroughs, and if my card is in it, I can only say that I must have given that card to the lady who owns the bag."

This seemed distinctly plausible, and also promised further information.

"Do you remember giving your card to any lady with such a bag?"

Mrs. Purvis smiled. "So many of your American women carry those bags," she said; "they seem to be almost universal this year. I have probably given my card to a score of ladies, who immediately put it into just such a bag."

"Could you tell me who they are?"

"No, indeed;" and Mrs. Purvis almost laughed outright, at what was doubtless a foolish question.

"But can't you help me in any way?" I pleaded.

"I don't really see how I can," she replied. "You see I have so many friends in New York, and they make little parties for me, or afternoon teas. Then I meet a great many American ladies, and we often exchange cards. But we do it so often that of course I can't remember every particular instance. Have you the card you speak of?"

I thanked my stars that I had been thoughtful enough to obtain the card before leaving West Sedgwick, and taking it from my pocket-book, I gave it to her.

"Oh, that one!" she said; "perhaps I can help you a little, Mr. Burroughs. That is an old-fashioned card, one of a few left over from an old lot. I have been using them only lately, because my others gave out. I have really gone much more into society in New York than I had anticipated, and my cards seemed fairly to melt away. I ordered some new ones here, but before they were sent to me I was obliged to use a few of these old-fashioned ones. I don't know that this would help you, but I think I can tell pretty nearly to whom I gave those cards."

It seemed a precarious sort of a chance, but as I talked with Mrs. Purvis, I felt more and more positive that she herself was not implicated in the Crawford case.

However, it was just as well to make certain. She had gone to her writing-desk, and seemed to be looking over a diary or engagement book.

"Mrs. Purvis," I said, "will you tell me where you were on Tuesday evening of last week?"

"Certainly;" and she turned back the leaves of the book. "I went to a theatre party with my friends, the Hepworths; and afterward, we went to a little supper at a restaurant. I returned here about midnight. Must I prove this?" she added, smiling; "for I can probably do so, by the hotel clerk and by my maid. And, of course, by my friends who gave the party."

"No, you needn't prove it," I answered, certain now that she knew nothing of the Crawford matter; "but I hope you can give me more information about your card."

"Why, I remember that very night, I gave my cards to two ladies who were at the theatre with us; and I remember now that at that time I had only these old-fashioned cards. I was rather ashamed of them, for Americans are punctilious in such matters; and now that I think of it, one of the ladies was carrying a gold-mesh bag."

"Who was she?" I asked, hardly daring to hope that I had really struck the trail.

"I can't seem to remember her name, but perhaps it will come to me. It was rather an English type of name, something like Coningsby."

"Where did she live?"

"I haven't the slightest idea. You see I meet these ladies so casually, and I really never expect to see any of them again. Our exchange of cards is a mere bit of formal courtesy. No, I can't remember her name, or where she was from. But I don't think she was a New Yorker."

Truly it was hard to come so near getting what might be vital information, and yet have it beyond my grasp! It was quite evident that Mrs. Purvis was honestly trying to remember the lady's name, but could not do so.

And then I had what seemed to me an inspiration. "Didn't she give you her card?" I asked.

A light broke over Mrs. Purvis's face. "Why, yes, of course she did! And I'm sure I can find it."

She turned to a card-tray, and rapidly running over the bits of pasteboard, she selected three or four.

"Here they are," she exclaimed, "all here together. I mean all the cards that were given me on that particular evening. And here is the name I couldn't think of. It is Mrs. Cunningham. I remember distinctly that she carried a gold bag, and no one else in the party did, for we were admiring it. And here is her address on the card; Marathon Park, New Jersey."

I almost fainted, myself, with the suddenness of the discovery. Had I really found the name and address of the owner of the gold bag? Of course there might be a slip yet, but the evidence seemed clear that Mrs. Cunningham, of Marathon Park, owned the bag that had been the subject of so much speculation.

I had no idea where Marathon Park might be, but that was a mere detail. I thanked Mrs. Purvis sincerely for the help she had given me, and I was glad I had not told her that her casual acquaintance was perhaps implicated in a murder mystery.

I made my adieux and returned at once to West Sedgwick.

As he had promised, Parmalee met me at the station, and I told him the whole story, for I thought him entitled to the information at once.

"Why, man alive!" he exclaimed, "Marathon Park is the very next station to West Sedgwick!"

"So it is!" I said; "I knew I had a hazy idea of having seen the name, but the trains I have taken to and from New York have been expresses, which didn't stop there, and I paid no attention to it."

"It's a small park," went on Parmalee, "of swagger residences; very exclusive and reserved, you know. You've certainly unearthed startling news, but I can't help thinking that it will be a wild goose chase that leads us to look for our criminal in Marathon Park!"

"What do you think we'd better do?" said I. "Go to see Mrs. Cunningham?"

"No, I wouldn't do that," said Parmalee, who had a sort of plebeian hesitancy at the thought of intruding upon aristocratic strangers. "Suppose you write her a letter and just ask her if she has lost her bag."

"All right," I conceded, for truth to tell, I greatly preferred to stay in West Sedgwick than to go out of it, for I had always the undefined hope of seeing Florence Lloyd.

So I wrote a letter, not exactly curt, but strictly formal, asking Mrs. Cunningham if she had recently lost a gold-mesh bag, containing her gloves and handkerchief.

Then Parmalee and I agreed to keep the matter a secret until we should get a reply to this, for we concluded there was no use in stirring up public curiosity on the matter until we knew ourselves that we were on the right trail.

CHAPTER 17: THE OWNER OF THE GOLD BAG

The next day I received a letter addressed in modish, angular penmanship, which, before I opened it, I felt sure had come from Mrs. Cunningham. It ran as follows,

Mr. HERBERT Burroughs,

Dear Sir: Yes, I have lost a gold bag, and I have known all along that it is the one the newspapers are talking so much about in connection with the Crawford case. I know, too, that you are the detective on the case, and though I can't imagine how you did it, I think it was awfully clever of you to trace the bag to me, for I'm sure my name wasn't in it anywhere. As I say, the bag is mine, but I didn't kill Mr. Crawford, and I don't know who did. I would go straight to you, and tell you all about it, but I am afraid of detectives and lawyers, and I don't want to be mixed up in the affair anyway. But I am going to see Miss Lloyd, and explain it all to her, and then she can tell you. Please don't let my name get in the papers, as I hate that sort of prominence.

Very truly yours,

ELIZABETH CUNNINGHAM.

I smiled a little over the femininity of the letter, but as Parmalee had prophesied, Marathon Park was evidently no place to look for our criminal.

The foolish little woman who had written that letter, had no guilty secret on her conscience, of that I was sure.

I telephoned for Parmalee and showed him the letter.

"It doesn't help us in one way," he said, "for of course, Mrs. Cunningham is not implicated. But the bag is still a clue, for how did it get into Mr. Crawford's office?"

"We must find out who Mr. Cunningham is," I suggested.

"He's not the criminal, either. If he had left his wife's bag there, he never would have let her send this letter."

"Perhaps he didn't know she wrote it."

"Oh, perhaps lots of things! But I am anxious to learn what Mrs. Cunningham tells Miss Lloyd."

"Let us go over to the Crawford house, and tell Miss Lloyd about it."

"Not this morning; I've another engagement. And besides, the little lady won't get around so soon."

"Why a little lady?" I asked, smiling.

"Oh, the whole tone of the letter seems to imply a little yellow-haired butterfly of a woman."

"Just the reverse of Florence Lloyd," I said musingly.

"Yes; no one could imagine Miss Lloyd writing a letter like that. There's lots of personality in a woman's letter. Much more than in a man's."

Parmalee went away, and prompted by his suggestions, I studied the letter I had just received. It was merely an idle fancy, for if Mrs. Cunningham was going to tell Miss Lloyd her story, it made little difference to me what might be her stature or the color of her hair. But, probably because of Parmalee's suggestion, I pictured her to myself as a pretty young woman with that air of half innocence and half ignorance which so well becomes the plump blonde type.

The broad veranda of the Sedgwick Arms was a pleasant place to sit, and I had mused there for some time, when Mr. Carstairs came out to tell me that I was asked for on the telephone. The call proved to be from Florence Lloyd asking me to come to her at once.

Only too glad to obey this summons, I went directly to the Crawford house, wondering if any new evidence had been brought to light.

Lambert opened the door for me, and ushered me into the library, where Florence was receiving a lady caller.

"Mrs. Cunningham," said Florence, as I entered, "may I present Mr. Burroughs—Mr. Herbert Burroughs. I sent for you," she added, turning to me, "because Mrs.

Cunningham has an important story to tell, and I thought you ought to hear it at once."

I bowed politely to the stranger, and awaited her disclosures.

Mrs. Cunningham was a pretty, frivolous-looking woman, with appealing blue eyes, and a manner half-childish, half-apologetic.

I smiled involuntarily to see how nearly her appearance coincided with the picture in my mind, and I greeted her almost as if she were a previous acquaintance.

"I know I've done very wrong," she began, with a nervous little flutter of her pretty hands; "but I'm ready now to 'fess up, as the children say."

She looked at me, so sure of an answering smile, that I gave it, and said,

"Let us hear your confession, Mrs. Cunningham; I doubt if it's a very dreadful one."

"Well, you see," she went on, "that gold bag is mine."

"Yes," I said; "how did it get here?"

"I've no idea," she replied, and I could see that her shallow nature fairly exulted in the sensation she was creating. "I went to New York that night, to the theatre, and I carried my gold bag, and I left it in the train when I got out at the station."

"West Sedgwick?" I asked.

"No; I live at Marathon Park, the next station to this."

"Next on the way to New York?"

"Yes. And when I got out of the train—I was with my husband and some other people—we had been to a little theatre party—I missed the bag. But I didn't tell Jack, because I knew he'd scold me for being so careless. I thought I'd get it back from the Lost and Found Department, and then, the very next day, I read in the paper about the—the—awful accident, and it told about a gold bag being found here."

"You recognized it as yours?"

"Of course; for the paper described everything in it—
even to the cleaner's advertisement that I'd just cut out
that very day."

"Why didn't you come and claim it at once?"

"Oh, Mr. Burroughs, you must know why I didn't!
Why, I was scared 'most to death to read the accounts of
the terrible affair; and to mix in it, myself—ugh! I
couldn't dream of anything so horrible."

It was absurd, but I had a desire to shake the silly
little bundle of femininity who told this really important
story, with the twitters and simpers of a silly school-girl.

"And you would not have come, if I had not written
you?"

She hesitated. "I think I should have come soon, even
without your letter."

"Why, Mrs. Cunningham?"

"Well, I kept it secret as long as I could, but yesterday
Jack saw that I had something on my mind. I couldn't fool
him any longer."

"As to your having a mind!" I said to myself, but I
made no comment aloud.

"So I told him all about it, and he said I must come at
once and tell Miss Lloyd, because, you see, they thought it
was her bag all the time."

"Yes," I said gravely; "it would have been better if you
had come at first, with your story. Have you any one to
substantiate it, or any proofs that it is the truth?"

The blue eyes regarded me with an injured
expression. Then she brightened again.

"Oh, yes, I can 'prove property'; that's what you mean,
isn't it? I can tell you which glove finger is ripped, and
just how much money is in the bag, and—and here's a
handkerchief exactly like the one I carried that night.
Jack said if I told you all these things, you'd know it's my
bag, and not Miss Lloyd's."

"And then, there was a card in it."

"A card? My card?"

"No, not your card; a card with another name on it. Don't you know whose?"

Mrs. Cunningham thought for a moment. Then, "Oh, yes!" she exclaimed. "Mrs. Purvis gave me her card, and I tucked it in the pocket of the bag. Was that the way you discovered the bag was mine? And how did that make you know it."

"I'll tell you about that some other time if you wish, Mrs. Cunningham; but just now I want to get at the important part of your story. How did your gold bag get in Mr. Crawford's office?"

"Ah, how did it?" The laughing face was sober now and she seemed appalled at the question. "Jack says some one must have found it in the car-seat where I left it, and he"—she lowered her voice—"he must be the—"

"The murderer," I supplied calmly. "It does look that way. You have witnesses, I suppose, who saw you in that train?"

"Mercy, yes! Lots of them. The train reaches Marathon Park at 12: 50, and is due here at one o'clock. Ever so many people got out at our station. There were six in our own party, and others besides. And the conductor knows me, and everybody knows Jack. He's Mr. John Le Roy Cunningham."

It was impossible to doubt all this. Further corroboration it might be well to get, but there was not the slightest question in my mind as to the little lady's truthfulness.

"I thank you, Mrs. Cunningham," I said, "for coming to us with your story. You may not be able to get your bag to-day, but I assure you it will, be sent to you as soon as a few inquiries can be made. These are merely for the sake of formalities, for, as you say, your fellow townspeople can certify to your presence on the train, and your leaving it at the Marathon Park station."

"Yes," she replied; "and"—she handed me a paper—"there's my husband's address, and his lawyer's address, and the addresses of all the people that were in our party that night. Jack said you might like to have the list. He would have come himself to-day, only he's fearfully busy. And I said I didn't mind coming alone, just to see Miss Lloyd. I wouldn't have gone to a jury meeting, though. And I'm in no hurry for the bag. In fact, I don't care much if I never get it. It wasn't the value of the thing that made me come at all, but the fear that my bag might make trouble for Miss Lloyd. Jack said it might. I don't see how, myself, but I'm a foolish little thing, with no head for business matters." She shook her head, and gurgled an absurd little laugh, and then, after a loquacious leave-taking, she went away.

"Well?" I said to Florence, and then, "Well?" Florence said to me.

It was astonishing how rapidly our acquaintance had progressed. Already we had laid aside all formality of speech and manner, and if the girl had not really discovered my mental attitude toward her, at least I think she must have suspected it.

"Of course," I began, "I knew it wasn't your bag, because you said it wasn't. But I did incline a little to the `woman visitor' theory, and now that is destroyed. I think we must conclude that the bag was brought here by the person who found it on that midnight train."

"Why didn't that person turn it over to the conductor?" she said, more as if thinking to herself than speaking to me.

"Yes, why, indeed?" I echoed. "And if he brought it here, and committed a criminal act, why go away and leave it here?"

I think it was at the same moment that the minds of both of us turned to Gregory Hall. Her eyes fell, and as for me, I was nearly stunned with the thoughts that came rushing to my brain.

If the late newspaper had seemed to point to Hall's coming out on that late train, how much more so this bag, which had been left on that very train.

We were silent for a time, and then, lifting her sweet eyes bravely to mine, Florence said,

"I have something to tell you."

"Yes," I replied, crushing down the longing to take her in my arms and let her tell it there.

"Mr. Hall had a talk with me this morning. He says that he and the others have searched everywhere possible for the will, and it cannot be found. He says Uncle Joseph must have destroyed it, and that it is practically settled that Uncle Philip is the legal heir. Of course, Mr. Philip Crawford isn't my uncle, but I have always called him that, and Phil and I have been just like cousins."

"What else did Mr. Hall say?" I asked, for I divined that the difficult part of her recital was yet to come.

"He said," she went on, with a rising color, "that he wished me to break our engagement."

I will do myself the justice to say that although my first uncontrollable thought was one of pure joy at this revelation, yet it was instantly followed by sympathy and consideration for her.

"Why?" I asked in a voice that I tried to keep from being hard.

"He says," she continued, with a note of weariness in her voice, "that he is not a rich man, and cannot give me the comforts and luxuries to which I have been accustomed, and that therefore it is only right for him to release me."

"Of course you didn't accept his generous sacrifice," I said; and my own hopes ran riot as I listened for her answer.

"I told him I was willing to share poverty with him," she said, with a quiet dignity, as if telling an impersonal tale, "but he insisted that the engagement should be broken."

"And is it?" I asked eagerly, almost breathlessly.

She gave me that look which always rebuked me— always put me back in my place—but which, it seemed to me, was a little less severe than ever before. "It's left undecided for a day or two," she said. Then she added hurriedly,

"I must see if he needs me. Do you suppose this story of Mrs. Cunningham's will in any way—well, affect him?"

"It may," I replied truthfully. "At any rate, he must be made to tell where he was and what he was doing Tuesday night. You have no idea, have you?"

Florence hesitated a moment, looked at me in a way I could not fathom, and then, but only after a little choking sound in her throat, she said,

"No, I have no idea."

It was impossible to believe her. No one would show such emotion, such difficulty of speech, if telling a simple truth. Yet when I looked in her troubled eyes, and read there anxiety, uncertainty, and misery, I only loved her more than ever. Truly it was time for me to give up this case. Whatever turn it took, I was no fit person to handle clues or evidence which filled me with deadly fear lest they turn against the one I loved.

And yet that one, already suspected by many, had been proved to have both motive and opportunity.

And I, I who loved her, knew that, in one instance, at least, she had been untruthful.

Yes, it was high time for me to give this case into other hands.

I looked at her again, steadily but with a meaning in my glance that I hoped she would understand. I wanted her to know, that though of course justice was my end and aim, yet I was sure the truth could not implicate her, and if it did implicate Mr. Hall, the sooner we discovered it the better.

I think she appreciated my meaning, for the troubled look in her own eyes disappeared, and she seemed suddenly almost willing to give me her full confidence.

I resolved to make the most of my opportunity.

"Of course you know," I said gently, "that I want to believe all you say to me. But, Miss Lloyd, your naturally truthful nature so rebels at your unveracity, that it is only too plain to be seen when you are not telling the truth. Now, I do not urge you, but I ask you to tell me, confidentially if you choose, what your surmise is as to Mr. Hall's strange reticence."

"It is only a surmise," she said, and though the troubled look came back to her eyes, she looked steadily at me. "And I have no real reason even to think it, but I can't help feeling that Gregory is interested in some other woman beside myself."

Again I felt that uncontrollable impulse of satisfaction at this disclosure, and again I stifled it. I endeavored to treat the matter lightly. "Is that all?" I asked; "do you mean that perhaps Mr. Hall was calling on some other lady acquaintance that evening?"

"Yes, that is what I do mean. And, as I say, I have no real reason to think it. But still, Mr. Burroughs, if it were true, I cannot agree with you that it is unimportant. Surely a man is not expected to call on one woman when he is betrothed to another, or at least, not to make a secret of it."

I thoroughly agreed with her, and my opinion that Hall was a cad received decided confirmation.

"My treating it as a light matter, Miss Lloyd, was not quite sincere. Indeed, I may as well confess that it was partly to cover the too serious interest I take in the matter."

She looked up, startled at this, but as my eyes told her a certain truth I made no effort to conceal, she looked down again, and her lip quivered.

I pulled myself together. "Don't think I am taking advantage of your confidence," I said gently; "I want only to help you. Please consider me an impersonal factor, and let me do all I can for you. For the moment, let us suppose your surmise is correct. This would, of course, free Mr. Hall from any implication of crime."

"Yes, and while I can't suspect him of anything like crime, I hate, also, to suspect him of disloyalty to me."

Her head went up with a proud gesture, and I suddenly knew that the thought of Hall's interest in another woman, affected her pride and her sense of what was due her, far more than it did her heart. Her fear was not so much that Hall loved another woman, as that his secrecy in the matter meant a slight to her own dignified position.

"I understand, Miss Lloyd, and I hope for the sake of all concerned, your surmise is not correct. But, with your permission, I feel it my duty to discover where Mr. Hall was that evening, even if to do this it is necessary to have professional assistance from headquarters."

She shuddered at this. "It is so horrid," she said, "to spy upon a gentleman's movements, if he is only engaged in his personal affairs."

"If we were sure of that, we need not spy upon him. But to the eye of justice there is always the possibility that he was not about his personal affairs that evening, but was here in West Sedgwick."

"You don't really suspect him, do you?" she said; and she looked at me as if trying to read my very soul.

"I'm afraid I do," I answered gravely; "but not so much from evidence against him, as because I don't know where else to look. Do you?"

"No," said Florence Lloyd.

CHAPTER 18: IN MR. GOODRICH'S OFFICE

As was my duty I went next to the district attorney's office to tell him about Mrs. Cunningham and the gold bag, and to find out from him anything I could concerning Gregory Hall. I found Mr. Porter calling there, and both he and Mr. Goodrich welcomed me as a possible bringer of fresh news. When I said that I did know of new developments, Mr. Porter half rose from his chair.

"I dare say I've no business here," he said; "but you know the deep interest I take in this whole matter. Joseph Crawford was my lifelong friend and near neighbor, and if I can be in any way instrumental in freeing Florence from this web of suspicion—"

I turned on him angrily, and interrupted him by saying,

"Excuse me, Mr. Porter; no one has as yet voiced a suspicion against Miss Lloyd. For you to put such a thought into words, is starting a mine of trouble."

The older man looked at me indulgently, and I think his shrewd perceptions told him at once that I was more interested in Miss Lloyd than a mere detective need be.

"You are right," he said; "but I considered this a confidential session."

"It is," broke in Mr. Goodrich, "and if you will stay, Mr. Porter, I shall be glad to have you listen to whatever Mr. Burroughs has to tell us, and then give us the benefit of your advice."

I practically echoed the district attorney's words, for I knew Lemuel Porter to be a clear-headed and well-balanced business man, and his opinions well worth having.

So it was to two very interested hearers that I related first the story of Florence's coming downstairs at eleven o'clock on the fatal night, for a final endeavor to gain her uncle's consent to her betrothal.

"Then it was her bag!" exclaimed Mr. Porter. "I thought so all the time."

I said nothing at the moment and listened for Mr. Goodrich's comment.

"To my mind," said the district attorney slowly, "this story, told now by Miss Lloyd, is in her favor. If the girl were guilty, or had any guilty knowledge of the crime, she would not have told of this matter at all. It was not forced from her; she told it voluntarily, and I, for one, believe it."

"She told it," said I, "because she wished to take the responsibility of the fallen rose petals upon herself. Since we are speaking plainly, I may assure you, gentlemen, that she told of her later visit to the office because I hinted to her that the yellow leaves might implicate Gregory Hall."

"Then," said Mr. Goodrich triumphantly, "she herself suspects Mr. Hall, which proves that she is innocent."

"It doesn't prove her innocent of collusion," observed Mr. Porter.

"Nor does it prove that she suspects Mr. Hall," I added. "It merely shows that she fears others may suspect him."

"It is very complicated," said the district attorney.

"It is," I agreed, "and that is why I wish to send for the famous detective, Fleming Stone."

"Stone! Nonsense!" exclaimed Mr. Goodrich. "I have every confidence in your skill, Mr. Burroughs; I would not insult you by calling in another detective."

"Surely not," agreed Mr. Porter. "If you need help, Mr. Burroughs, confer with our local man, Mr. Parmalee. He's a pretty clever chap, and I don't know why you two don't work more together."

"We do work together," said I. "Mr. Parmalee is both clever and congenial, and we have done our best in the matter. But the days are going by and little of real importance has been discovered. However, I haven't told you as yet, the story of the gold bag. I have found its owner."

Of course there were exclamations of surprise at this, but realizing its importance they quietly listened to my story.

With scarcely a word of interruption from my hearers, I told them how I had found the card in the bag, how I had learned about Mrs. Purvis from headquarters, how I had gone to see her, and how it had all resulted in Mrs. Cunningham's visit to Miss Lloyd that morning.

"Well!" exclaimed Mr. Porter, as I concluded the narrative. "Well! Of all things! Well, I am amazed! Why, this gives a wide scope of possibilities. Scores of our people come out on that theatre train every night."

"But not scores of people would have a motive for putting Joseph Crawford out of the way," said Mr. Goodrich, who sat perplexedly frowning.

Then, by way of a trump card, I told them of the "extra" edition of the evening paper I had found in the office.

The district attorney stared at me, but still sat frowning and silent.

But Mr. Porter expressed his wonderment.

"How it all fits in!" he cried. "The bag, known to be from that late train; the paper, known to have been bought late in New York! Burroughs, you're a wonder! Indeed, we don't want any Fleming Stone, when you can do such clever sleuthing as this."

I stared at him. Nothing I had done seemed to me "clever sleuthing," nor did my simple discoveries seem to me of any great significance.

"I don't like it," said Mr. Goodrich, at last. "Everything so far known, both early and late information, seems to me to point to Gregory Hall and Florence Lloyd in collusion."

"But you said," I interrupted, "that Miss Lloyd's confession that she did go down-stairs late at night was in her favor."

"I said that before I knew about this bag story. Now I think the case is altered, and the two who had real motive are undoubtedly the suspects."

"But they had no motive," said Mr. Porter, "since Florence doesn't inherit the fortune."

"But they thought she did," explained the district attorney, "and so the motive was just as strong. Mr. Burroughs, I wish you would confer with Mr. Parmalee, and both of you set to work on the suggestions I have advanced. It is a painful outlook, to be sure, but justice is inexorable. You agree with me, Mr. Porter?"

Mr. Porter started, as if he, too, had been in a brown study.

"I do and I don't," he said. "Personally, I think both those young people are innocent, but if I am correct, no harm will be done by a further investigation of their movements on Tuesday night. I think Mr. Hall ought to tell where he was that night, if only in self-defense. If he proves he was in New York, and did not come out here, it will not only clear him, but also Florence. For I think no one suspects her of anything more than collusion with him."

Of course I had no mind to tell these men what Florence had told me confidentially about Mr. Hall's possible occupation Tuesday evening. They were determined to investigate that very question, and so, if her surmise were correct, it would disclose itself.

"Very well," I said, after listening to a little further discussion, which was really nothing but repetition, "then I will consult with Mr. Parmalee, and we will try to make further investigation of Mr. Hall's doings. But I'm ready to admit that it does not look easy to me to discover anything of importance. Mr. Hall is a secretive man, and unless we have a definite charge against him it is difficult to make him talk."

"Well, you can certainly learn something," said Mr. Goodrich. "At any rate devote a few days to the effort. I have confidence in you, Mr. Burroughs, and I don't think you need call in a man whom you consider your superior. But if you'll excuse me for making a suggestion, let me ask you to remember that a theory of Hall's guilt also possibly implicates Miss Lloyd. You will probably discover this for yourself, but don't let your natural chivalry toward a woman, and perhaps a personal element in this case, blind you to the facts."

Although he put it delicately, I quite understood that he had noticed my personal interest in Florence Lloyd, and so, as it was my duty to disregard that interest in my work, I practically promised to remember his injunction.

It was then that I admitted to myself the true state of my mind. I felt sure Florence was innocent, but I knew appearances were strongly against her, and I feared I should bungle the case because of the very intensity of my desire not to. And I thought that Fleming Stone, in spite of evidence, would be able to prove what I felt was the truth, that Florence was guiltless of all knowledge of or complicity in her uncle's death.

However, I had promised to go on with the quest, and I urged myself on, with the hope that further developments might clear Florence, even if they more deeply implicated Gregory Hall.

I went back to the inn, and spent some time in thinking over the matter, and methodically recording my conclusions. And, while I thought, I became more and more convinced that, whether Florence connived or not, Hall was the villain, and that he had actually slain his employer because he had threatened to disinherit his niece.

Perhaps when Hall came to the office, late that night, Mr. Crawford was already engaged in drawing up the new will, and in order to purloin it Hall had killed him, not knowing that the other will was already destroyed. And destroyed it must be, for surely Hall had no reason to steal or suppress the will that favored Florence.

As a next move, I decided to interview Mr. Hall.

Such talks as I had had with him so far, had been interrupted and unsatisfactory. Now I would see him alone, and learn something from his manner and appearance.

I found him, as I had expected, in the office of his late employer. He was surrounded with papers, and was evidently very busy, but he greeted me with a fair show of cordiality, and offered me a chair.

"I want to talk to you plainly, Mr. Hall," I said, "and as I see you're busy, I will be as brief as possible."

"I've been expecting you," said he calmly. "In fact, I'm rather surprised that you haven't been here before."

"Why?" said I, eying him closely.

"Only because the inquiries made at the inquest amounted to very little, and I assumed you would question all the members of the household again."

"I'm not sure that's necessary," I responded, following his example in adopting a light, casual tone. "I have no reason to suspect that the servants told other than the exact truth. I have talked to both the ladies, and now I've only a few questions to put to you."

He looked up, surprised at my self-satisfied air.

"Have you nailed the criminal?" he asked, with a greater show of interest than he had before evinced.

"Not exactly nailed him, perhaps. But we fancy we are on the scent."

"Resent what?" he asked, looking blank.

"I didn't say `resent.' I said, we are on the scent."

"Oh, yes. And in what direction does it lead you?"

"In your direction," I said, willing to try what effect bluntness might have upon this composed young man.

"I beg your pardon?" he said, as if he hadn't heard me.

"Evidences are pointing toward you as the criminal," I said, determined to disturb his composure if I could.

Instead of showing surprise or anger, he gave a slight smile, as one would at an idea too ridiculous to be entertained for an instant. Somehow, that smile was more convincing to me than any verbal protestation could have been.

Then I realized that the man was doubtless a consummate actor, and he had carefully weighed the value of that supercilious smile against asseverations of innocence. So I went on:

"When did you first learn of the accident to the Atlantic liner, the North America?"

"I suppose you mean that question for a trap," he said coolly; "but I haven't the least objection to answering it. I bought a late 'extra' in New York City the night of the disaster."

"At what hour did you buy it?"

"I don't know exactly. It was some time after midnight."

Really, there was little use in questioning this man. If he had bought his paper at half-past eleven, as I felt positive he did, and if he had come out to Sedgwick on the twelve o'clock train, he was quite capable of answering me in this casual way, to throw me off the track.

Well, I would try once again.

"Excuse me, Mr. Hall, but I am obliged to ask you some personal questions now. Are you engaged to Miss Lloyd?"

"I beg your pardon?"

His continued requests for me to repeat my questions irritated me beyond endurance. Of course it was a bluff to gain time, but he did it so politely, I couldn't rebuke him.

"Are you engaged to Miss Lloyd?" I repeated.

"No, I think not," he said slowly. "She wants to break it off, and I, as a poor man, should not stand in the way of her making a brilliant marriage. She has many opportunities for such, as her uncle often told me, and I should be selfish indeed, now that she herself is poor, to hold her to her promise to me."

The hypocrite! To lay on Florence the responsibility for breaking the engagement. Truly, she was well rid of him, and I hoped I could convince her of the fact.

"But she is not so poor," I said. "Mr. Philip Crawford told me he intends to provide for her amply. And I'm sure that means a fair-sized fortune, for the Crawfords are generous people."

Gregory Hall's manner changed.

"Did Philip Crawford say that?" he cried. "Are you sure?"

"Of course I'm sure, as he said it to me."

"Then Florence and I may be happy yet," he said; and as I looked him straight in the eye, he had the grace to look ashamed of himself, and, with a rising color, he continued: "I hope you understand me, Mr. Burroughs. No man could ask a girl to marry him if he knew that meant condemning her to comparative poverty."

"No, of course not," said I sarcastically. "Then I assume that, so far as you are concerned, your engagement with Miss Lloyd is not broken?"

"By no means. In fact, I could not desert her just now, when there is a—well, a sort of a cloud over her."

"What do you mean?" I thundered. "There is no cloud over her."

"Well, you know, the gold bag and the yellow rose leaves..."

"Be silent! The gold bag has been claimed by its owner. But you are responsible for its presence in this room! You, who brought it from the midnight train, and left it here! You, who also left the late city newspaper here! You, who also dropped two yellow petals from the rose in your buttonhole."

Gregory Hall seemed to turn to stone as he listened to my words. He became white, then ashen gray. His hands clinched his chair-arms, and his eyes grew glassy and fixed.

I pushed home my advantage. "And therefore, traced by these undeniable evidences, I know that you are the slayer of Joseph Crawford. You killed your friend, your benefactor, your employer, in order that he might not disinherit the girl whose fortune you wish to acquire by marrying her!"

Though I had spoken in low tones, my own intense emotion made my words emphatic, and as I finished I was perhaps the more excited of the two.

For Hall's composure had returned; his face resumed its natural color; his eyes their normal expression—that of cold indifference.

"Mr. Burroughs," he said quietly, "you must be insane."

"That is no answer to my accusations," I stormed. "I tell you of the most conclusive evidence against yourself, and instead of any attempt to refute it you mildly remark, 'you are insane.' It is you who are insane, Mr. Hall, if you think you can escape arrest and trial for the murder of Joseph Crawford."

"Oh, I think I can," was his only answer, with that maddening little smile of his.

"Then where were you on Tuesday night?"

"Excuse me?"

"Where were you on Tuesday night?"

"That I refuse to tell—as I have refused before, and shall always refuse."

"Because you were here, and because you have too much wisdom to try to prove a false alibi."

He looked at me half admiringly. "You are right in that," he said. "It is extremely foolish for any one to fake an alibi, and I certainly never should try to do so."

"That's how I know you were here," I replied triumphantly.

"You do, do you? Well, Mr. Burroughs, I don't pretend to misunderstand you—for Miss Lloyd has told me all about Mrs. Cunningham and her bag that she left in the train. But I will say this if you think I came out on that midnight train, go and ask the conductor. He knows me, and as I often do come out on that train, he may remember that I was not on it that night. And while you're about it, and since you consider that late newspaper a clue, also ask him who was on the train that might have come here afterward."

If this was bluffing, it was a very clever bluff, and magnificently carried out. Probably his hope was that the conductor could not say definitely as to Hall's presence on the late train, and any other names he might mention would only complicate matters.

But before I left I made one more attempt to get at this man's secret.

"Mr. Hall," I began, "I am not unfriendly. In fact, for Miss Lloyd's sake as well as your own, I should like to remove every shadow of suspicion that hovers near either or both of you."

"I know that," he said quickly. "Don't think I can't see through your `friendliness' to Miss Lloyd! But be careful there, Mr. Burroughs. A man does not allow too many `friendly' glances toward the girl he is engaged to."

So he had discovered my secret! Well, perhaps it was a good thing. Now I could fight for Florence more openly if necessary.

"You are right, Mr. Hall," I went on. "I hold Miss Lloyd in very high esteem, and I assure you, as man to man, that so long as you and she are betrothed, neither of you will have cause to look on me as other than a detective earnest in his work in your behalf."

"Thank you," said Hall, a little taken aback by my frankness.

I went away soon after that, and without quizzing him any further, for, though I still suspected him, I realized that he would never say anything to incriminate himself.

The theory that the criminal was some one who came in on that midnight train was plausible indeed; but what a scope it offered!

Why, a total stranger to Sedgwick might have come and gone, entirely unobserved, in the crowd.

It was with little hope, therefore, that I arranged for an interview with the conductor of the train.

He lived in Hunterton, a few stations from West Sedgwick, and, after ascertaining by telephone that he could see me the next day, I went to his house.

"Well, no," he replied, after thinking over my query a bit; "I don't think Mr. Hall came out from New York that night. I'm 'most sure he didn't, because he usually gives me his newspaper as he steps off the train, and I didn't get any `extra' that night."

Of course this wasn't positive proof that Hall wasn't there, so I asked him to tell me all the West Sedgwick people that he did remember as being on his train that night.

He mentioned a dozen or more, but they were nearly all names unknown to me.

"Do you remember the Cunninghams being on the train?" I asked.

"Those Marathon Park people? Oh, yes. They were a gay party,—coming back from a theatre supper, I suppose. And that reminds me: Philip Crawford sat right behind the Cunninghams. I forgot him before. Well, I guess that's all the West Sedgwick people I can remember."

I went away not much the wiser, but with a growing thought that buzzed in my brain.

It was absurd, of course. But he had said Philip Crawford had sat right behind Mrs. Cunningham. How, then, could he help seeing the gold bag she left behind, when she got out at the station just before West Sedgwick? Indeed, who else could have seen it but the man in the seat directly behind? Even if some one else had picked it up and carried it from the car, Mr. Crawford must have seen it.

Moreover, why hadn't he said he was on that train? Why conceal such a simple matter? Again, who had profited by the whole affair? And why had Gregory Hall said: "Ask the conductor who did get off that train?"

The rose petals were already explained by Florence. If, then, Philip Crawford had, much later, come to his brother's with the gold bag and the late newspaper, and had gone away and left them there, and had never told of all this, was there not a new direction in which to look?

But Philip Crawford! The dead man's own brother!

CHAPTER 19: THE MIDNIGHT TRAIN

The enormity of suspecting Philip Crawford was so great, to my mind, that I went at once to the district attorney's office for consultation with him.

Mr. Goodrich listened to what I had to say, and then, when I waited for comment, said quietly:

"Do you know, Mr. Burroughs, I have thought all along that Philip Crawford was concealing something, but I didn't think, and don't think now, that he has any guilty secret of his own. I rather fancied he might know something that, if told, would be detrimental to Miss Lloyd's cause."

"It may be so," I returned, "but I can't see how that would make him conceal the fact of his having been on that late train Tuesday night. Why, I discussed with him the possibility of Hall's coming out on it, and it would have been only natural to say he was on it, and didn't see Hall."

"Unless he did see him," remarked the district attorney.

"Yes; there's that possibility. He may be shielding Hall for Miss Lloyd's sake—and—"

"Let's go to see him," suggested Mr. Goodrich. "I believe in the immediate following up of any idea we may have."

It was about five in the afternoon, an hour when we were likely to find Mr. Crawford at home, so we started off at once, and on reaching his house we were told that Mr. Randolph was with him in the library, but that he would see us. So to the library we went, and found Mr. Crawford and his lawyer hard at work on the papers of the Joseph Crawford estate.

Perhaps it was imagination, but I thought I detected a look of apprehension on Philip Crawford's face, as we entered, but he greeted us in his pleasant, simple way, and asked us to be seated.

"To come right to the point, Mr. Crawford," said the district attorney, "Mr. Burroughs and I are still searching for new light on the tragedy of your brother's death. And now Mr. Burroughs wants to put a few questions to you, which may help him in his quest."

Philip Crawford looked straight at me with his piercing eyes, and it seemed to me that he straightened himself, as for an expected blow.

"Yes, Mr. Burroughs," he said courteously. "What is it you want to ask?"

So plain and straightforward was his manner, that I decided to be equally direct.

"Did you come out in that midnight train from New York last Tuesday night?" I began.

"I did," he replied, in even tones.

"While on the train did you sit behind a lady who left a gold bag in the seat when she got out?"

"I did."

"Did you pick up that bag and take it away with you?"

"I did."

"Then, Mr. Crawford, as that is the gold bag that was found in your brother's office, I think you owe a more detailed explanation."

To say that the lawyer and the district attorney, who heard these questions and answers, were astounded, is putting it too mildly. They were almost paralyzed with surprise and dismay.

To hear these condemning assertions straight from the lips of the man they incriminated was startling indeed.

"You are right," said Philip Crawford. "I do owe an explanation, and I shall give it here and now."

Although what he was going to say was doubtless a confession, Mr. Crawford's face showed an unmistakable expression of relief. He seemed like a man who had borne a terrible secret around with him for the past week, and was now glad that he was about to impart it to some one else.

He spoke very gravely, but with no faltering or hesitation.

"This is a solemn confession," he said, turning to his lawyer, "and is made to the district attorney, with yourself and Mr. Burroughs as witnesses."

Mr. Randolph bowed his head, in acknowledgment of this formal statement.

"I am a criminal in the eyes of the law," said Mr. Crawford, in an impersonal tone, which I knew he adopted to hide any emotion he might feel. "I have committed a dastardly crime. But I am not the murderer of my brother Joseph."

We all felt our hearts lightened of a great load, for it was impossible to disbelieve that calm statement and the clear gaze of those truthful, unafraid eyes.

"The story I have to tell will sound as if I might have been my brother's slayer, and this is why I assert the contrary at the outset."

Pausing here, Mr. Crawford unlocked the drawer of a desk and took out a small pistol, which he laid on the table.

"That," he said, "is my revolver, and it is the weapon with which my brother was killed."

I felt a choking sensation. Philip Crawford's manner was so far removed from a sensational—or melodramatic effect, that it was doubly impressive. I believed his statement that he did not kill his brother, but what could these further revelations mean? Hall? Florence? Young Philip? Whom would Philip Crawford thus shield for a whole week, and then, when forced to do so, expose?

"You are making strange declarations, Mr. Crawford," said Lawyer Randolph, who was already white-faced and trembling.

"I know it," went on Philip Crawford, "and I trust you three men will hear my story through, and then take such measures as you see fit.

"This pistol, as I said, is my property. Perhaps about a month ago, I took it over to my brother Joseph. He has always been careless of danger, and as he was in the habit of sitting in his office until very late, with the long windows open on a dark veranda, I often told him he ought to keep a weapon in his desk, by way of general protection. Then, after there had been a number of burglaries in West Sedgwick, I took this pistol to him, and begged him as a favor to me to let it stay in his desk drawer as a precautionary measure. He laughed at my solicitude, but put it away in a drawer, the upper right-hand one, among his business papers. So much for the pistol.

"Last Tuesday night I came out from New York on that midnight train that reaches West Sedgwick station at one o'clock. In the train I did not notice especially who sat near me, but when I reached our station and started to leave the car, I noticed a gold bag in the seat ahead. I picked it up, and, with a half-formed intention of handing it to the conductor, I left the train. But as I stepped off I did not see the conductor, and, though I looked about for him, he did not appear, and the train moved on. I looked in the station, but the ticket agent was not visible, and as the hour was so late I slipped the bag into my pocket, intending to hand it over to the railroad authorities next morning. In fact, I thought little about it, for I was very much perturbed over some financial considerations. I had been reading my newspaper all the way out, from the city. It was an `extra,' with the account of the steamship accident."

Here Mr. Crawford looked at me, as much as to say, "There's your precious newspaper clue," but his manner was indicative only of sadness and grief; he had no cringing air as of a murderer.

"However, I merely skimmed the news about the steamer, so interested was I in the stock market reports. I needn't now tell the details, but I knew that Joseph had a `corner' in X.Y. stock. I was myself a heavy investor in it, and I began to realize that I must see Joseph at once, and learn his intended actions for the next day. If he threw his stock on the market, there would be a drop of perhaps ten points and I should be a large loser, if, indeed, I were not entirely wiped out. So I went from the train straight to my brother's home. When I reached the gate, I saw there was a low light in his office, so I went round that way, instead of to the front door. As I neared the veranda, and went up the steps, I drew from my overcoat pocket the newspaper, and, feeling the gold bag there also, I drew that out, thinking to show it to Joseph. As I look back now, I think it occurred to me that the bag might be Florence's; I had seen her carry one like it. But, as you can readily understand, I gave no coherent thought to the bag, as my mind was full of the business matter. The French window was open, and I stepped inside."

Mr. Crawford paused here, but he gave way to no visible emotion. He was like a man with an inexorable duty to perform, and no wish to stop until it was finished.

But truth was stamped unmistakably in every word and every look.

"Only the desk light was turned on, but that gave light enough for me to see my brother sitting dead in his chair. I satisfied myself that he was really dead, and then, in a sort of daze, I looked about the room. Though I felt benumbed and half unconscious, physically, my thoughts worked rapidly. On the desk before him I saw his will."

An irrepressible exclamation from Mr. Randolph was the only sound that greeted this astonishing statement.

"Yes," and Mr. Crawford took a document from the same drawer whence he had taken the pistol; "there is Joseph Crawford's will, leaving all his property to Florence Lloyd."

Mechanically, Mr. Randolph took the paper his client passed to him, and, after a glance at it, laid it on the table in front of him.

"That was my crime," said Philip Crawford solemnly, "and I thank God that I can confess it and make restitution. I must have been suddenly possessed of a devil of greed, for the moment I saw that will, I knew that if I took it away the property would be mine, and I would then run no danger of being ruined by my stock speculations. I had a dim feeling that I should eventually give all, or a large part, of the fortune to Florence, but at the moment I was obsessed by evil, and I—I stole my brother's will."

It was an honest confession of an awful crime. But under the spell of that strong, low voice, and the upright bearing of that impressive figure, we could not, at the moment, condemn; we could only listen and wait.

"Then," the speaker proceeded, "I was seized with the terrific, unreasoning fear that I dare say always besets a malefactor. I had but one thought, to get away, and leave the murder to be discovered by some one else. In a sort of subconscious effort at caution, I took my pistol, lest it prove incriminating evidence against me, but in my mad frenzy of fear, I gave no thought to the gold bag or the newspaper. I came home, secreted the will and the revolver, and ever since I have had no doubts as to the existence of a hell. A thousand times I have been on the point of making this confession, and even had it not been brought about as it has, I must have given way soon. No mortal could stand out long under the pressure of remorse and regret that has been on me this past week. Now, gentlemen, I have told you all. The action you may take in this matter must be of your own choosing. But, except for the stigma of past sin, I stand again before the world, with no unconfessed crime upon my conscience. I stole the will; I have restored it. But my hands are clean of the blood of my brother, and I am now free to add my efforts to yours to find the criminal and avenge the crime."

He had not raised his voice above those low, even tones in which he had started his recital; he had made no bid for leniency of judgment; but, to a man, his three hearers rose and held out friendly hands to him as he finished his story.

"Thank you," he said simply, as he accepted this mute token of our belief in his word. "I am gratified at your kindly attitude, but I realize, none the less, what this will all mean for me. Not only myself but my innocent family must share my disgrace. However, that is part of the wrongdoer's punishment—that results fall not only on his own head, but on the heads and hearts of his loved ones."

"Mr. Goodrich," said Mr. Randolph, "I don't know how you look upon this matter from your official viewpoint, but unless you deem it necessary, I should think that this confidence of Mr. Crawford's need never be given to the public. May we not simply state that the missing will has been found, without any further disclosures?"

"I am not asking for any such consideration," said Philip Crawford. "If you decide upon such a course, it will be entirely of your own volition."

The district attorney hesitated.

"Speaking personally," he said, at last, "I may say that I place full credence in Mr. Crawford's story. I am entirely convinced of the absolute truth of all his statements. But, speaking officially, I may say that in a court of justice witnesses would be required, who could corroborate his words."

"But such witnesses are manifestly impossible to procure," said Mr. Randolph.

"Certainly they are," I agreed, "and I should like to make this suggestion: Believing, as we do, in Mr. Crawford's story, it becomes important testimony in the case. Now, if it were made public, it would lose its importance, for it would set ignorant tongues wagging, and give rise to absurd and untrue theories, and result in blocking our best-meant efforts. So I propose that we keep the matter to ourselves for a time—say a week or a fortnight—keeping Mr. Crawford under surveillance, if need be. Then we can work on the case, with the benefit of the suggestions offered by Mr. Crawford's revelations; and I, for one, think such benefit of immense importance."

"That will do," said Mr. Goodrich, whose troubled face had cleared at my suggestion. "You are quite right, Mr. Burroughs. And the `surveillance' will be a mere empty formality. For a man who has confessed as Mr. Crawford has done, is not going to run away from the consequences of his confession."

"I am not," said Mr. Crawford. "And I am grateful for this respite from unpleasant publicity. I will take my punishment when it comes, but I feel with Mr. Burroughs that more progress can be made if what I have told you is not at once generally known."

"Where now does suspicion point?"

It was Mr. Randolph who spoke. His legal mind had already gone ahead of the present occasion, and was applying the new facts to the old theories.

"To Gregory Hall," said the district attorney.

"Wait," said I. "If Mr. Crawford left the bag and the newspaper in the office, we have no evidence whatever that Mr. Hall came out on that late train."

"Nor did he need to," said Mr. Goodrich, who was thinking rapidly. "He might have come on an earlier train, or, for that matter, not by train at all. He may have come out from town in a motor car."

This was possible; but it did not seem to me probable. A motor car was a conspicuous way for a man to come out from New York and return, if he wished to keep his visit secret. Still, he could have left the car at some distance from the house, and walked the rest of the way.

"Did Mr. Hall know that a revolver was kept in Mr. Crawford's desk drawer?" I asked.

"He did," replied Philip Crawford. "He was present when I took my pistol over to Joseph."

"Then," said Mr. Goodrich, "the case looks to me very serious against Mr. Hall. We have proved his motive, his opportunity, and his method, or, rather, means, of committing the crime. Add to this his unwillingness to tell where he was on Tuesday night, and I see sufficient justification for issuing a warrant for his arrest."

"I don't know," said Philip Crawford, "whether such immediate measures are advisable. I don't want to influence you, Mr. Goodrich, but suppose we see Mr. Hall, and question him a little. Then, if it seems to you best, arrest him."

"That is a good suggestion, Mr. Crawford," said the district attorney. "We can have a sort of court of inquiry by ourselves, and perhaps Mr. Hall will, by his own words, justify or relieve our suspicions."

I went away from Mr. Crawford's house, and went straight to Florence Lloyd's. I did this almost involuntarily. Perhaps if I had stopped to think, I might have realized that it did not devolve upon me to tell her of Philip Crawford's confession. But I wanted to tell her myself, because I hoped that from her manner of hearing the story I could learn something. I still believed that in trying to shield Hall, she had not yet been entirely frank with me, and at any rate, I wanted to be the one to tell her of the important recent discovery.

When I arrived, I found Mr. Porter in the library talking with Florence. At first I hesitated about telling my story before him, and then I remembered that he was one of the best of Florence's friends and advisers, and moreover a man of sound judgment and great perspicacity. Needless to say, they were both amazed and almost stunned by the recital, and it was some time before they could take in the situation in all its bearings. We had a long, grave conversation, for the three of us were not influenced so much by the sensationalness of this new development, as by the question of whither it led. Of course the secret was as safe with these two, as with those of us who had heard it directly from Philip Crawford's lips.

"I understand Philip Crawford's action," said Mr. Porter, very seriously. "In the first place he was not quite himself, owing to the sudden shock of seeing his brother dead before his eyes. Also the sight of his own pistol, with which the deed had evidently been committed, unnerved him. It was an almost unconscious nervous action which made him take the pistol, and it was a sort of subconscious mental working that resulted in his abstracting the will. Had he been in full possession of his brain faculty, he could not have done either. He did wrong, of course, but he has made full restitution, and his wrong-doing should not only be forgiven but forgotten."

I looked at Mr. Porter in unfeigned admiration. Truly he had expressed noble sentiments, and his must be a broadly noble nature that could show such a spirit toward his fellow man.

Florence, too, gave him an appreciative glance, but her mind seemed to be working on the possibilities of the new evidence.

"Then it would seem," she said slowly, "that as I, myself, was in Uncle's office at about eleven o'clock, and as Uncle Philip was there a little after one o'clock, whoever killed Uncle Joseph came and went away between those hours."

"Yes," I said, and I knew that her thoughts had flown to Gregory Hall. "But I think there are no trains in and out again of West Sedgwick between those hours."

"He need not have come in a train," said Florence slowly, as if simply voicing her thoughts.

"Don't attempt to solve the mystery, Florence," said Mr. Porter in his decided way. "Leave that for those who make it their business. Mr. Burroughs, I am sure, will do all he can, and it is not for you to trouble your already sad heart with these anxieties. Give it up, my girl, for it means only useless exertion on your part."

"And on my part too, I fear, Mr. Porter," I said. "Without wishing to shirk my duty, I can't help feeling I'm up against a problem that to me is insoluble. It is my desire, since the case is baffling, to call in talent of a higher order. Fleming Stone, for instance."

Mr. Porter gave me a sudden glance, and it was a glance I could not understand. For an instant it seemed to me that he showed fear, and this thought was instantly followed by the impression that he feared for Florence. And then I chid myself for my foolish heart that made every thought that entered my brain lead to Florence Lloyd. With my mind in this commotion I scarcely heard Mr. Porter's words.

"No, no," he was saying, "we need no other or cleverer detective than you, Mr. Burroughs. If, as Florence says, the murderer was clever enough to come between those two hours, and go away again, leaving no sign, he is probably clever enough so to conceal his coming and going that he may not be traced."

"But, Mr. Porter," I observed, "they say murder will out."

Again that strange look came into his eyes. Surely it was an expression of fear. But he only said, "Then you're the man to bring that result about, Mr. Burroughs. I have great confidence in your powers as a detective."

He took his leave, and I was not sorry, for I wanted an opportunity to see Florence alone.

"I am so sorry," she said, and for the first time I saw tears in her dear, beautiful eyes, "to hear that about Uncle Philip. But Mr. Porter was right, he was not himself, or he never could have done it."

"It was an awful thing for him to find his brother as he did, and go away and leave him so."

"Awful, indeed! But the Crawfords have always been strange in their ways. I have never seen one of them show emotion or sentiment upon any occasion."

"Now you are again an heiress," I said, suddenly realizing the fact.

"Yes," she said, but her tone indicated that her fortune brought in its train many perplexing troubles and many grave questions.

"Forgive me," I began, "if I am unwarrantably intrusive, but I must say this. Affairs are so changed now, that new dangers and troubles may arise for you. If I can help you in any way, will you let me do so? Will you confide in me and trust me, and will you remember that in so doing you are not putting yourself under the slightest obligation?"

She looked at me very earnestly for a moment, and then without replying directly to my questions, she said in a low tone, "You are the very best friend I have ever had."

"Florence!" I cried; but even as she had spoken, she had gone softly out of the room, and with a quiet joy in my heart, I went away.

That afternoon I was summoned to Mr. Philip Crawford's house to be present at the informal court of inquiry which was to interrogate Gregory Hall.

Hall was summoned by telephone, and not long after he arrived. He was cool and collected, as usual, and I wondered if even his arrest would disturb his calm.

"We are pursuing the investigation of Mr. Joseph Crawford's death, Mr. Hall," the district attorney began, "and we wish, in the course of our inquiries, to ask some questions of you."

"Certainly, sir," said Gregory Hall, with an air of polite indifference.

"And I may as well tell you at the outset," went on Mr. Goodrich, a little irritated at the young man's attitude, "that you, Mr. Hall, are under suspicion."

"Yes?" said Hall interrogatively. "But I was not here that night."

"That's just the point, sir. You say you were not here, but you refuse to say where you were. Now, wherever you may have been that night, a frank admission of it will do you less harm than this incriminating concealment of the truth."

"In that case," said Hall easily, "I suppose I may as well tell you. But first, since you practically accuse me, may I ask if any new developments have been brought to light?"

"One has," said Mr. Goodrich. "The missing will has been found."

"What?" cried Hall, unable to conceal his satisfaction at this information.

"Yes," said Mr. Goodrich coldly, disgusted at the plainly apparent mercenary spirit of the man; "yes, the will of Mr. Joseph Crawford, which bequeaths the bulk of his estate to Miss Lloyd, is safe in Mr. Randolph's possession. But that fact in no way affects your connection with the case, or our desire to learn where you were on Tuesday night."

"Pardon me, Mr. Goodrich; I didn't hear all that you said."

Bluffing again, thought I; and, truly, it seemed to me rather a clever way to gain time for consideration, and yet let his answers appear spontaneous.

The district attorney repeated his question, and now Gregory Hall answered deliberately,

"I still refuse to tell you where I was. It in no way affects the case; it is a private matter of my own. I was in New York City from the time I left West Sedgwick at six o'clock on Monday, until I returned the next morning. Further than that I will give no account of my doings."

"Then we must assume you were engaged in some occupation of which you are ashamed to tell."

Hall shrugged his shoulders. "You may assume what you choose," he said. "I was not here, I had no hand in Mr. Crawford's death, and knew nothing of it until my return next day."

"You knew Mr. Crawford kept a revolver in his desk. You must know it is not there now."

Hall looked troubled.

"I know nothing about that revolver," he said. "I saw it the day Mr. Philip Crawford brought it there, but I have never seen it since."

This sounded honest enough, but if he were the criminal, he would, of course, make these same avowals.

"Well, Mr. Hall," said the district attorney, with an air of finality, "we suspect you. We hold that you had motive, opportunity, and means for this crime. Therefore, unless you can prove an alibi for Tuesday night, and bring witnesses to grove where you, were, we must arrest you, on suspicion, for the murder of Joseph Crawford."

Gregory Hall deliberated silently for a few moments, then he said:

"I am innocent. But I persist in my refusal to allow intrusion on my private and personal affairs. Arrest me if you will, but you will yet learn your mistake."

I can never explain it, even to myself, but something in the man's tone and manner convinced me, even against my own will, that he spoke the truth.

CHAPTER 20: FLEMING STONE

The news of Gregory Hall's arrest flew through the town like wildfire.

That evening I went to call on Florence Lloyd, though I had little hope that she would see me.

To my surprise, however, she welcomed me almost eagerly, and, though I knew she wanted to see me only for what legal help I might give her, I was glad even of this.

And yet her manner was far from impersonal. Indeed, she showed a slight embarrassment in my presence, which, if I had dared, I should have been glad to think meant a growing interest in our friendship.

"You have heard all?" I asked, knowing from her manner that she had.

"Yes," she replied; "Mr. Hall was here for dinner, and then—then he went away to—"

"To prison," I finished quietly. "Florence, I cannot think he is the murderer of your uncle."

If she noticed this, my first use of her Christian name, she offered no remonstrance, and I went on,

"To be sure, they have proved that he had motive, means, opportunity, and all that, but it is only indefinite evidence. If he would but tell where he was on Tuesday night, he could so easily free himself. Why will he not tell?"

"I don't know," she said, looking thoughtful. "But I cannot think he was here, either. When he said good-by to me to-night, he did not seem at all apprehensive. He only said he was arrested wrongfully, and that he would soon be set free again. You know his way of taking everything casually."

"Yes, I do. And now that you are your uncle's heiress, I suppose he no longer wishes to break the engagement between you and him."

I said this bitterly, for I loathed the nature that could thus turn about in accordance with the wheel of fortune.

To my surprise, she too spoke bitterly.

"Yes," she said; "he insists now that we are engaged, and that he never really wanted to break it. He has shown me positively that it is my money that attracts him, and if it were not that I don't want to seem to desert him now, when he is in trouble—"

She paused, and my heart beat rapidly. Could it be that at last she saw Gregory Hall as he really was, and that his mercenary spirit had killed her love for him? At least, she had intimated this, and, forcing myself to be content with that for the present, I said:

"Would you, then, if you could, get him out of this trouble?"

"Gladly. I do not think he killed Uncle Joseph, but I'm sure I do not know who did. Do you?"

"I haven't the least idea," I answered honestly, for there, in Florence Lloyd's presence, gazing into the depths of her clear eyes, my last, faint suspicion of her wrong-doing faded away. "And it is this total lack of suspicion that makes the case so simple, and therefore so difficult. A more complicated case offers some points on which to build a theory. I do not blame Mr. Goodrich for suspecting Mr. Hall, for there seems to be no one else to suspect."

Just then Mr. Lemuel Porter dropped in for an evening call. Of course, we talked over the events of the day, and Mr. Porter was almost vehement in his denunciation of the sudden move of the district attorney.

"It's absurd," he said, "utterly absurd. Gregory Hall never did the thing. I've known Hall for years, and he isn't that sort of a man. I believe Philip Crawford's story, of course, but the murderer, who came into the office after Florence's visit to her uncle, and before Philip arrived, was some stranger from out of town—some man whom none of us know; who had some grievance against Joseph, and who deliberately came and went during that midnight hour."

I agreed with Mr. Porter. I had thought all along it was some one unknown to the Sedgwick people, but some one well known to Joseph Crawford. For, had it been an ordinary burglar, the victim would at least have raised a protecting hand.

"Of course Hall will be set free at once," continued Mr. Porter, "but to arrest him was a foolish thing to do."

"Still, he ought to prove his alibi," I said.

"Very well, then; make him prove it. Give him the third degree, if necessary, and find out where he was on Tuesday night."

"I doubt if they could get it out of him," I observed, "if he continues determined not to tell."

"Then he deserves his fate," said Mr. Porter, a little petulantly. "He can free himself by a word. If he refuses to do so it's his own business."

"But I'd like to help him," said Florence, almost timidly. "Is there no way I can do so, Mr. Burroughs?"

"Indeed there is," I said. "You are a rich woman now; use some of your wealth to employ the services of Fleming Stone, and I can assure you the truth will be discovered."

"Indeed I will," said Florence. "Please send for him at once."

"Nonsense!" said Mr. Porter. "It isn't necessary at all. Mr. Burroughs here, and young Parmalee, are all the detectives we need. Get Hall to free himself, as he can easily do, and then set to work in earnest to run down the real villain."

"No, Mr. Porter," said Florence, with firmness; "Gregory will not tell his secret, whatever it is. I know his stubborn nature. He'll stay in prison until he's freed, as he is sure he will be, but he won't tell what he has determined not to divulge. No, I am glad I can do something definite at last toward avenging Uncle

Joseph's death. Please send for Mr. Stone, Mr. Burroughs, and I will gladly pay his fees and expenses." Mr. Porter expostulated further, but to no avail. Florence insisted on sending for the great detective.

So I sent for him.

He came two days later, and in the interval nothing further had been learned from Gregory Hall. The man was an enigma to me. He was calm and impassive as ever. Courteous, though never cordial, and apparently without the least apprehension of ever being convicted for the crime which had caused his arrest.

Indeed, he acted just as an innocent man would act; innocent of the murder, that is, but resolved to conceal his whereabouts of Tuesday night, whatever that resolve might imply.

To me, it did not imply crime. Something he wished to conceal, certainly; but I could not think a criminal would act so. A criminal is usually ready with an alibi, whether it can be proved or not.

When Fleming Stone arrived I met him at the station and took him at once to the inn, where I had engaged rooms for him.

We first had a long conversation alone, in which I told him, everything I knew concerning the murder.

"When did it happen?" he asked, for, though he had read some of the newspaper accounts, the date had escaped him.

I told him, and added, "Why, I was called here just after I left you at the Metropolis Hotel that morning. Don't you remember, you deduced a lot of information from a pair of shoes which were waiting to be cleaned?"

"Yes, I remember," said Stone, smiling a little at the recollection.

"And I tried to make similar deductions from the gold bag and the newspaper, but I couldn't do it. I bungled matters every time. My deductions are mostly from the witnesses' looks or tones when giving evidence."

"On the stand?"

"Not necessarily on the stand. I've learned much from talking to the principals informally."

"And where do your suspicions point?"

"Nowhere. I've suspected Florence Lloyd and Gregory Hall, in turn, and in collusion; but now I suspect neither of them."

"Why not Hall?"

"His manner is too frank and unconcerned."

"A good bluff for a criminal to use."

"Then he won't tell where he was that night."

"If he is the murderer, he can't tell. A false alibi is so easily riddled. It's rather clever to keep doggedly silent; but what does he say is his reason?"

"He won't give any reason. He has determined to keep up that calm, indifferent pose, and though it is aggravating, I must admit it serves his purpose well."

"How did they find him the morning after the murder?"

"Let me see; I believe the coroner said he telephoned first to Hall's club. But the steward said Hall didn't stay there, as there was no vacant room, and that he had stayed all night at a hotel."

"What hotel?"

"I don't know. The coroner asked the steward, but he didn't know."

"Didn't he find out from Hall, afterward?"

"I don't know, Stone; perhaps the coroner asked him, but if he did, I doubt if Hall told. It didn't seem to me important."

"Burroughs, my son, you should have learned every detail of Hall's doings that night."

"But if he were not in West Sedgwick, what difference could it possibly make where he was?"

"One never knows what difference anything will make until the difference is made. That's oracular, but it means more than it sounds. However, go on."

I went on, and I even told him what Florence had told me concerning the possibility of Hall's interest in another woman.

"At last we are getting to it," said Stone; "why in the name of all good detectives, didn't you hunt up that other woman?"

"But she is perhaps only a figment of Miss Lloyd's brain."

"Figments of the brains of engaged young ladies are apt to have a solid foundation of flesh and blood. I think much could be learned concerning Mr. Hall's straying fancy. But tell me again about his attitude toward Miss Lloyd, in the successive developments of the will question."

Fleming Stone was deeply interested as I rehearsed how, when Florence was supposed to be penniless, he wished to break the engagement. When Philip Crawford offered to provide for her, Mr. Hall was uncertain; but when the will was found, and Florence was known to inherit all her uncle's property, then Gregory Hall not only held her to the engagement, but said he had never wished to break it.

"H'm," said Stone. "Pretty clear that the young man is a fortune-hunter."

"He is," I agreed. "I felt sure of that from the first."

"And he is now under arrest, calmly waiting for some one to prove his innocence, so he can marry the heiress."

"That's about the size of it," I said. "But I don't think Florence is quite as much in love with him as she was. She seems to have realized his mercenary spirit."

Perhaps an undue interest in my voice or manner disclosed to this astute man the state of my own affections, for he gave me a quizzical glance, and said, "O-ho! sits the wind in that quarter?"

"Yes," I said, determined to be frank with him. "It does. I want you, to free Gregory Hall, if he's innocent. Then if, for any reason, Miss Lloyd sees fit to dismiss him, I shall most certainly try to win her affections. As I came to this determination when she was supposed to be penniless, I can scarcely be accused of fortune-hunting myself."

"Indeed, you can't, old chap. You're not that sort. Well, let's go to see your district attorney and his precious prisoner, and see what's to be done."

We went to the district attorney's office, and, later, accompanied by him and by Mr. Randolph, we visited Gregory Hall.

As I had expected, Mr. Hall wore the same unperturbed manner he always showed, and when Fleming Stone was introduced, Hall greeted him coldly, with absolutely no show of interest in the man or his work.

Fleming Stone's own kindly face took on a slight expression of hauteur, as he noticed his reception, but he said, pleasantly enough,

"I am here in an effort to aid in establishing your innocence, Mr. Hall."

"I beg your pardon?" said Hall listlessly.

I wondered whether this asking to have a remark repeated was merely a foolish habit of Hall's, or whether, as I had heretofore guessed, it was a ruse to gain time.

Fleming Stone looked at him a little more sharply as he repeated his remark in clear, even tones.

"Thank you," said Hall, pleasantly enough. "I shall be glad to be free from this unjust suspicion."

"And as a bit of friendly advice," went on Stone, "I strongly urge that you, reveal to us, confidentially, where you were on Tuesday night."

Hall looked the speaker straight in the eye.

"That," he said, "I must still refuse to do."

Fleming Stone rose and walked toward the window.

"I think," he said, "the proof of your innocence may depend upon this point."

Gregory Hall turned his head, and followed Stone with his eyes.

"What did you say, Mr. Stone?" he asked quietly.

The detective returned to his seat.

"I said," he replied, "that the proof of your innocence might depend on your telling this secret of yours. But I begin to think now you will be freed from suspicion whether you tell it or not."

Instead of looking glad at this assurance, Gregory Hall gave a start, and an expression of fear came into his eyes.

"What do you mean?" he said,

"Have you any letters in your pocket, Mr. Hall?" went on Fleming Stone in a suave voice.

"Yes; several. Why?"

"I do not ask to read them. Merely show me the lot."

With what seemed to be an unwilling but enforced movement, Mr. Hall drew four or five letters from his breast pocket and handed them to Fleming Stone.

"They've all been looked over, Mr. Stone," said the district attorney; "and they have no bearing on the matter of the crime."

"Oh, I don't want to read them," said the detective.

He ran over the lot carelessly, not taking the sheets from the envelopes, and returned them to their owner.

Gregory Hall looked at him as if fascinated. What revelation was this man about to make?

"Mr. Hall," Fleming Stone began, "I've no intention of forcing your secret from you. But I shall ask you some questions, and you may do as you like about answering them. First, you refuse to tell where you were during the night last Tuesday. I take it, you mean you refuse to tell how or where you spent the evening. Now, will you tell us where you lodged that night?"

"I fail to see any reason for telling you," answered Hall, after a moment's thought. "I have said I was in New York City, that is enough."

"The reason you may as well tell us," went on Mr. Stone, "is because it is a very simple matter for us to find out. You doubtless were at some hotel, and you went there because you could not get a room at your club. In fact, this was stated when the coroner telephoned for you, the morning after the murder. I mean, it was stated that the club bed-rooms were all occupied. I assume, therefore, that you lodged at some hotel, and, as a canvass of the city hotels would be a simple matter, you may as well save us that trouble."

"Oh, very well," said Gregory Hall sullenly; "then I did spend the night at a hotel. It was the Metropolis Hotel, and you will find my name duly on the register."

"I have no doubt of it," said Stone pleasantly. "Now that you have told us this, have you any objection to telling us at what time you returned to the hotel, after your evening's occupation, whatever it may have been?"

"Eh?" said Hall abstractedly. He turned his head as he spoke, and Fleming Stone threw me a quizzical smile which I didn't in the least understand.

"You may as well tell us," said Stone, after he had repeated his question, "for if you withhold it, the night clerk can give us this information."

"Well," said Hall, who now looked distinctly sulky, "I don't remember exactly, but I think I turned in somewhere between twelve and one o'clock."

"And as it was a late hour, you slept rather late next morning," suggested Stone.

"Oh, I don't know. I was at Mr. Crawford's New York office by half-past ten."

"A strange coincidence, Burroughs," said Fleming Stone, turning to me.

"Eh? Beg pardon?" said Hall, turning his head also.

"Mr. Hall," said Stone, suddenly facing him again, "are you deaf? Why do you ask to have remarks repeated?"

Hall looked slightly apologetic. "I am a little deaf," he said; "but only in one ear. And only at times—or, rather, it's worse at times. If I have a cold, for instance."

"Or in damp weather?" said Stone. "Mr. Hall, I have questioned you enough. I will now tell these gentlemen, since you refuse to do so, where you were on the night of

Mr. Crawford's murder. You were not in West Sedgwick, or near it. You are absolutely innocent of the crime or any part in it."

Gregory Hall straightened up perceptibly, like a man exonerated from all blame. But he quailed again, as Fleming Stone, looking straight at him, continued: "You left West Sedgwick at six that evening, as you have said. You registered at the Metropolis Hotel, after learning that you could not get a room at your club. And then—you went over to Brooklyn to meet, or to call on, a young woman living in that borough. You took her back to New York to the theatre or some such entertainment, and afterward escorted her back to her home. The young woman wore a street costume, by which I mean a cloth gown without a train. You did not have a cab, but, after leaving the car, you walked for a rather long distance in Brooklyn. It was raining, and you were both under one umbrella. Am I correct, so far?"

At last Gregory Hall's calm was disturbed. He looked at Fleming Stone as at a supernatural being. And small wonder. For the truth of Stone's statements was evident from Hall's amazement at them.

"You—you saw us!" he gasped.

"No, I didn't see you; it is merely a matter of observation, deduction, and memory. You recollect the muddy shoes?" he added, turning to me.

Did I recollect! Well, rather! And it certainly was a coincidence that we had chanced to examine those shoes that morning at the hotel.

As for Mr. Randolph and the district attorney, they were quite as much surprised as Hall.

"Can you prove this astonishing story, Mr. Stone?" asked Mr. Goodrich, with an incredulous look.

"Oh, yes, in lots of ways," returned Stone. "For one thing, Mr. Hall has in his pocket now a letter from the young lady. The whole matter is of no great importance except as it proves Mr. Hall was not in West Sedgwick that night, and so is not the murderer."

"But why conceal so simple a matter? Why refuse to tell of the episode?" asked Mr. Randolph.

"Because," and now Fleming Stone looked at Hall with accusation in his glance—"because Mr. Hall is very anxious that his fiancee shall not know of his attentions to the young lady in Brooklyn."

"O-ho!" said Mr. Goodrich, with sudden enlightenment. "I see it all now. Is it the truth, Mr. Hall? Did you go to Brooklyn and back that night, as Mr. Stone has described?"

Gregory Hall fidgeted in an embarrassed way. But, unable to escape the piercing gaze of Stone's eyes, he admitted grudgingly that the detective had told the truth, adding, "But it's wizardry, that's what it is! How could he know?"

"I had reason for suspicion," said Stone; "and when I found you were deaf in your right ear, and that you had in your pocket a letter addressed in a feminine hand, and postmarked `Brooklyn,' I was sure."

"It's all true," said Hall slowly. "You have the facts all right. But, unless you have had me shadowed, will you tell me how you knew it all?"

And then Fleming Stone told of his observations and deductions when we noticed the muddied shoes at the Metropolis Hotel that morning.

"But," he said, as he concluded, "when I hastily adjudged the young lady to be deaf in the left ear, I see now I was mistaken. As soon as I realized Mr. Hall himself is deaf in the right ear, especially so in damp or wet weather, I saw that it fitted the case as well as if the lady had been deaf in her left ear. Then a note in his pocket from a lady in Brooklyn made me quite sure I was right."

"But, Mr. Stone," said Lawyer Randolph, "it is very astonishing that you should make those deductions from those shoes, and then come out here and meet the owner of the shoes."

"It seems more remarkable than it really is, Mr. Randolph," was the response; "for I am continually observing whatever comes to my notice. Hundreds of my deductions are never verified, or even thought of again; so it is not so strange that now and then one should prove of use in my work."

"Well," said the district attorney, "it seems wonderful to me. But now that Mr. Hall has proved his alibi, or, rather, Mr. Stone has proved it for him, we must begin anew our search for the real criminal."

"One moment," said Gregory Hall. "As you know, gentlemen, I endeavored to keep this little matter of my going to Brooklyn a secret. As it has no possible bearing on the case of Mr. Crawford, may I ask of you to respect my desire that you say nothing about it?"

"For my part," said the district attorney, "I am quite willing to grant Mr. Hall's request. I have put him to unnecessary trouble and embarrassment by having him arrested, and I shall be glad to do him this favor that he asks, by way of amends."

But Mr. Randolph seemed reluctant to make the required promise, and Fleming Stone looked at Hall, and said nothing.

Then I spoke out, and, perhaps with scant courtesy, I said:

"I, for one, refuse to keep this revelation a secret. It was discovered by the detective engaged by Miss Lloyd. Therefore, I think Miss Lloyd is entitled to the knowledge we have thus gained."

Mr. Randolph looked at me with approval. He was a good friend of Florence Lloyd, and he was of no mind to hide from her something which it might be better for her to know.

Gregory Hall set his lips together in a way which argued no pleasant feelings toward me, but he said nothing then. He was forthwith released from custody, and the rest of us separated; having arranged to meet that evening at Miss Lloyd's home to discuss matters.

Except the half-hour required for a hasty dinner, Fleming Stone devoted the intervening time to looking over the reports of the coroner's inquest, and in asking me questions about all the people who were connected with the affair.

"Burroughs," he said at last, "every one who is interested in Joseph Crawford's death has suspected Gregory Hall, except one person. Not everybody said they suspected him, but they did, all the same. Even Miss Lloyd wasn't sure that Hall wasn't the criminal. Now, there's just one person who declares that Hall did not do it, and that he is not implicated. Why should this person feel so sure of Hall's innocence? And, furthermore, my boy, here are a few more important questions. In which drawer of the desk was the revolver kept?"

"The upper right-hand drawer," I replied.

"I mean, what else was in that drawer?"

"Oh, important, valuable memoranda of Mr. Crawford's stocks and bonds."

"Do you mean stock certificates and actual bonds?"

"No; merely lists and certain data referring to them. The certificates themselves were in the bank."

"And the will—where had that been kept?"

"In a drawer on the other side of the desk. I know all these things, because with the lawyer and Mr. Philip Crawford, I have been through all the papers of the estate."

"Well, then, Burroughs, let us build up the scene. Mr. Joseph Crawford, after returning from his lawyer's that night, goes to his office. Naturally, he takes out his will, that he thinks of changing, and—we'll say—it is lying on his desk when Mr. Lemuel Porter calls. He talks of other matters, and the will still lies there unheeded. It is there when Miss Lloyd comes down later. She has said so. It remains there until much later—when Philip Crawford comes, and, after discovering that his brother is dead, sees the will still on the desk and takes it away with him, and also sees the pistol on the desk, and takes that, too. Now, granting that the murderer came between the time Miss Lloyd left the office and the time Philip Crawford came there, then it was while the murderer was present that the drawer which held the pistol was opened, the pistol taken out, and the murder committed, Since Mr. Joseph Crawford showed no sign of fear of violence, the murderer must have been, not a burglar or an unwelcome intruder, but a friend, or an acquaintance, at least. His visit must have been the reason for opening that drawer, and that not to get the pistol, but to look at or discuss the papers contained in that drawer. The pistol, thus disclosed, was temptingly near the hand of the visitor, and, for some reason connected with the papers in that drawer, the pistol was used by the visitor—suddenly, unpremeditatedly, but with deadly intent at the moment."

"But who—" I began.

"Hush," he said, "I see it all now—or almost all. Let us go to Philip Crawford's at once—before it is time to go to Miss Lloyd's."

We did so, and Fleming Stone, in a short business talk with Mr. Crawford, learned all that he wanted to know. Then we three went over to Florence Lloyd's home.

Awaiting us were several people. The district attorney, of course, and Lawyer Randolph. Also Mr. Hamilton and Mr. Porter, who had been asked to be present. Gregory Hall was there, too, and from his crestfallen expression, I couldn't help thinking that he had had an unsatisfactory interview with Florence.

As we all sat round the library, Fleming Stone was the principal speaker.

He said: "I have come here at Miss Lloyd's request, to discover, if possible, the murderer of her uncle, Mr. Joseph Crawford. I have learned the identity of the assassin, and, if you all wish me to, I will now divulge it."

"We do wish you to, Mr. Stone," said Mr. Goodrich, and his voice trembled a little, for he knew not where the blow might fall. But after Fleming Stone's wonderful detective work in the case of Gregory Hall, the district attorney felt full confidence in his powers.

Sitting quietly by the library table, with the eyes of all the company upon him, Fleming Stone said, in effect, to them just what he had said to me. He told of the revolver in the drawer with the financial papers. He told how the midnight visitor must have been some friend or neighbor, whose coming would in no way startle or alarm Mr. Crawford, and whose interest in the question of stocks was desperate.

And then Fleming Stone turned suddenly to Lemuel Porter, and said: "Shall I go on, Mr. Porter, or will you confess here and now?"

It was as if a thunderbolt had fallen. Hitherto unsuspected, the guilt of Lemuel Porter was now apparent beyond all doubt. White-faced and shaking, his burning eyes glared at Fleming Stone.

"What are you?" he whispered, in hoarse, hissing tones. "I feared you, and I was right to fear you. I have heard of you before. I tried to prevent your coming here, but I could not. And I knew, when you came, that I was doomed—doomed!

"Yes," he went on, looking around at the startled faces. "Yes, I killed Joseph Crawford. If I had not, he would have ruined me financially. Randolph knows that—and Philip Crawford, too. I had no thought of murder in my heart. I came here late that night to renew the request I had made in my earlier visit that evening— that Joseph Crawford would unload his X.Y. stock gradually, and in that way save me. I had overtraded; I had pyramided my paper profits until my affairs were in such a state that a sudden drop of ten points would wipe me out entirely. But Joseph Crawford was adamant to my entreaties. He said he would see to it that at the opening of the market the next morning X.Y. stock should be hammered down out of sight. Details are unnecessary. You lawyers and financial men understand. It was in his power to ruin or to save me and he chose to ruin me. I know, why, but that concerns no one here. Then, as by chance, he moved a paper in the drawer, and I saw the pistol. In a moment of blind rage I grasped it and shot him. Death was instantaneous. Like one in a dream, I laid down the pistol, and came away. I was saved, but at what a cost! No one, I think, saw me come or go. I was afterward puzzled to know what became of the pistol, and of the will which lay on the desk when I was there. These matters have since been explained. Philip Crawford is as much a criminal as I. I shot a man, but he robbed the dead. He has confessed and made restitution, so he merits no punishment. In the nature of things, I cannot do that, but I can at least cheat the gallows."

With these words, Mr. Porter put something into his mouth and swallowed it.

Several people started toward him in dismay, but he waved them back, saying:

"Too late. Good-by, all. If possible, do not let my wife know the truth. Can't you tell her—I died of heart failure—or—something like that?"

The poison he had taken was of quick effect. Though a doctor was telephoned for at once, Mr. Porter was dead before he came.

Everything was now made clear, and Fleming Stone's work in West Sedgwick was done.

I was chagrined, for I felt that all he had discovered, I ought to have found out for myself.

But as I glanced at Florence, and saw her lovely eyes fixed on me, I knew that one reason I had failed in my work was because of her distracting influence on it.

"Take me away from here," she said, and I gently led her from the library.

We went into the small drawing-room, and, unable to restrain my eagerness, I said,

"Tell me, dear, have you broken with Hall?"

"Yes," she said, looking up shyly into my face. "I learned from his own lips the story of the Brooklyn girl. Then I knew that he really loves her, but wanted to marry me for my fortune. This knowledge was enough for me. I realize now that I never loved Gregory, and I have told him so."

"And you do love somebody else?" I whispered ecstatically. "Oh, Florence! I know this is not the time or the place, but just tell me, dear, if you ever love any one, it will be—"

"You" she murmured softly, and I was content.

THE END

Other Resurrected Press Mysteries From Carolyn Wells

A Chain of Evidence
Anybody But Anne
In The Onyx Lobby
Raspberry Jam
Spooky Hollow
The Clue
The Curved Blades
The Diamond Pin
The Gold Bag
The Man Who Fell Through the Earth
The Mystery Girl
The Mystery of the Sycamore
The Room With The Tassels
The Vanishing of Betty Varian
The White Alley
Vicky Van

Resurrected Press Mysteries From Louis Tracy

The Albert Gate Mystery

Four men murdered and a fortune in diamonds belonging to the Turkish Sultan stolen, while the Foreign Office official in charge has gone missing. Was it a common jewelry theft or was it a case of international intrigue? This is the question that barrister detective Reginald Brett must solve.

The Bartlett Mystery

When Ronald Tower is murdered on his way to a bridge game on the yacht Sans Souci it at first appears a common crime. But as Rex Carshaw finds, a tragic case of mistaken identity leads to political scandal among the rich and powerful of New York.

The Strange Case of Mortimer Fenley

When the wealthy Mortimer Fenley is struck down by a shot from an express rifle on the steps of his mansion, detectives Winter and Furneaux of Scotland Yard must find the culprit. Was it the artist who claimed he was painting a picture at the time of the shot? The disaffected younger son? Or is there another suspect?

The Stowmarket Mystery

For five generations the Fergus-Hume family has been cursed. Each of the baronets has met a violent end. When the fifth baronet is found slain by a ceremonial Japanese dagger, suspicion falls on his cousin David. It falls to barrister detective Reginald Brett to prove his innocence and find the real murder in a case that spans two continents and as many centuries.

Resurrected Press Mysteries by J. S. Fletcher

The Orange-Yellow Diamond
When an elderly pawnbroker is murdered in the London parish of Paddington, a young, down on his luck writer is accused of the crime. But then it's found the pawnbroker had had in his possession an extraordinary South African diamond worth over eighty-thousand pounds —a diamond that's now missing. It falls to Melky Rubenstein to unravel the mystery and prove the young man's innocence.

The Middle Temple Murder
When an elderly man's body is found on the steps of chambers in the Midde Temple, one of the Inns of Court, it falls to newspaperman Frank Spargo and Detective-Sergeant Rathbury to solve the crime. The murdered man, for indeed it was murder, was found with no money or identification on his person except for a piece of paper with the name and address of a young barrister. Who is the victim? Why was he killed? Who is the murderer?

Scarhaven Keep
Bassett Oliver, the famed actor, has gone missing. When Oliver fails to show for a rehearsal, aspiring playwright Richard Copplestone finds himself sent to the small village of Scarhaven on the northern coast of England to track down the actors movements. What he finds is mystery. Find the answers as Copplestone unravels the mystery of Scarhaven Keep.

Visit www.resurrectedpress.com

Resurrected Press Mysteries by Fergus Hume

The Green Mummy

Professor Braddock hoped to compare the burial practices of the Egyptians with those of the ancient Peruvians with his latest acquisition, the mummy of the last Inca, Caxas. But on arrival, the packing case proved to hold not the mummy, but the body of his assistant Sidney Bolton. It falls to Archie Hope to discover the murderer if he is to marry the professors step-daughter, Lucy Kendal. Who killed Bolton and where is the mummy? Was it the sea captain Hervey? The mysterious Don Pedro? Cockatoo the Polynesian servant? The professor, himself? And what has become of the emeralds? These are the questions that Hope must answer amongst the secrets of the past in The Green Mummy.

The Mystery of a Hansom Cab

"Truth is said to be stranger than fiction, and certainly the extraordinary murder which took place in Melbourne Friday morning goes a long way towards verifying that saying." Thus opens The Mystery of a Hansom Cab, the best selling mystery of the nineteenth century. When a man is found dead in a hansom cab one of Melbourne's leading citizens is accused of the murder. He pleads his innocence, yet refuses to give an alibi. It falls to a determined lawyer and an intrepid detective to find the truth, revealing long kept secrets along the way. Fergus Hume's first and perhaps most famous mystery... The Mystery Of A Hansom Cab.

Visit www.resurrectedpress.com

Resurrected Press Mysteries from the Dr. John Thorndyke Series

Dr. John Thorndyke Lecturer on Medical Jurisprudence and Forensic Medicine. Before Bones, before CSI, before Quincy, M.E– there was Dr. John Thorndyke solving the most baffling cases of Edwardian London using the latest tools of medical science. Read about his cases in:

The Eye of Osiris
John Bellingham, noted Egyptologist has vanished not once but twice in the same day. Now Dr, Thorndyke must unravel the tangled claims on his estate, solve the riddle of the missing man and find the "Eye of Osiris".

The Mystery of 31 New Inn
When Dr. Jervis is whisked away in a coach with no windows to an unknown location to treat a man in a coma from undivulged causes it is Dr. Thorndyke who must come up with the solution.

The Red Thumb Mark
The first of Dr. Thorndyke's cases finds him trying to prove the innocence of a young man accused of being a diamond thief despite the fact that his finger print was found at the scene of the crime.

John Thorndyke's Cases
More cases of medical mysteries as told by his trusted assistant Jervis, M.D. Eight stories of crime and deduction in Edwardian London.

Visit www.resurrectedpress.com

Resurrected Press Mysteries by John R. Watson & Arthur J. Rees

The Hampstead Mystery

High Court Justice Sir Horace Fewbanks found shot dead in his Hampstead home, a butler with a criminal past, a scorned lover and a hint of scandal. These are the elements of the Hampstead Mystery that Detective Inspector Chippenfield of Scotland Yard must unravel with the assistance of the ambitious Detective Rolfe. But will he be able to sort out the tangled threads of this case and arrest the culprit before he is upstaged by the celebrated gentleman detective Crewe. Follow the details of this amazing case at it plays out across Hampstead, London and Scotland until it reaches a stunning conclusion in the courts of the Old Bailey.

The Mystery of the Downs

When Harry Marsland was caught in a sudden down pour he sought shelter at Cliff Farm. Met at the door by a young woman clearly expecting someone else he is only too glad to get inside to wait out the storm. When they hear a noise upstairs in the deserted house they investigate only to discover the body of the farm's owner, Frank Lumsden, dead of a gunshot wound. Who then, killed Lumsden, and why? Who was the woman expecting and did she have any roll in the murder? These are the questions that private detective Crewe must answer in The Mystery of the Downs.

Visit www.resurrectedpress.com

Other Resurrected Press Mysteries

Mysteries on a Train

Before the Orient Express there was:

The Rome Express by Arthur Griffiths
A man is found dead in his first class sleeping compartment on the express from Rome to Paris. Who was his murderer? The Countess? The English General? His brother the clergy man? The maid who has disappeared? Is the French justice system up to solving the crime? Read about it in The Rome Express.

The Passenger from Calais by Arthur Griffiths
Colonel Basil Annesley finds he is the only passenger on the train from Calais to Lucerne. That is until a mysterious woman shows up at the last minute to book a compartment. Who is after her? What is her secret? Is she a criminal or a victim? Read about it in The Passenger from Calais

Visit us at www.resurrectedpress.com

About Resurrected Press

A division of Intrepid Ink, LLC, Resurrected Press is dedicated to bringing high quality, vintage books back into publication. See our entire catalogue and find out more at www.ResurrectedPress.com.

About Intrepid Ink, LLC

Intrepid Ink, LLC provides full publishing services to authors of fiction and non-fiction books, eBooks and websites. From editing to formatting, from publishing to marketing, Intrepid Ink gets your creative works into the hands of the people who want to read them. Find out more at www.IntrepidInk.com.